CHARLOTTE STUART

RAVEN'S LEGACY

Praise for *Raven's Legacy*:

"I highly recommend *Raven's Legacy* as a great detective story and a thought-provoking commentary on cultural heritage."
—*Gabriel Santos for Readers' Favorite*

"A police procedural steeped in immersive detail and a magnetic cast of believable players, Stuart strikes a fine balance between suspenseful sleuthing and rich cultural storytelling."
—*SPR Reviews*

"Charlotte Stuart delivers a gripping story . . . great settings and cultural revelations."
—*Matt Pechey, for Reedsy Discovery*

"The writing is flawless and had me reading late into the night. A truly spectacular mystery."
—*N.N. Light's Book Heaven*

"I'd especially recommend it to fans of Dana Stabenow or those who love stories that blend culture, community, and quiet suspense."
—*Literary Titan*

Praise for *Raven's Grave*:

Listed in *Kirkus Reviews* as one of "28 Indies Worth Discovering" (November 5, 2024)

"…in the tradition of Dana Stabenow's beloved Kate Shugak novels. St. Clair emerges as a stolid, self-possessed rock of a hero …"
—*Kirkus Reviews*

"Charlotte Stuart's evocation of the power of Alaska's untamed wilderness on its inhabitants and her readers is palpable and profound."
—*Gerald Elias, musician and author of the Daniel Jacobus mystery series*

"Teeming with authenticity and rich cultural detail. A wonderfully satisfying novel."
—*James W. Ziskin, author of the Anthony, Barry, and Macavity award-winning Ellie Stone mysteries*

"…masterfully woven mystery… haunting images of the past."
—*Kathi Daley, USA Today Bestselling Author*

"Every scene is detailed with cultural nuances and folklore, so the reader is immersed in the story. It's also emotional and full of intrigue."
—*NN Light's Book Heaven*

"…a very enjoyable, easy to read and well-spun mystery that kept me intrigued right up to the end."
—*LoveReading*

"If you like deep crime dramas with well-developed and compelling characters, you will love *Raven's Grave*."
—*Tammy Ruggles for Reader Views*

To the legacy of Mary Reeves Leber,
and to her daughter Elizabeth,
son-in-law Andrew, and her grandchildren Peter and Kat

"*Time flies over us, but leaves its shadow behind.*"
Nathaniel Hawthorne

PROLOGUE

Jonah St. Clair was ten years old when he first saw the Raven House screen. It spanned the back wall of the cedar log longhouse in Koloshan, bookended by two clan corner posts. On the left, the stylistic representation of the coho salmon clan, L'uknax̲.ádi. On the right, the beaver clan, Deisheetaan. The outside of the longhouse was in disrepair, and the raised platforms around the perimeter of the room had collapsed in places. But the imagery on the Raven House screen was still vivid, the carved detail beneath the red and black paint intensifying its geometric mysticism.

A Tlingit elder explained to him how the interconnected forms on the screen should be viewed both as distinct elements and as a part of the whole. But to the young boy, it was like looking at an optical illusion where your eyes see first one image then another, back and forth until eventually the complete picture emerges. What impressed him most at the time, however, was the way the screen dominated the space, demanding attention. How unlike the tiny, sterile altar in the local church his mother had introduced him to a few years earlier.

During that same visit he was told about Yéil the Raven for the first time. Known as the trickster because Yéil is mischievous and cunning; he is said to have stolen the sun and given it to the people.

In the years following Jonah's introduction to Tlingit culture, he would be told many stories about the Raven and other legends. Life lessons, like Grimm's Fairy Tales, only linked to animals and nature in a way he found endlessly fascinating. He carried these stories within him when he returned to L.A., then to Viet Nam, and finally, when he found his way back to Koloshan.

During his absence, the Raven House screen was moved to a warehouse space, and the longhouse had collapsed. Over time, the cedar logs and planks ended up in fireplaces throughout the village, leaving behind an empty plot of ground and many fond memories.

Little did Jonah suspect that one day the Raven House screen would divide villagers, pitting tradition against greed and a waning culture against modern-day aspirations.

A clash that would result in death.

PART I

The Investigation

TLÉIX'

(ONE)

Koloshan, AK—1980

The small, one-story jail stood alone at a bend in the dirt street, a short sprint away from the bay that connected them to other parts of Alaska. From the outside it looked like a rustic hunter's cabin, square and weathered. There was no sign to indicate that this was Koloshan's jail. No sign was needed; everyone in the village knew what it was.

You couldn't get to Koloshan by road, so not many strangers came to town, except in summer. Then, an occasional pleasure boat stopped in the harbor, or a small cruise ship dropped off a dozen or so passengers for a couple hours. There was a landing strip referred to as the "airport," although the runway was too short for commercial airplanes. Unscheduled flights by small private planes accommodated resident needs and brought in a few visitors. But most out-of-towners in Koloshan were fishermen who came in to sell their catch.

There was also a ferry from Juneau that came twice a week on a loop route that included a number of small villages. Unless the weather got in the way, the Tuesday stop was in the late morning when the ferry was on its way *from* Juneau. The Thursday stop in Koloshan was at midnight when the ferry was *returning* to Juneau. In both instances, the boat only paused long enough to load and unload. So, for the most part, the predominantly native village of about 800 residents remained isolated. And that was just the way most villagers liked it.

Jonah St. Clair, Koloshan's only police officer, was sitting at his desk, contemplating a crack in the small window to the left of the door. Only last year he had replaced the glass after having the window boarded up for the two years before that. And now it was broken again.

When his telephone rang, he picked up the receiver and said: "St. Clair."

"Jonah, you'd better get over to the Center right away!" The urgency of the statement shocked Jonah into action. He didn't bother asking what the problem was; he'd find out soon enough.

He could have walked to the Center, but the locals expected their only police officer to wear a uniform and to drive a vehicle with an emblem on the side. They were all aware he had spent six years on the L.A. police force after a tour in Vietnam, but they hadn't known him then. Without the uniform, the badge, the sidearm, and his official pickup truck with the village eagle and mountain logo on its door, he was just plain Jonah, someone who had spent a lot of his youth in Koloshan, someone everyone called by his first name. The uniform symbolized his office in the same way the ornamental robe and headdress signified the chief of the village at ceremonial gatherings.

When his aging, dust-streaked official vehicle wouldn't start, Jonah cursed and angrily pumped the gas pedal. Once the engine finally caught, he didn't wait for it to warm up. Ignoring its uneven sputtering, he kept pressure on the gas as he drove up the dusty hill road. Despite the panic in the caller's voice, he didn't anticipate it would be anything too serious. Most police calls for assistance in Koloshan were fairly routine. A fight. Vandalism. An accident. Still, the caller had sounded like it was something more pressing than usual.

Jonah could see the Center in the distance as he maneuvered around the bumps and ruts in the poorly maintained road. The official title was the Koloshan Native Arts Center. It had been built a few years earlier with a state grant acquired by a local teacher. Her goal was to display the Raven House screen and any other artifacts village residents could be persuaded to donate. Tlingits had lived in the area for centuries. The collection in the Center was a tribute to their local heritage.

Although the community was proud of the Center and what it represented, few locals bothered to stop by. But since it was on several tourist brochures, it got a handful of visitors from time to time. In one corner of the Center's main room, there was a table where locals were able to sell their crafts. Not everything on the table was native art, but the occasional tourists who purchased memorabilia didn't seem to mind.

As he pulled up in front of the Center, a modern structure by village standards, Jonah noted that it was already looking shabby. Koloshan's long winters were hard on buildings. He also noted that there were more cars than usual in the small parking area. The large bay window in front visually linked the parking lot with the main display area inside. Jonah could see a crowd gathered, kids running around, weaving in and out among the adults. Faces peering anxiously through the dirt streaking windows, obviously waiting for him to arrive. As he got out of his truck, the double doors in front of the Center opened wide, and several individuals energetically waving him inside. "Jonah," one shouted. "Come see what they've done!"

Murmured complaints echoed around the room as the crowd parted to let him through. Then, suddenly, everything became quiet. Even the young children stood still, staring up at Jonah as he made his way to the center of the room. At

6'4", Jonah towered over everyone there. His height set him apart, but it also gave him status, a mixed blessing at times. Without saying anything, he looked around, noting who was there, reading sorrow and anger on their faces. At the same time, something registered at the back of his mind: there was something wrong, something terribly wrong.

The Raven Screen was gone.

The glass display cases empty.

Ending the silence, someone said, "Can you believe it? We've been robbed." At that declaration, the room erupted into a cacophony of outrage as everyone slowly turned toward the huge wall where the Raven House screen used to dominate the room. Jonah followed their gaze. Once the centerpiece of the collection, only a few hooks remained, dangling from bent nails on the bare wood wall.

Suddenly, kids were back in motion with everyone talking at once. Jonah forced his eyes away from the wall where the screen used to be and began walking around the perimeter of the room, feeling as empty as the display cases. All the artifacts that had been so carefully labeled and put on display were all gone. Jonah did not have Tlingit ancestors, but after years living and working in Koloshan, he still felt their absence as a personal loss, accompanied by a sharp-edged anger at those responsible for the theft.

He turned his attention to the individuals gathered there, taking in their distress, their incredulity about what had happened. They were all waiting for his reaction. He knew he needed to push his personal feelings aside and start treating the Center as a crime scene.

"When was this discovered?" Jonah asked one of the Center's volunteers. It had obviously been a hurried job, pedestals overturned, display cloth trampled, one glass case smashed, its padlock still intact. A hurried but thorough job. Whoever had done it had left nothing behind.

"About an hour ago. Stella found it when she came to work." Stella was standing quietly at the back of the group, a small, older woman with graying hair in a long braid wrapped around her head Norwegian fashion. There wasn't much to do at the Center; Stella held the one paid position funded by the state. She usually opened the Center by ten o'clock during the week, although sometimes a bit later, and if she had something else that needed doing, she might miss a day here and there. But she always showed up for cruise ship arrivals, no matter what day they came.

Jonah looked around, mentally making a list of names of those present. There would be time later to admonish those responsible for not calling him before potentially messing up any physical evidence that might help him track the thieves. For now, he needed to send most of the villagers on their way so he could take a close, unhurried look at the room.

"Stella. Jack. Ray. Earl. Harold." Jonah called out the names of those he wanted to stay. The four men were Tlingit elders, influential members of the community; he hoped they would be able to give him some insight into what had happened. He could question the others later. "Everyone else, please leave," he said. "And would you mind staying on the path alongside the building instead of going into the parking area." It was an order, not a question. "You can pick up your cars later, after I've had a chance to have a look around. Okay?"

There were a few mumbled protests, but no real resistance to his request. They would obviously have preferred to remain and watch what Jonah did next. But Jonah was the law, and, for the most part, they were law-abiding citizens.

The kids were rounded up and everyone obediently made for the exit. "Remember, stay away from the parking lot," Jonah called after them, adding "I may want to talk to some of you later." He didn't have to tell anyone that they shouldn't leave town. He knew all of them. And, unless they went by boat or airplane, they weren't going anywhere.

Three of the Tlingit elders Jonah had asked to stay stood near a smashed case, reading aloud the plaques for the missing objects, their voices filled with emotion. "Eineit shá" or horn spoon. "Yoo katan lítaa." Curved knife. "Shí s'aatée wutsaagáyi." Dance staff.

Jonah and Stella watched as the three men began working their way methodically around the room, pausing at each empty space to read the small card stating what had been there. It felt like a memorial for the artifacts. Although few in the village spoke Tlingit, it seemed appropriate to mourn the pieces using their Tlingit names.

"Káa yooka.óot' x'óow." Button blanket.

"Naaxein." Chilkat blanket.

"X'uskeit." Leggings

"Sheishóox." Rattle.

As he listened to the unique cadence of the words, Jonah felt overwhelmed by the enormity of the theft. When the Center first opened, he had come here with his adopted grandfather, Dennis Gray. He remembered Dennis proudly pointing out the dagger with the carved bear head pommel with its abalone eyes. Before being donated to the Center, it had been in the Gray family for generations.

Crest hats, bentwood boxes, paddles, button blankets, baskets, halibut hooks, frontlets, bowls, headdresses, pipes, rattles, masks—Koloshan had never been a rich village, but its approximately 500 native residents had inherited these artifacts from ancestors and kept them through all the cultural changes that had altered their daily lives. The donations were made to safeguard the collective community heritage and to share that heritage with future generations.

And now those treasured objects were gone. All of them. Gone.

One elder had not joined the other three as they made their pilgrimage around the room. Harold stood off to the side, his face etched with mixed emotions. Jonah wasn't sure what was going on with him, but that could wait. His most urgent need was to talk with Stella. He motioned for her to join him at the back of the room.

"I will need a list of what was taken, and a brief description of the artifacts. Can you put that together for me?"

"Yes, it will take a while though. I'm in the process of consolidating our records."

"That's fine—maybe just identify some of the more valuable pieces for now and get that to me as soon as possible. I want to let officials know what to keep an eye out for. But first, I understand you discovered this when you got here this morning. What time was that?"

Stella glanced around, and her mouth quivered as she tried to respond. "I . . . I . . . got here a little after 10:00."

"Were the doors locked when you arrived?"

"No, they weren't." Jonah had observed that the lock had not been forced, and there were no broken windows. But he also knew this was not a casual burglary, someone simply taking advantage of an unlocked entrance. The screen was at least fifteen feet by eight feet. And the two carved corner posts were heavy and would have been awkward to handle. Then there were the smaller artifacts, many of them fragile. Moving all that had taken a lot of planning.

"How many keys to the building are there?"

"Three. I have two. I keep one in my purse and one in my desk drawer. The archeologist, Austin Mann, has the third. He's using one of the back rooms as a temporary office." She paused, then said, "You don't think . . ." She suddenly seemed to consider that what had happened might be due to her own negligence.

"No, Stella. Not your fault. It wasn't someone who found an unlocked door and snatched a few items. This was a professional job." He looked around at the empty space. Many of the items taken were valuable if sold on the black market, but the idea that something like this could happen in Koloshan hadn't been on anyone's radar. No one in the village worried much about security. Most businesses locked their doors, but the only break-in Jonah could remember was a group of half-drunk teenagers noisily smashing a window in the liquor store. But even without a key to the Center or smashing a window, it would have been relatively easy for someone with the right skills to have gained access by picking the lock on the front door.

"Stella, what was the first thing you did after you saw what had happened?"

"I called Harold." She pointed at one of the three elders surveying their losses. Jonah knew that Harold had fought for the grant for the Center and had spearheaded the collection and organization of the artifacts. "He said to stay put and he would be right over."

"Did you see anyone near the building when you arrived? Any cars or trucks in the area?"

She shook her head "no."

"And did you try to clean anything up while you waited for Harold?"

"No . . . I called my mother."

That explained all the people. Stella's mother, quick-witted and with time on her hands, had undoubtedly called friends and relatives to tell them about the robbery. In the small, isolated village, word traveled fast. The family-and-friends network was as effective as any big-business communications system.

Jonah motioned Harold over. He was in his late sixties, black hair streaked with gray, square chin beneath obsidian eyes. When Harold wore traditional dress for participation in ceremonies, he was the poster child for Tlingit ancestry. "Did you tell anyone about what happened?" Jonah asked.

"Just my wife."

"And, as far as you know, did she tell anyone?"

"She might have."

Knowing Harold's wife, that "might have" was a certainty. Between her and Stella's mom, almost everyone in Koloshan probably knew about the theft by now. Jonah would have preferred being able to ask questions before everyone had time to massage facts by consciously or unconsciously merging what they knew with what someone told them.

Jonah called to the other three men, interrupting the naming of missing artifacts. "Thanks for staying. I need to get on this as quickly as possible." Before he could say more, Ray interrupted. Known for being outspoken, he tossed out an accusation like someone lobbing a grenade.

"We all know who's responsible." He looked meaningfully at Harold.

"You accusing me of something, Ray?" Harold's voice loud in the empty room. "Go ahead, spit it out."

Jonah could have stopped the confrontation, but he didn't. Sometimes you learned more if you held back.

"You've been trying to get us to sell the Raven House screen from the beginning." He pointed to the empty wall where the screen had been displayed. "You have no feeling for the past, no understanding of what it means to the community to be able to see what our ancestors made and valued . . ."

When Ray paused, Jonah jumped in. "Ray, do you have reason to suspect that Harold might be involved in the theft? Any *evidence*?"

Harold glared at Ray, daring him to make the accusation official. All four men were in their 60s and had known each other all their lives. If an outsider had said something against any one of them, they would have stood together no matter what the issue. But in this village dispute over whether they should sell or keep some or all of the Center's artifacts, sides had been taken, friendships set aside, old resentments rekindled.

"Who else?" Ray said angrily.

"Why you—." The lines around Harold's mouth deepened with rage.

"I asked if you have any *evidence*," Jonah said firmly but calmly.

Ray hedged, "Well, nothing specific. But it was him that got that museum interested in the screen. It was him that wanted to sell it, sell our heritage." Jonah knew they had once been offered a half-million dollars for the screen and corner posts by a wealthy collector, an almost incomprehensible amount by Koloshan standards.

Jonah looked Harold in the eyes and asked, "Were you involved in this?"

"Of course not. I've never said we should sell 'everything.' Just the screen. We can't care for it properly here. It will only deteriorate. We ought to sell it before—."

He stopped and glanced up at the empty wall where the screen had been mounted, as if suddenly realizing that arguments for and against selling the screen were no longer relevant.

"Does anyone have anything specific they can tell me?" Jonah's dark eyes rested briefly on each of the five individuals he'd asked to stay. "Can you think of someone who may have done this? Or suggest somewhere to look for the missing items?"

Five sets of eyes returned his gaze. But silence hung in the air like the calm after a storm. It was Stella who finally spoke. "There have been a number of outsiders who've shown interest in purchasing the screen. A few dealers, a couple of collectors. A museum or two."

"Can you get me those names?"

Stella nodded.

Jonah stared at the others, willing them to know something, anything, no matter how small, that might be a lead. But still none of the men responded.

"There must be rumors, someone who knows something . . ."

The four men shook their heads in defeat.

"Ask around, okay? And remember, this isn't about money, or clans, or blame. It's a police matter. And we could be dealing with some organized criminals, most likely outsiders. So, I don't want any of you trying to follow up on your own if you get a lead. If you learn anything that you think might be helpful, *anything,* even something that seems insignificant, come to me and I'll deal with it. Understood?"

They all nodded in agreement, not looking at each other. Lines had been drawn before the break-in, hardened in place by lack of clarity around who actually owned the screen. Initially it may have been made for a family or group of families belonging to the Raven moiety, one of two groups of clans. But its lineage before being installed in the longhouse at the new Koloshan site had been forgotten, partly because, at the time, no one considered "ownership" important; it had belonged to the community.

Nor did anyone know who the original artist was. It was even possible that several artists had worked on the screen and the corner posts. Written records were vague; official records non-existent. The lack of provenance was muddied further by conflicting stories supporting different chains of ownership. That was one of the arguments against selling the screen. Who had the right to make the decision? Who would receive the payment? Having the Center acquire the screen had stilled the controversy temporarily, but now the theft was about to revive old grievances. Jonah knew it wasn't going to be easy to function both as a member of the community and as their police officer in this instance. But he had no choice. He had to try.

When no one seemed to have anything to add, Jonah suggested they leave, by the same path the others had taken. All except for Stella. He asked her to stay and work on the lists she'd promised him.

He watched them go, moving single file down the dirt path. For an instant he imagined them as they might have looked 200 years ago, dressed in deerskin clothes with their straight dark hair pulled back and secured with leather thongs. Then the sunlight skittered across the bright plaid shirts and denim jeans, and the image vanished.

Jonah stood there a moment after they disappeared from sight and let the silence wash over him, remembering the lilt of the Tlingit language as the missing artifacts were acknowledged one by one by the descendants of the original artists. So little was left of their culture. A complex and half-forgotten language, only a few of the traditional crafts, bits and pieces of an oral tradition, stories and legends of the past held fast by a handful of elders, and a collection of artifacts . . . This theft was going to be a spike into the heart of this village—a violation of the personal identity of its residents.

If he failed to find the thief or thieves, everyone in the village would suffer. And as a non-native committed to serving the community . . . well, failure wasn't a possibility he wanted to face.

DÉIX

(TWO)

It was very still in the parking lot. Jonah looked up when he heard the melodious *kloo-klock* of a raven in flight. The bird disappeared into the thicket bordering the path that meandered down the hill from the Center. Although he didn't consider himself to be superstitious, it crossed his mind that the raven's presence might be somehow significant. Then he chided himself for the thought. Ravens were as common in Koloshan as gulls had been along the beach where he had often walked in L.A. A raven flying overhead wasn't some symbolic event. The fact was that some very valuable property had been stolen; there was nothing mystical about it.

There weren't more than five miles of road in Koloshan, unless you counted the logging roads that stretched into the surrounding hills. Even so, a lot of residents owned vehicles. It seemed like no one wanted to walk anymore. There was status in owning a car or truck no matter how old or rusty it was. Seven cars and a pickup had found their way into the unpaved parking lot that morning, making Jonah's job more difficult. There had been a few sprinkles during the night, so the dirt lot was crisscrossed with visible tire marks and shoeprints from those who had come in cars and those who appeared to have come from down the road, people walking or running to the scene of the crime.

Careful to avoid stepping on the prints that were already there, Jonah studied the barely visible impressions in the dirt. It didn't take long to find what he was looking for: some large tracks that indicated a sizable vehicle had been backed up to the front of the building not that long ago. A lot of villagers drove trucks, usually ones with worn tread. But these tracks had been made by good tires with enough tread to leave deep groove marks. Another smaller truck had been alongside it, its tracks almost completely obscured by recent traffic. The significant factor was that both sets of prints indicated that these two vehicles also drove *out* of the parking area, the only ones to do so recently.

Jonah followed the tracks of the larger truck to the road where it had headed downhill. He lost them when the side road intersected with the main route into town. A lot of traffic had passed by that morning. Despite a little rain, the mostly dry, packed ground didn't hold onto many secrets.

At the bottom of the hill, he paused to say good morning to the two older men seated on the porch of a ramshackle house. They looked much alike—T-shirts showing through open flannel shirts, shoulder length dark hair pushed back from aging faces, relaxed and friendly, enjoying the occasional passer-by. Both were former commercial fishermen, retired and living off incomes that wouldn't have been nearly adequate in the lower 48. They spent time most days sitting on Phil's front porch or in The Cafe, reminiscing about the past.

"Morning, Phil, Randy," Jonah said, pausing to chat. It wasn't polite to rush off too quickly. And it was possible they might know something useful.

"Heard about the theft," Phil offered before he could ask.

"You tracking them down?" Randy nodded toward the road. The two men had obviously seen him studying the ground on his way down the hill.

"Trying to. You see any trucks go by earlier?"

"Sorry. Didn't see or hear a thing," Phil said, Randy nodding agreement.

Jonah only knew Randy well enough to pass the time of day, but Phil had played an important role in his early years in Koloshan. The first season he and his father had come to Alaska to fish, Phil had been generous with his time and the information he shared. There had been a lot to learn about local customs, including how to position your boat when fishing in locations where you had to take your turn for a beach pass to get to the fish milling near the shore. He had also given Jonah some invaluable tips on how to clean a fish while balancing against the roll of the boat as it was tossed around by wind and waves. And he'd shown them some places to fish that they would have been unlikely to discover on their own. Jonah had a warm spot in his heart for the man.

"Well, enjoy the sunshine," Jonah said as he continued following the tracks the truck had left behind.

"Good luck," Phil called after him.

He didn't run into anyone else as he worked his way toward the waterfront and the cluster of buildings that made up the commercial district of the village beyond the jail: a Presbyterian Church, a bank, two grocery stores, post office, liquor store, cold storage plant, café, city hall, ANB hall—Alaska Native Brotherhood, a fire-gutted laundromat, and on the hillside above the last building, a Russian Orthodox Church. Beyond, a row of houses was tucked up against the hillside, facing outward onto the sound. A few older houses built on piling extending out over the water were still occupied, but many had long since deteriorated, leaning at precarious angles, boards missing, debris from past residents left to rot, the occasional fragment dropping into the water and eventually either washing up on shore or drifting out to the inlet.

Many of the residents lived on the slope above the village, dirt side streets curving along the hillside, some in what locals referred to as the "new" homes built with government money after a major earthquake had destroyed many of the original houses. The government-built dwellings all looked alike, a boxy cookie-cutter design that could be put up quickly, totally lacking in charm or character. Not that Koloshan had ever been known for its picturesque buildings. But with water on one side, treed hills on the other, and mountains in the distance, there was a rugged Alaskan feel to the locale that appealed to those who valued the lifestyle more than appearances.

Once past the main part of the village, Jonah walked briskly toward the ferry terminal. It would have been faster by car, but you never knew what you might find or who you might run into when on foot. It had occurred to him that it was possible the thieves had chosen Thursday evening for the theft to coincide with the ferry schedule. If so, he might pick up the tracks again near there. It would have been a logical way to get the screen out of town in a hurry. There was, however, also the possibility that everything had been loaded onto a private boat. Maybe the choice of Thursday evening for the theft had been an intentional ruse to divert suspicion from a boat departure from the marina or from the docks at the cannery on the point. Although in such a small community filled with fishing boats that came and went at all hours, they would have risked being seen loading a boat with such conspicuous cargo.

He wasn't surprised when he picked up the tracks near the ferry terminal, and at the same time, he felt let down. At the back of his mind, he'd hoped the screen and other artifacts were still on the island. Now he would have to face the probability that they were indeed gone. A blackboard hanging on the terminal door listed the arrival and departure times for the ferry. Not that they varied much, except when impacted by weather conditions. If the truck had left on the midnight ferry for Juneau, by now the screen and artifacts could easily have been transferred to a private boat or another truck or hidden away somewhere.

Jonah jogged back to the Center. He considered trying to follow the tracks of the smaller truck, but decided it was more important to follow up quickly on the larger one, the one that most likely took away the screen. He got in his truck and drove to the jail. The next step was to make some calls to alert the authorities about the theft and ask for their assistance.

The note on the jail door looked like it had been written in a hurry: "Jonah—urgent—call me." It was signed Matt. Jonah quickly went inside and dialed the familiar number of the owner of the village cold storage plant on the waterfront. Maybe Matt had seen or heard something from a fisherman about the theft. He felt a surge of hope.

Matt answered on the first ring. "It's me," Jonah said.

"We've got a problem," Matt said.

"I know."

"You do?"

There was something about his tone that made Jonah think they might be talking about two different things. "Is this about the theft at the Center?"

"I heard about that. But no, we've got another problem. A wounded bear."

Jonah quickly switched gears. "Arrow or gunshot?" There was a local guide who occasionally accommodated hunters who wanted to try taking down a bear with a bow and arrow. A daunting undertaking that did not always go well. But a surprising number of people were willing to pay big bucks for the opportunity.

"Gunshot. It was some kids. They were out hunting early this morning on the east ridge. They surprised a big brown, and it turned on them. One of the kids got off a shot that they think hit him in the shoulder. But the bear ran away before anyone could finish him off. They followed the trail of blood, but they never caught up with him."

"They were damn lucky that bear ran off."

"I know."

"Anyone out looking for it?"

"The boys' fathers and a few friends just left. I'm going to spread the word to stay away from the area until they get him. I know you're caught up in looking for the Center thieves, but I thought you should know."

As Koloshan's only police officer, Jonah was technically responsible for the safety of the community, and sometimes that responsibly included dealing with wildlife issues. The east ridge was close to the island village, so an unpredictable wounded grizzly bear fell within his jurisdiction. But he was comfortable letting others handle the hunt for the wounded animal. He thanked Matt, hung up, and dialed the ferry terminal manager. When Ed answered and said he was home, Jonah told him to stay there; he would be right over; he had a few questions about who was on the midnight ferry leaving Koloshan.

Ed answered his door within seconds of Jonah's light rapping on the weathered door. The house was small and square with a living room that looked like it had been furnished in the 1950s. There were antimacassars on the arms and backs of the overstuffed couch and chairs and rows of knickknacks on ornate shelves on the walls. Ed's wife was in the kitchen fixing something to eat. She called out to Jonah and asked if he wanted some coffee.

"Yes, thanks," he called back. "That would be good."

The two men sat across from each other in the antiquated but comfortable room. Ed had lived in Koloshan for as long as Jonah could remember, but he wasn't a native and apparently not on the family-and-friends network because he hadn't heard about the theft. Jonah quickly filled him in, noting that Ed was just as appalled by the theft as those with more direct connections to the collection. Ed's wife came in with a mug of coffee but didn't join the two men. Jonah took a sip before getting to the point of his visit.

"I'm looking for someone, maybe more than one person. They would have been on the midnight ferry."

Ed looked thoughtful. "I've been thinking about it since you called. Not too many got on that ferry."

"I'm not necessarily interested in foot passengers," Jonah said. "Were there any trucks that you remember?"

"Trucks? Nooo. Two or three cars."

"No trucks?" Jonah suddenly felt hopeful. Maybe the truck had continued past the terminal. The haul could be stashed in the abandoned cannery or in the woods somewhere, hidden but traceable. Or, more likely, its contents could be on a boat headed who knew where.

"No." Ed shook his head with certainty. "That is, unless you're thinking of the co-op truck. It came in Tuesday afternoon and went out last night. Its usual schedule."

The co-op truck was a large, windowless truck used to bring groceries from Juneau once or twice a month, sometimes more often, depending on the season. The driver went to the school to unload. Anyone who had ordered groceries picked them up there. The local grocery was the largest customer, but the school and quite a few private individuals also participated. The truck was then parked in a vacant lot near the ferry terminal to wait for the return ferry to Juneau. The driver rented a small trailer for the nights spent in town and sometimes did odd jobs for the cold storage while waiting for the return trip. It wasn't an ideal arrangement for the driver, but jobs other than fishing weren't easy to come by.

As soon as Ed mentioned the co-op truck, Jonah pictured how perfect it would have been for transporting something big and heavy like the screen, although it seemed unlikely that anyone working for the co-op would be involved. Still, you never knew. He would need to check out the truck's tires. And he wasn't going to wait until it returned next week to do that.

"Heard about the bear," Ed said, as Jonah finished off his coffee and stood to leave. "Hope they catch up with him soon."

After leaving Ed's, Jonah drove to the jail to schedule a flight to Juneau. Then he headed to the school. One of the teachers was responsible for co-op deliveries. She could tell him about the driver and how to locate the truck in town. With luck, he could be in Juneau by about 2:00 p.m.

The school was on the main road, set back from the street away from traffic, but close enough for easy access during the winter. It was a modern building, built with state oil tax money during the oil boom a few years earlier. Unfortunately, when the oil revenues dried up, state funding for maintenance and equipment had been cut, leaving Koloshan with an Olympic-sized pool that it couldn't afford to maintain and operate. The pool was drained and useless, with a crack along one side that should have been repaired at the time by the out-of-town government contractor. And now probably never would be.

It was lunch hour. Kids were pouring out of the school when Jonah arrived, hurrying off to do whatever it was they did during that brief escape from classes. "Hi, Jonah," a young boy called as he ran past. "Hi, Jonah," several others echoed. Jonah was well known at the school. He gave talks on drugs and three-wheel and snowmobile safety. He also made it a point to drop by for a game of basketball from time to time. It was a popular sport in the village, and no one, besides Jonah—not even the athletic director—had played college ball. The kids were always eager to try out their skills against him and get tips on how to improve their game.

He found Mary Jo in the teacher's lounge. She looked up from her lunch when he came in, smiled, then turned back to the book she'd been reading. Jonah poured himself a cup of coffee in a Styrofoam cup, dug a quarter out of his pocket and tossed it into the saucer next to the coffee pot.

"Hello, Mary Jo," he said as he pulled up a chair across the table from her.

She looked up, cheeks suddenly flushed with color. "Hello, Jonah." She was very blond, with a pale complexion that he thought probably burned easily in the sun. On more than one occasion, Jonah had considered asking her out, but he wasn't sure he wanted the scrutiny that dating Mary Jo would inevitably bring about. And if the relationship didn't go anywhere, then what?

"I need some information," he said, getting immediately to the point.

Mary Jo's cheeks lightened a shade. "This is a business visit, then."

"Yes." Jonah was aware that several other teachers had surreptitiously glanced in their direction.

"Ask away." She set her book aside.

"Would you mind if we talked in private?"

"No, of course not." She got up and led him into the hall. "Is this private enough?"

"This is fine." The hallway was dimly lit, lined with historic pictures of Koloshan. Jonah knew that one was a picture of the Raven House screen taken by one of the early white settlers in the area, but he couldn't spot it without looking more closely. The doors nearby were all closed. Still, he kept his voice low. "What's your arrangement with the co-op?"

"I coordinate delivery requests. And we use the parking lot for pickups. The whole operation is subsidized by the state; otherwise, it would never pay for itself."

"Did you talk to the co-op driver on Tuesday?"

"Yes." She hesitated, then added "It was a new driver, someone I didn't know. Why?"

"Can you tell me his name?"

"He said it was Larry."

"There was something about the way she phrased the response that made him ask: "Do you have any reason to suspect that his name wasn't Larry?"

"I have no reason to think he would lie about his own name. I mean, after all, why should he?"

"Because it's possible the truck was used in a theft last night."

"Not the art center theft?" She sounded not only surprised, but shocked.

"Yes. So, I need to know everything you can tell me about this 'Larry.' I take it he didn't give you a last name."

"No. He was very flip when I asked who he was. All he said was 'You can call me Larry.'"

"Did he say what happened to your usual driver?"

"I assumed Gary was sick."

"What does this Larry look like?"

"Very average—late thirties, brown hair, medium height and weight, nothing that stood out."

"What was he wearing?"

"Jeans. And a brown jacket, I think. Something lightweight."

"Would you recognize him again?"

"Yes, I'm sure I would."

"And was there anyone with him."

"Not that I saw."

Jonah paused. "Think back. Is there anything at all that you can tell me that might help me identify him?"

Mary Jo thought a moment, then shook her head. "No. Sorry."

"Any mannerisms? Was he smoking? Chewing gum?"

"No. He wasn't from Alaska though."

"Why do you say that?"

"He asked me about the no-see-ums. He said something about never seeing so many bugs in his life." She frowned. "They *were* pretty bad on Tuesday. But if he'd been in Southeast for long, he would have come across them before, right?"

"That's good," Jonah said. "Anything else?"

"I don't think so. I wish I could remember something helpful."

"If you think of anything, give me a call, okay? And I need the address where I can find the co-op truck in Juneau. I'm going there this afternoon."

"I can't believe the co-op truck may have been involved in stealing all those wonderful artifacts. I should have followed my instincts and asked about the new driver."

"Don't beat yourself up—you had no way of knowing someone would try something like that."

When Mary Jo went to get the address, he walked up and down the school hall, sipping his cold coffee and looking at the pictures. It was the Koloshan of the grandfathers and great grandfathers of his local friends. But even in those pictures, the traditional native culture showed signs of being influenced by outsiders. There were native men in jeans, women selling local crafts along a newly constructed boardwalk, a tall church steeple rising high above the dwellings that lined the shore.

In one very early faded photograph of the old town there were totems proudly proclaiming the clan affiliations of those residing within hand-built, plank houses. But totems had not been compatible with the Christian beliefs. With the arrival of outsiders, they had been taken down and destroyed. Totem design was a craft that was re-emerging, but owing to how much had been lost, it was now as much an art form as a depiction of family lineage.

Mary Jo returned and handed Jonah a piece of paper. "We are all so sad about what happened," she said.

"I know everyone will be talking about the theft, but I would appreciate it if you didn't mention the role the co-op truck may have played; not until I know for sure."

"I'm hoping you find out someone else is responsible. Until then, I'll keep quiet. You have my word."

Jonah thanked her for the information and hurried off. He had just enough time to swing by his place and pick up an overnight bag before hopping the small float plane to Juneau.

NÁS'K

(THREE)

It was a clear day. Jonah sat next to the pilot. Another passenger, a visitor, was in the back with the luggage and a stack of boxes. He told Jonah he'd been staying at the Lodge while on a guided hunting trip, hoping to bag a bear, either a black or a brown. But he hadn't even seen one, let alone get a chance to shoot. "It was still a great experience," he said. "Went on a boat to a spot bears frequent. Camped out a couple of nights. Saw a lot of eagles. Ate fresh salmon."

The pilot was a young man in his late twenties who had once told Jonah that he hoped someday to get a job with a large airline. Meanwhile, he swooped around Southeast Alaska, hauling people and supplies to and from small towns located near water. Flying in a ramshackle float plane that bounced and twitched like a living thing could be unnerving if you weren't used to it. Trees and mountains appeared out of nowhere, barriers to be maneuvered around while the engine noises sounded like the plane was struggling to stay in the air.

Not long after they were airborne, the pilot turned to Jonah with a grin and mouthed "let's take a closer look at what's down there, okay?" Jonah knew what to expect, but he bet the guy in back would be surprised.

As the plane turned sideways and dipped down toward the beach, the man in back yelled "What's happening?" It was hard to talk over the noise of the engine, so Jonah turned and gave him a thumb's up to indicate things were fine. He didn't disapprove of the pilot's bit of fun, but he still sympathized with the passenger. He remembered how he had felt his first time in an aging Huey chopper in Vietnam. The experience had been an assault on his senses, everything closer and louder than he'd expected, and all the time the threat of instantaneous extinction.

The trees that lined the narrow strip of beach loomed large, almost close enough to touch. Then the plane banked and pulled away from the rocky hillside that had appeared from behind the trees. Jonah was sure the other passenger was probably scared out of his mind, but it would make a great story when he got home. Maybe it would make up a little for not getting his bucket-list kill.

They flew away from the beach, following the water highway. Twenty minutes later they were approaching Juneau. He could see Auke Bay below, the harbor sprinkled with boats. Houses and new construction followed the shoreline. Mendenhall Glacier shimmered bluish white in the distance as they swung low over a wide marsh. Then, abruptly, they were landing. Moments later they were safely on the water, gliding to a float.

It was two miles from the float to his destination. Jonah could have walked, but he was short on time and had called ahead for a taxi. They drove through the heart of Juneau, the capital of Alaska, a moderately small town of about 20,000. He loved Juneau's scenic setting, its surrounding mountains usually topped with snow well into June. The town began at the water's edge and pushed its way up against the tall mountains. Steep stairways linked the waterside buildings with those on hillsides, the rugged terrain only tenuously tamed by development.

The address Mary Jo had given him was on the other side of town. It was a small trucking service in a narrow building sandwiched between an auto repair shop and a deli. Jonah was relieved to see the truck out front, its roll-up door padlocked shut. Before going in, Jonah stooped to examine the truck's tires. He was in the right place, but no doubt far too late.

The woman at the desk facing the front door smiled at Jonah from behind an old, manual typewriter. In contrast to her typewriter, she was young and modern looking, with long red fingernails and matching lipstick. "Can I help you?"

"I need some information."

"Yes?"

"Can you give me the name and address of the driver of the truck out front? The one who brought it from Koloshan last night."

"Is there a problem?" The smile faded.

Jonah took out his identification and placed it next to the typewriter on her desk.

She glanced at his ID. "Was the truck involved in an accident?"

"No."

The woman blinked, watching Jonah as he put his identification away.

"It's a simple request," Jonah pointed out.

"It's just that . . ." She paused. "I don't want to get anyone in trouble." Her eyes probed Jonah's as if looking for reassurance.

"Someone's already in trouble. But I doubt it has anything to do with you." He waited, hoping he wouldn't have to get officious to get her to give him the information.

"Look, I've known Gary for a long time. I can't believe he would be involved in anything . . . well . . . I mean, I can't believe he would be in trouble with the law."

"Gary is your usual driver, right?"

"Yes."

"But he didn't drive last night, did he?"

"He was supposed to."

"But he didn't."

"He was scheduled to drive," she said firmly.

"But you know he didn't."

She shook her head in defeat. "I saw him on the sidewalk near his house about seven. When I asked why he wasn't out getting the co-op truck ready, he got real upset. He said he didn't want our boss to know he hadn't gone to Koloshan as planned. He said he'd had a family problem and that a friend had driven for him. He was worried that our boss would be mad if he found out."

"And would he? Have been mad, that is."

"I'm not sure. But Gary seemed to think so. He made me promise not to tell anyone."

"I appreciate how difficult this is for you, but I need Gary's address. I want to talk with him about the substitute driver."

"Is Gary in trouble?"

"I don't know yet. That's why I need to talk with him."

She picked up a file and pulled out a sheet of paper with names and addresses. As she was writing down the driver's information, Jonah said: "I would also like to take a look inside the truck. Do you have the keys?"

She paused and looked up. "What happened? What's this all about?"

"I'm sorry, but I can't say much at this point because I just don't have enough facts yet. If you could give me the keys?"

After just a brief hesitation, she said, "There's a spare set in the back room. I'll go get them." She got up, handed Jonah the address, and disappeared into the other room. Jonah listened, hoping he wouldn't hear her on the phone.

He should have cautioned her against calling Gary or her boss. Fortunately, she came back right away and handed him the keys.

"It would be best if you don't talk to anyone about this," Jonah said. "In case it turns out to be nothing. And do not call Gary to let him know I'm going to drop in on him." He tried to sound and look stern, acting like the police officer he was even though he didn't have any real authority in Juneau.

"I just can't believe Gary has done anything wrong."

"I'm not saying he did."

"He's a really good guy."

"I'm sure he is." Jonah thought but didn't add that sometimes good guys do bad things. "Is the truck scheduled for use today?" he asked as he turned to leave.

"No, not until tomorrow morning."

"Good. I'll bring back the keys, but after that, I'd like you to keep the truck locked up until I give you the okay, got that?"

"Yes." She looked and sounded distressed.

Jonah didn't like to tell someone that everything would be okay when he didn't necessarily think it would be, so he simply nodded goodbye and went to check out the truck. He didn't expect to find anything inside, but he still felt a rush of disappointment when he surveyed the empty interior. He took out the penlight he always carried with him and ran it around the inside of the truck. Unless there was evidence invisible to the eye, the truck wasn't going to be of much help. After he talked with the driver, he'd decide whether to ask the Juneau police to send someone to check for fingerprints.

Before he returned the keys, he also checked out the front cab area, careful not to leave any of his own fingerprints. Nothing of interest there, either.

On the next street over from the trucking service, Jonah caught a bus that took him within about six blocks of his destination. He climbed the steps up the side of the hill and walked briskly up the sidewalk that followed the drop-off until he reached the street he was looking for. Then he took a right into a modest residential community. Most of the houses had fenced yards with bushes and plants that were just beginning to show signs of life. It had been a hard winter, and everything was slow to blossom this year.

The house he was looking for had been recently painted. It stood out from those on either side of it like a bright new penny. Someone had planted a row of flowers along the front of the house, and a few were blooming. Jonah didn't recognize them by name, but he was impressed by the effort it must have taken to add color so early in the season.

As he opened the gate and started toward the house, he caught a glimpse of a small boy peering around some bushes at the corner of the house. "Hello there," he said. The boy promptly withdrew. When Jonah reached the front steps, he saw the boy sneak another look. This time Jonah pretended not to notice.

The door was opened almost immediately by a thin woman in jeans and a baggy pink sweatshirt. The woman looked past Jonah and called, "Billy? Billy, where are you?" She sounded nervous.

"He's over there." Jonah pointed in the direction he had last seen the boy.

"Billy, come inside this instant." It sounded like a very serious command. Jonah saw the boy slowly come around the corner and hesitate.

Jonah stepped to one side to give him some room, and the boy streaked past him into the house. The woman turned back toward her fleeing son and said, "I thought I told you not to go outside." Then, still obviously tense, she looked at Jonah. "What can I do for you?"

"I need to speak to your husband."

For a moment Jonah thought she was going to close the door in his face. Instead, she said: "He isn't here."

"Do you know when he'll be back?"

"No." She blinked as a look of concern washed across her face. Maybe she regretted admitting she was alone with her son. Whatever the reason, there was something wrong; Jonah was sure of it.

He took out his identification. "I really do need to talk with him, Mrs. Brock. And I have the feeling that you know why—" He left the comment hanging, watching her reaction.

"Is he in trouble?" she asked, obviously struggling to remain calm.

It crossed Jonah's mind that her husband may have kept her in the dark while saying or doing just enough to make her nervous. "I'm here to talk with him, not to arrest him. Now, can you give me some idea about where he is? It's a time sensitive situation."

Her eyes flicked from one side to the other, as if trying to make up her mind about what to do. Finally, she said: "He's painting a house about a mile from here. I'll get you the address." She went inside, leaving the door open a crack. Jonah leaned forward and listened, hoping she wasn't taking this opportunity to call her husband. He didn't hear anything though, and just a few minutes later she returned. As she handed him the address she said, "Gary wouldn't do anything dishonest. Never."

"You do know that he let someone else drive the co-op truck for him this week . . ."

She seemed reluctant to acknowledge it, but she slowly nodded.

"Do you know why?"

She turned away, a tear rolling down one gaunt check.

"I need to know why," Jonah said softly.

They could hear Billy in the other room, talking to himself as he played. The sound of his voice seemed to help her come to a decision. "He wouldn't have done it, but they threatened him. Threatened *us*. He had to let them take the truck. We've been worried sick ever since. I mean, what did they want it for? Why couldn't they just rent another truck? Did they do something bad?"

"Yes. They did something illegal and very bad." He decided to tell her the truth; it would soon be in the news anyway. "If I'm right about this, they stole some valuable native artifacts that required a large truck for transport. If you know anything that would help me find them, it would be in your best interest to speak up now." He paused, giving her time to make up her mind.

"Native artifacts?"

"Worth a lot of money."

"Oh no. I'm sure Gary had no idea—"

"But you said they threatened him."

"I heard him on the phone, telling someone to stay away from his family. When I asked him about it, he tried to pretend everything was fine. But I knew it wasn't. That's why I'm afraid to let Billy go outside alone."

"Well, they got what they wanted, but it still might be a good idea to keep an eye on your son for now."

"Will Gary be arrested? He only did it to protect his family."

Jonah didn't want to scare her more, nor did he want to give her false hope.

"If he helps me catch the guys who did this, he can probably make a deal with the prosecution. But he should have gone to the police when they first approached him."

As he stepped back, she closed the door quickly, and Jonah heard the lock click shut.

In addition to finding the artifacts, Jonah now had another reason to find the thieves. He didn't want anything to happen to Gary or his family. Whoever did this might consider them loose ends. Even Mary Jo might be in danger. Although they must have thought they would be long gone before anyone had a chance to identify the driver.

He jogged the mile to the house Gary was painting. Some of the distance was uphill, and Jonah was pleased that he was able to make it without breaking into a sweat. The previous year he had felt like he was getting soft. During the winter, he had shunned snowmobiles in lieu of walking and had worked out in the school gym at least three times a week. To further test himself, he had spent a week camping in the snow with a friend who was running some trap lines. It had been a great week, being outside, close to nature, with time to reflect and just "be."

Gary was on a scaffold, painting the eaves of the house with a spray gun. Slender like his wife, his overalls hung on him as though they had been purchased for someone much larger. The bottoms of his pantlegs were rolled up. His overalls and shoes were spattered with paint.

"Gary Brock?" Jonah called while staying several feet away from the scaffold, trying to avoid getting paint on his clothes.

The man stopped painting and looked down at him. His nondescript face was speckled with white spots.

"Who wants to know?" The man's voice failed to convey the belligerence his words implied.

"I'm Jonah St. Clair. I just talked to your wife—"

Before he could finish his sentence, the man leapt off the scaffold and was in his face. "What right do you have to bother my wife?" he demanded.

"I didn't 'bother' her. I just wanted to find you before you get yourself any deeper into this mess."

The man took a step back. "What mess?" His demeanor suggested he couldn't decide whether to be angry or frightened.

Jonah took out his ID and held it up for Brock to read. "I think you know what I want to talk to you about."

Brock scanned Jonah's credentials. "I have nothing to say." He took another step back.

"Come on, Brock. If someone *threatened* your family, you need my help to keep them safe. You're not going to be able to do this on your own. Not now that the police know about the truck and how you supplied it to the thieves."

"I didn't 'supply' it to anyone."

"Time is critical here," Jonah said firmly. "I'm trying to track down a truckload of very valuable native artifacts. And you know who stole them. So, are you going to cooperate, or do I need to arrest you as an accomplice?"

"Oh my God. What did they do?" He leaned away, his eyes widening as one hand covered his mouth.

"They used the co-op truck to transport stolen goods from Koloshan to Juneau. And, if it's at all possible, I need to catch up with them before they leave the area. Now, are you going to tell me who I'm looking for and where to find them?"

Brock's shoulders drooped, and his whole body sagged a little. "What did my wife tell you?"

"She doesn't seem to know many details. But she knows you're afraid, and she's afraid too. Frightened for you and for Billy. And if you don't help me, she'll be facing that fear on her own. And I think she—and you—are justified in being afraid. Do I make myself clear?"

"I have nothing to say," he said slowly.

"I don't have much time or I'd run you in right now." He hoped Brock didn't realize how much rigamarole was involved in arresting someone outside of his jurisdiction. "All I want to know is the name of the person who ⁿⁿproached you and whether you knew him before. If not, ₒw do you think he got your name?" He paused. When Brock didn't respond, he added, "If you don't care about what happens to you, think about your family."

"I can take care of them." His voice sounded less certain than his words.

"May I point out that you aren't with them *now*. Even if I don't arrest you, how do you take care of them at a distance? You going to quit working and guard them 24/7? For how long? We *will* catch them, you know. But trials take time. You'll be a prime witness whether you want to be or not. Or . . . maybe you'll be a co-defendant."

Jonah almost felt sorry for Brock. It seemed fairly obvious that he hadn't been a willing participant. But he was a link and, as such, possibly a target.

"I don't have anything to tell you," Brock repeated, sounding less certain than before.

"Maybe you don't realize how much trouble you're in. These men you're protecting, they didn't steal a few TVs or VCRs. A low estimate for the artifacts they stole is $1.5 million. *Irreplaceable* artifacts." He paused to let the gravity of the situation sink in. Brock had turned pale and looked like he needed to sit down before he collapsed. "If you help,

I may be able to convince the courts that you were a victim, not an accomplice."

"I didn't know what they were going to do. I swear I didn't."

"Then tell me what you can, and I promise to try and help you after they're caught."

"They told me they had some stuff in Koloshan that they needed a truck for. How was I supposed to know they were going to steal something?"

"If you thought they were on the up-and-up, then why did they have to threaten you to keep quiet?"

"They . . . they weren't all that specific; there was just something about how they made the . . . ah, request. They really wanted to use the co-op truck. And they gave me $200 to let them do my job. I . . . I couldn't afford to turn that down. You know how bills pile up when you have a family." He looked at Jonah, eyes pleading for understanding.

"Just tell me their names. I'll take it from there. And I'll do my best to keep you out of this." He wasn't sure he could overlook Brock's role in what had happened; it depended on how things evolved. The important thing was to track down the stolen goods and, if possible, get them back.

"There were two of them," Brock confirmed. "I'd never seen them before, and they didn't give me their names. And they didn't bring the keys back like they said they would. But they did drop off the truck. I checked." Jonah didn't point out that returning the truck had been a tactic to delay pursuit.

"Can you describe them?"

"Yes, I can give you a pretty good description." He took a deep breath. "If you catch them, do they have to know I told you all this?"

"I'm not sure," Jonah said. "But, as I said, I'll do what I can to keep you out of it. Not just for you, but for your family. Meanwhile, you keep an eye on your wife and son and maintain a low profile. As the only person who links them to the crime they committed, the thieves could consider you an *inconvenience*. And they won't know for sure how much you shared with your wife. You get that, don't you?"

DAAX'OON

(FOUR)

Jonah was surprised how good Gary Brock had been at describing the two men who had approached him about "borrowing" the truck. Maybe deep down he knew that at some point in the future he would have to tell someone what they looked like. Although he'd obviously hoped they would do whatever it was they wanted to do and disappear. And that no one would trace their actions back to him. He would have been $200 to the good and no one the wiser. But once you get mixed up with criminals, nothing is ever that simple. That was a lesson Brock was learning the hard way.

Although he'd told the Brocks to maintain vigilance, Jonah's instincts said they weren't really in danger. If the thieves were outsiders, they were either long gone or trying to get out of town. Still, it made sense to let the local police know there might be an issue. He could also pass along the descriptions of the two men. And maybe suggest they question some of the locals who could have taken the two men to Koloshan by boat or plane in the weeks before the theft. The men had undoubtedly needed to do some reconnaissance in advance. Of course, they could have come by ferry and stayed for a few days. Unless there was an insider who planned the heist for them.

Jonah called a cab to take him to police headquarters. It was far enough out of town that he didn't want to waste time by walking or waiting for a bus. Koloshan didn't have much of a budget for things of that sort, so, as he often did, Jonah was paying most expenses out of his own pocket.

The Alaska State Troopers supported policing in small villages that either didn't have their own police or in situations where more help was needed. They had a Property Crimes Unit whose resources Jonah could call on, but their main office was in Anchorage. Besides, the thieves had either passed through or were still in Juneau. If the Juneau police were willing to help, they could get on it right away with less red tape.

Jonah had known Lieutenant Ned Jacobson for about five years. They had an uncomfortable relationship, although on the surface it remained cordial. When Jonah had been hired as Koloshan's police officer, Jacobson apparently assumed that Jonah would flaunt his six years with the LAPD, and they'd bumped egos right from the start. In addition, Jacobson was short, and having Jonah tower over him didn't help their relationship. To top it off, Jacobson seemed to consider small villages as backwaters filled with people who couldn't make it elsewhere. Jonah also suspected there was a hint of racism in his attitude toward Native American villages.

Jacobson's secretary was pushing fifty, and the years were not treating her kindly. At the same time, she dressed for "the city" with every hair stiffly in place. Juneau was the center of her universe, and she made it clear that Koloshan was a small speck at the far edge. As usual, she acted as though she'd never met Jonah before.

"Name, please," she said in her perfunctory office demeanor.

"Jonah St. Clair." He fought to keep the impatience out of his voice.

"I'll see if Lieutenant Jacobson is available," she said.

Jonah stood at attention as she pushed several buttons on the intercom. She tried to wave him to a seat across the room, but he ignored the suggestion. "Officer St. Clair from Koloshan would like to see you when you have the time," she said into the receiver. Then she glanced up at Jonah with a patronizing smile. "Alright." She hung up and said to Jonah, "Please take a seat. Lieutenant Jacobson will be with you as soon as he can."

But Jonah wasn't about to "take a seat." Without a word, he headed down the hall to Jacobson's office.

"You can't do that," the secretary warned. Her voice was ruffled, but her hair remained perfectly in place.

He was inside Jacobson's office before his secretary had a chance to warn him. Jacobson was behind his desk with a coffee cup halfway to his lips. He checked his surprise at the intrusion and forced a genial grin. "Hello, St. Clair. I was just going to ask you to come in."

"Glad I could save you the trouble," Jonah said.

"Have a seat."

Jonah stood in front of the gray metal desk with its immaculate Formica top. With deliberate calm, he put his hands on the edge of the desk and leaned forward. From his chair, Jacobson had to tilt his head back to look at Jonah.

"This morning I called in an APB on the truck used by the co-op. Do you have any information on it yet?" He already knew the answer and was feeling irritated; hence his power play with Jacobson.

"As soon as we do, we'll let you know." Jacobson inched his chair away from his desk so he could look at Jonah without craning his neck.

"Has anything been done to trace its movements? Anything at all?"

"We've followed procedures," Jacobson said. "Now, why don't you sit down so we can discuss this like civilized men."

Jonah straightened up but did not sit down. "I'd think *procedures* might include trying to actually find the vehicle in question."

"Of course."

"Well, for your information, it's parked in its 'usual' spot. You might alert whoever is in charge and suggest they check it for fingerprints. Here's the address." He took the piece of paper he'd written the address on for himself and tossed it on the desk in front of Jacobson. "It needs to be done right away, so I'll wait while you make the call. When you're done, I have more to talk with you about." He knew he sounded hostile, but just the sight of Jacobson irritated him. And there was too much at stake to play power games.

The features on Jacobson's face seemed to be searching for the appropriate response. His thick eyebrows moved up and down as his mouth hovered between a frown and a neutral straight line. Jonah wondered if maybe this time he had gone too far. Maybe this time Jacobson's measured politeness would give way to real feelings. He almost welcomed the confrontation; he was tired of all the phony civility.

After a brief hesitation, Jacobson picked up his telephone. As soon as he started giving orders about the truck, Jonah sat down. He was prepared to hang around until he had enlisted all the help he could get from Jacobson. He also needed to contact the State Troopers. After all, there wasn't much that he personally could do if the artifacts were already in transit. Alaska was a vast place. He didn't have the resources or the clout to conduct a proper investigation on his own.

"All right," Jacobson said as he put down the phone. "Now . . ." He looked directly at Jonah. "Would you care to explain?"

"Sorry for getting in your face," Jonah said. "But in the message requesting the APB I noted that artifacts have been stolen from the Native Arts Center in Koloshan. They could be worth as much as 1.5 million." He paused when he saw the stricken look on Jacobson's face. He obviously hadn't realized the extent of the theft. "They were brought here by ferry in the co-op truck. If we don't act quickly, they will be on their way to who knows where. That's why I need your help."

"Have you contacted the State Troopers?"

"That's my next step. I started in Juneau because the truck is from here."

"What else do you want me to do?" He was obviously getting the message that Juneau might have some responsibility for at least part of the investigation.

"Send a team to find out if anyone was seen loading a large, wood screen on a boat this morning. The Raven House screen is about fifteen by eight feet. There were also two tall corner posts. That's why they needed the co-op truck. If anyone saw anything like that, find out if they know who owns the boat and where it was headed. Even if the boat has already left, maybe it can be tracked. Also, check trucks leaving by ferry. The Raven House screen won't be easy to hide. And timing is critical."

"Unless they broke it down, it probably didn't leave by air, right?"

"It would lessen the value if they took it apart, so I think it's more likely they shipped it somewhere by boat or truck."

"Okay. Anything else?"

"Yes, you can send out descriptions of two suspects. They either organized or helped execute the theft. They may even still be in possession of some or all of the artifacts." He handed Jacobson a sheet of paper on which he had written out the descriptions.

Jacobson read them aloud: "One thin but muscular, the other heavy set. Both average heights. Both white. Both with short brown hair. One may be wearing a brown jacket. Late 30s. No distinguishing scars, tattoos, or birthmarks on either, although the heavy-set man had a raised mole on his forehead. Possibly armed." He stopped and looked up. "Pretty average in every way, except for a mole. Not much to go on. And this is fishing season. As you well know, there are big boats from out of state, coming and going everywhere. Lots of strangers around."

"I didn't say it was going to be easy." Jonah looked directly at Jacobson. "This isn't just about Koloshan, you know. Every native in Alaska is going to relate to the loss. The press is going to be all over it." Jonah knew the latter would be important to Jacobson. And if his team found the artifacts, they would get the credit. It would be a big win for his department.

"Okay, I'll do my best."

It was getting late. Jonah called the State Troopers from the lobby of police headquarters and brought them up to speed on what had happened and what was being done so far. After getting the Juneau police and the State Troopers involved, he felt somewhat relieved yet not particularly hopeful. The truck would be checked for fingerprints, officers would ask around at marinas and search trucks at the ferry dock, State Troopers would send out alerts to possible transport sites. Everyone would be on the lookout for the two men, although given their average looks, unless they were discovered with the artifacts, it was doubtful they would be identified.

The thieves had done everything right so far, and they had a head start. Still, in Jonah's experience, you never knew when you would get a break in a criminal investigation. Although usually it was the result of hard work as well as a pinch of luck. He was willing to give it everything he had, but he wasn't feeling lucky.

He took a cab to Aurora Basin, one of the two main boat harbors in Juneau. In addition to the Juneau marinas, there was a marina across the channel at Douglas and another not too far away on the road at Auke Bay. There were also numerous large and small private docks up and down the channel. Jacobson would be sending out officers to investigate, but there was a lot of ground to cover, and Jonah had a couple of hours to spare before his return flight to Koloshan.

During the summer there was always a lot of boat activity, boats coming and going in Juneau—fishermen, vacationers, tourists. Still, it was a fairly close community. Fishermen and yachtsmen tended to keep an eye on other boats in the area, both for safety reasons and out of curiosity.

Aurora Basin was crowded with boats, and there were a fair number of people around. Nice days always brought boaters down to the docks. There were hulls to be painted, rails to oil, repairs to make—jobs that couldn't be done when the weather was bad. There were also stories to swap—what had happened during the winter and what they were looking forward to. Then there were the gawkers, the people who didn't own boats but enjoyed looking at them.

When Jonah interrupted people working on their boats to ask a few questions, they seemed to welcome taking a short break. And those strolling the docks were more than willing to talk. Unfortunately, no one had noticed anyone loading a large object on a boat that morning.

He left Aurora Basin and hiked along Egan Drive the short distance to Harris Harbor. The tide grid along the shore was lined with boats, impatient owners waiting for the last few feet of tide to go out so they could start work. All work had to be completed before the tide came in again, so the time pressure was absolute. Jonah made his way across the rocky slope between the grid and the road, pausing to talk to anyone willing to answer his questions. Again, no one could remember seeing anything as large as the Raven House screen being loaded onto a boat any time that day.

He left the grid area and wandered the docks in Harris Harbor until he decided his remaining time might better be spent elsewhere. The museum was only a short walk away, a walk that helped relieve the tension in his muscles, a tension he knew was caused by the stress of his unproductive search.

As he walked, he thought about the artifacts. What would happen to the screen? Would it disappear into some storeroom, preserved but unavailable for viewing, awaiting a time when the controversy over its acquisition had faded from memory? Or would it end up in a private collection, never to be shared with the public, nor with the people whose ancestors had created it? Jonah knew there were any number of unscrupulous collectors out there. Maybe even someone on the list of people who had expressed interest in purchasing the screen in the past. That's why he needed to talk to someone who knew how these under-the-radar purchases were made.

Once inside the museum he started toward the offices, then impulsively changed his mind. Instead, he wandered into the room where many native artifacts were on display. It was a dimly lit space, perhaps intentionally to hint at the mystery of the past. To Jonah, the white view of native life was often seen through a haze—smoke-filled longhouses and firelit ceremonies under dark skies. A romanticized lifestyle created by movies and stories that glossed over the day-to-day challenges of survival. Reality in the past had not been so kind, but then, reality seldom was. He confessed to having these images in his own head. Including people in traditional dress like the ones isolated in glass cases in the museum, their humanity removed by the way in which they were stiffly posed for viewing.

One of the centerpieces in the museum's Native American collection was a replica of a longhouse. As Jonah stooped to get through the low, narrow opening, the lure of ancient voices momentarily reached out to him. The chanting of the elders, the delicate ocean sounds of the Shaman's rattle, the pounding of dancing feet, the imposing presence of clan totems. In that instant he could envision the Raven House screen as it had been when it was a vital part of community life. Then the wonder of the moment passed, and he left the longhouse, stepping back into the present.

It had been a long time since Jonah had been in the museum. One of his favorite exhibits was still there though. He had caught sight of it when he first came in. Now he paused to take a longer look.

Eagles were common in and around Koloshan, but the bird's eye view of an eagle's nest as seen from the stairway of the museum was stunning. They were magnificent birds, aggressively majestic. And although as a rule he didn't like to look at stuffed animals, the museum eagles in their huge nest were an impressive sight.

He knew he was wasting precious time, but he'd found the brief visit to the longhouse and the glimpse of the eagle's nest motivating. A reminder of why he needed to try everything he could to track the stolen artifacts. He left the exhibits and hurried to the museum offices. He had met the curator on a couple of occasions and found him to be knowledgeable and approachable.

The door to the curator's office was closed. Jonah knocked, and a voice said, "Come in."

Dr. Edison was standing next to a desk covered with piles of books and papers. A small man, his immaculate dress in contrast to the untidy office—a beige sweater vest over a blue dress shirt, brown slacks, and polished leather shoes. Motioning Jonah to a chair, he continued flipping through one of the books on his desk. "I must be getting old," he said. "I can't seem to remember anything anymore. Oh well." He closed the book. "Jonah St. Clair, what brings you here?" He smiled and reached out to shake Jonah's hand.

"I need information."

He waved a hand around his office. "Well, I'm sure it's here somewhere . . . if I can find it." He appeared to be only half joking.

"Well, what I want to know is how a museum goes about acquiring artifacts, specifically native artifacts."

"What kind of artifacts?"

"Large artifacts, like screens and clan posts."

"The Art Center isn't considering selling the Raven House screen, is it?" His eyes lit up with interest.

"Not exactly. You see, the screen was stolen last night, along with all of the smaller artifacts in the Center."

Dr. Edison abruptly sat down. "Stolen? How is that possible?"

"That's what I'm investigating."

"No," he said, shaking his head. "What a tragedy. The screen is a lovely piece. Absolutely priceless."

"Someone is trying to put a price on it," Jonah said. "It's very important to the village that we get it back."

"I should think so! Well, what can I do to help?"

"You can give me some background on museums that might be interested in acquiring the screen and how they would go about it. Both legally and *unofficially*."

"You don't think some museum is responsible for the theft, do you?"

"It has crossed my mind that some museum director might not be too scrupulous about where particular works of art came from. Especially if they were willing to wait a while before putting them on display. That's why I want to know more about the process, how much discretion directors have to make large purchases, who monitors purchases, how and where such items might be stored, and how carefully provenance and ownership is tracked. That sort of thing."

"I see." He seemed to be considering his response as if reluctant to admit a museum might cut a few corners to purchase something they wanted for their collection.

"It seems to me I remember reading about other instances where museums have been sued for illegal purchases, including native relics and artifacts."

"Yes, that's true. But I don't know of any museum that's been accused of 'stealing' something. It's usually a question of 'buying' items from people whose legal right to them was questioned by someone objecting to the sale."

"That's a fine line."

"Provenance can be faked. Museum personnel aren't infallible."

"What if the ownership is disputed, what then?"

"Whoever wants to buy it would have to decide whether they are willing to engage in a legal conflict over ownership. That is, if they know at the time of purchase that ownership is disputed."

"Doesn't a museum have an ethical responsibility as well as a legal one to investigate ownership before buying something?"

Dr. Edison smiled. "Another gray area. For instance, I admit that I would rather see the Raven House screen in a controlled environment. It deserves to be preserved. If I didn't feel a connection to the local villagers and know how important the screen is to them, I might be tempted to rationalize buying it on the grounds that I was saving it." He paused. "On the other hand, some museums are simply competitive and want to acquire special pieces."

"Like the Raven House screen."

"Yes, I would put it in that category. But if they did so, at some point they'd want to show it—not hide it."

"And they might cut ethical or legal corners in pursuit of acquisition?"

"People are people whether a museum director or the CEO of an oil company."

"If, however, a curator purchases something and is unaware of its history, you would assume they would respond honestly to inquiries, right?"

"I would like to think so. Although once their money is gone, they might be tempted to let the dust settle in the hope that they would be able to hang onto their purchase."

Jonah looked very hard at Dr. Edison. Was his response hypothetical? The museum had a notable native art collection already, and the screen and other artifacts would greatly enhance its reputation. But even though Dr. Edison admitted that he thought the screen should be in a better environment, the purchase was a little too close to home and probably too pricey for a small museum—his response was likely hypothetical.

"Any idea where someone in possession of the screen might try to sell it? Assuming there are phony papers that could convince potential buyers that it would be a legitimate purchase."

"I'll give that some thought. Make some inquiries . . ."

"I would appreciate that. I'll send you a list of what was taken in case some of the smaller objects show up too."

"And if there is anything else I can do, don't hesitate to ask. The loss of an entire collection in a small village—" He left the sad thought hanging between them, an almost palpable shared pain.

On the way out, Jonah took one last look at the methodically displayed native artifacts on the main floor. Was this where history belonged, he asked himself? Where it could best be preserved for future generations? Or did the descendants of the creators of the artifacts have the right to let them deteriorate? If, for example, the families in Koloshan had refused to donate their treasures to the Center, they would have remained in homes, on shelves, in drawers or baskets, hidden away in closets. No one would have invaded their privacy to accuse them of not taking proper care of their property. Did the public acquire some kind of claim over these objects once they were on display? And, more importantly, were the artifacts of a people so inextricably linked to their past that their theft also robbed them of an integral part of their culture?

KEIJÍN

(FIVE)

It was almost 9:30 p.m. when Jonah's float plane touched down in the Koloshan harbor. Although it was late, it was not completely dark. By the end of May dusky twilights replaced the Alaskan winter darkness. Until August there would be varying degrees of visibility throughout the night; then darkness would return.

They taxied over to the end of the airplane float. The pilot pulled in close, and Jonah leapt out. There was a breeze that held the airplane against the dock, so Jonah had to help push off. Then he stood and watched the small aircraft as it took flight and headed back toward the strait, the engine noise slowly fading as it gathered speed for its ascent before disappearing into the distance, lost in the shadows of water and wilderness.

Jonah noticed a dark cluster of no-see-ums hovering at the bottom of the ramp that led to shore. They never bothered him, but he knew that many residents and fishermen considered them worse than a nuisance. To some, their bites triggered extreme itching and easily became infected. Jonah was glad he didn't have to wear bug repellant or the popular alternative, Avon Body Lotion, to keep them away. It always made him smile to catch the sweet scents of lotion mingling with the lingering smell of fish on a fisherman.

As he walked down the dock, he automatically checked the floats for anything suspicious. An outboard motor had been stolen the week before, but he had quickly traced it to one of the locals who claimed he had borrowed it for a boat ride. Let him tell that to their local magistrate—Jonah's job was to identify and apprehend the guilty, not to convict or to sentence them.

Instead of heading for home, Jonah stopped by the jail to see if there were any messages. He left thumbtacks on the door in case someone wanted to leave him a note. Some managed to stuff messages under the door during the summer when the wood dried and shrank just enough to allow a piece of paper through. Otherwise, when he was gone, anyone who wanted to get in touch left word with Matt Clark at Clark Cold Storage. Matt had been running the cold storage for a couple years when Jonah and his dad started fishing out of Koloshan. Fifteen years older than Jonah, he was both mentor and friend. Matt was the only other person with a key to the jail. Jonah was hoping to see a message from Matt on his desk that said the wounded bear had been dispatched.

There were no messages tacked to his door, but there were two notes from Matt inside. The one on top said that Austin Mann, the archeologist from the University who was temporarily working out of the Center while on an assignment, was trying to get in touch with him. The other message was about the bear—it was still out there somewhere. They were going to hunt for him again tomorrow.

Jonah dialed Matt's home number, and Matt answered on the first ring. "No luck on the bear, huh?"

"Not even a sighting. Maybe he went off into the woods and died."

"That's possible, but doubtful if he was only hit in the shoulder. I'm glad they're going to keep looking."

"Any news on the screen?" Matt asked.

"A few leads, but nothing too promising."

"What do you think of the odds for recovery?"

"Not sure. Probably not good, but I'm going to keep trying. And the Juneau police and State Troopers are on it too."

"Is there's anything I can do?"

"Thanks. Not now, maybe later. I'll let you know. But the reason I called was to ask if Mann said what he wanted?" Mann had been hired by the state to supervise the excavation near an old native burial site where a new stretch of road was going in. He was supposed to prevent the workers from destroying any remains or relics they might uncover. In recent years, the state had become more concerned about preserving antiquities and not upsetting locals, and they were providing funds to see to it that things were done properly.

"I don't think it's about the robbery, if that's what you're wondering. He mentioned something about a trip to the old village site. He asked if I thought you know its location."

"I once mentioned to him that I did. He doesn't believe me, huh?"

"Well, you aren't native, so he has his doubts." Matt laughed.

"Dennis took me and Dan there back when I was living with him." Dan and Jonah had been best friends when he was fishing with his father out of Koloshan. Jonah's mother died unexpectedly during a fishing season when Jonah was thirteen, and his father had been devastated, unable to cope with his own grief let alone Jonah's. It was decided that Jonah would remain in Koloshan for a while. There was no room with Dan's family, so Jonah ended up staying with Dennis Gray, Dan's grandfather. It was supposed to be a short-term arrangement, but the weeks had turned into months, and the months into two and a half years. As sad as he'd been to lose a parent, and in some ways both parents, Jonah had treasured his time with Dennis.

"Since he's thinking about you as a guide rather than a local, I'm a bit suspicious about his intentions."

"You think he wants to dig around to see what he can find?"

"We didn't discuss it, but that wouldn't surprise me. And what if he does want to dig for relics or artifacts? I mean, just because he's been given the authority to oversee the road project doesn't mean he has blanket permission to mess with other native sites."

"I don't think there's any law that keeps him or anyone else from *visiting* the site. After all, it was abandoned over sixty years ago. But if he wants to do more than look, I think he should talk with the village council. I'm just sorry I ever admitted knowing about it."

After Jonah hung up, he thought about what he would do if Mann asked for directions to the site. Or worse yet, if he wanted Jonah to take him there. He would, of course, tell Mann he needed to get permission from the council, but it was possible the council would say "yes," and Jonah would still be on the hook to help Mann out. Then he reminded himself that it wasn't something he should even be thinking about now. One of the lessons Dennis had emphasized during the time Jonah spent with him was that you didn't worry about problems that hadn't occurred yet; you were supposed to focus on being in the moment because you couldn't control the future until it was the present.

How different the Tlingit philosophy was from the carefully scheduled and planned lives of the people he came in contact with in L.A. He'd often thought that was one of the reasons his father had turned to fishing. You needed to do *some* planning to succeed as a fisherman, but for the most part you lived in the moment, responding to the elements and learning how to enjoy fishing when it was good and figuring out where the fish were when it wasn't. Time spent with Dennis had shaped much of Jonah's view of the world and continued to be an anchor for his life.

Jonah glanced at the monthly calendar on his desk. He hadn't flipped the page from last month, and it was already the second week of the new month. There wasn't much on last month's calendar. But he had underlined a notation to check into prices of telephone answering machines. That had been on the previous month's to-do list too. Maybe even the one before that. It made more sense to get an answering machine than to continue relying on Matt to pass along messages. Matt was willing, but it was unfair to put that burden on him when a machine could do the job. Another option was to have the secretary at city hall take his messages, but then they became public. On the other hand, having Matt help out like that was in some ways a symbol of their friendship. Hell, maybe he shouldn't be in a hurry to get an answering machine.

He flipped the calendar page to the current month.

As he stood up his eyes were drawn to the framed photograph on the wall next to the door. He had borrowed it from the school's collection. It was an aerial shot of Koloshan taken about thirty years ago. The village looked much the same as it did now. The native culture didn't seem to place importance on progress or change for the sake of change. Villagers usually waited until they really needed a new house or a better car or to replace something on the brink of failure. To Jonah, this seemed to provide a material continuity you didn't feel in all-white communities. Of course, there had been minor changes, a few houses destroyed by fire, an old shack he remembered from his youth that had finally collapsed, some improvements to the marina. But the main difference was all the logging roads and cleared areas not too far from the village. Maybe that was why they'd had more trouble with bears lately.

Jonah switched off the light and went out to his official pickup. The engine turned over a few times but wouldn't start. It was possible the battery terminals were dirty or the battery itself was ready to give up the ghost. It might be the starter. He got out and headed for home on foot.

The village was quiet. There weren't many people about, no cars slicing the silence with engine noise, no hum of commercial activity, no sounds of nightlife revelry; only dim elongated squares of light from homes to indicate there were people inside going about their lives. This was something he had missed in L.A.—peaceful evenings when it felt like everyone was settled in, lives at rest, problems at bay. At least for the moment.

He turned down the familiar street and started up the hill. It was reassuring to know who lived in each house he passed. Many of the families had been part of the community for generations, their numbers relatively stable since the purchase of Alaska from the Russians in 1867. The non-natives who came to Koloshan to work also tended to stay. Most came seeking a simpler existence and a return-to-the-land lifestyle. Some came to teach in the school. Others came to pursue easy money and hung around even after those dreams died.

The house Jonah had purchased when he returned to Koloshan looked like most of the other houses in the village, square and plain. The front yard stwas overgrown, and there was a long-neglected vegetable garden out back. But it was home.

As he drew near, he could make out someone sitting on his front porch—Ellen Williams. Something must be wrong or she wouldn't be waiting for him at his home. "Ellen," he said as he drew near. "What's up?"

She stood and said, "Jonah, I need to talk to you." In the shadowy light she could almost have been lifted directly from one of the historic photos in the school hallway. She had wide, dark eyes set in a broad face with her long, dark hair pulled back and gathered at her neck. But her pastel-colored slacks and bulky sweater conflicted sharply with that image. He had known Ellen for a long time, since he first came fishing with his dad, when they were both carefree youngsters.

"Sure. Come on in." Jonah went in ahead of her and switched on the lights. The room was tidy but spare. The minimal furniture had been purchased for comfort and for his height. There was a bookshelf against one wall. Except for a few photos, the walls were bare. He'd been meaning to buy some pictures, maybe a Winslow Homer. He liked the one of a man and boy pulling a herring net into a skiff on a dark, lively sea.

"Please, sit down. Can I get you something to drink? I'm going to fix myself a cup of instant coffee. And I have tea."

"Instant coffee would be good."

Jonah went into the kitchen and put on the water. It struck him that Ellen was nervous about something. Was it about the screen? Her husband was a fisherman. He would be going out for halibut again soon; Jonah remembered seeing his boat at the dock, piled high with gear and markers. Maybe she had a family problem that she wanted to talk to him about. Sometimes villagers treated Jonah almost like a counselor or a social worker.

When he handed her the mug, she took it in two hands, her fingers trembling slightly. "Thank you."

He sat down and leaned forward, "What's wrong, Ellen?"

"It's Will." She took a sip before setting the mug down on Jonah's hand-made, wood coffee table. "I was afraid you weren't coming back tonight." She looked down at her hands. "You've been trying to track the missing artifacts, haven't you?"

"Yes, I just got back from Juneau."

She looked up at him. "Have you found out anything?"

"Not yet." He waited for her to say something more. She picked up her coffee, took another sip and choked on it. After she recovered, she put the mug down again.

"Oh, Jonah," she said, her voice tight with emotion. "I don't know what to do."

"Tell me about it. Maybe I can help."

"It's Will. He's disappeared."

"What do you mean, *disappeared*?"

"He left sometime last night, and . . . I haven't seen him since." She wrapped her arms around her body and leaned back. "I'm so scared."

"Ellen, I have to ask—was Will mixed up in the theft of the artifacts?"

"No. He couldn't be—" She shook her head, then looked down. "I don't know. I just don't know."

"But he left sometime last night, what time?"

"A little before eleven. He tried to slip out without me knowing, but I heard him. I asked where he was going. He said he couldn't sleep and was going out to take a walk."

"Has he done that before?"

"No, never. But . . . well, I was tired, and I thought he'd had too much coffee or something. I fell back asleep. It wasn't until this morning that I realized he hadn't returned. He'd taken the pickup and gone somewhere."

"You've checked the boat?"

"Uh huh."

"And you've talked to his parents and anyone else he might be with?"

"Yes."

"Did anyone say they'd seen him today."

"No." Her voice lapsed into a low whisper. "No one has seen him all day."

"And you didn't see his truck anywhere . . ."

"No. He promised to help Randy's son with his engine today and never showed up."

"Okay, Ellen. I know this is painful, but I need to know who you've talked to and what they've said." He took out a notepad, and as she went over her conversations with people about if they'd seen Will, he jotted down names and conversation highlights. She had covered a lot of ground, talking to everyone he would have talked to. When she finished, he asked, "Is there anyone you haven't contacted that you want me to get in touch with?"

"There's no one else I can think of." She slowly shook her head again.

"Was there anyone he spent time with this week or talked to more than usual?"

She stiffened visibly, her voice suddenly stronger. "You mean like someone he was planning a theft with?"

"It's the timing, Ellen. It's obvious that it's crossed your mind."

"Look, Will was in favor of selling the screen and some of the other artifacts, but that doesn't make him a thief."

"That's not what I'm saying. If I remember right, Will's grandfather believed he had legal claim to the screen." Jonah needed to talk with Dennis about these disputes. Make sure he had the facts right. When the Center opened, there had been a rush of contributions, everyone trying to outdo the other. Like a Potlatch. No one had worried about ownership claims. Afterwards, however, when the question of whether to sell some of the artifacts was brought up, there were sharp divisions of opinion about who had the right to make such decisions and who should benefit financially from a sale.

"Yes, but Will wouldn't do something like that, even though . . ."

"Even though?"

"Well, we could use the money. I guess you know that. But Will wouldn't steal. I know he wouldn't."

Jonah suddenly recalled that Ellen and Will's last child had been born with multiple birth defects. Very few in the village had health insurance; he doubted Ellen and Will did. And not only were operations expensive, but the logistics of getting to a hospital from Koloshan added to the cost.

"Maybe he didn't think of it as stealing," Jonah suggested gently. "Maybe he thought of it as taking what rightfully belonged to him."

Ellen looked at the empty wall behind Jonah, then directly at him. "That's what I'm afraid of. I'm afraid he got mixed up in something awful and . . . oh, I just want him to be alright."

So did Jonah. No matter what Will had done. He liked Will. "I want to find him, too. For your sake, and for his. But I need something to go on, somewhere to start."

"I'm not sure. But not with his father. He's really angry about what happened." Two concentration lines creased her forehead. "Maybe go see Lou. Or Mike. I talked to them briefly, but maybe they've learned something. Or maybe they'll tell you something they didn't want me to know."

"Okay. I'll get on it right away. You go on home and try to get some rest." He walked her to the door. "And if you hear anything or think of anyone else you want me to talk to, let me know."

After she was gone, he poured himself another cup of coffee and got out the telephone. It was going to be a long night.

Like Will, his buddies Lou and Mike were fishermen. Lou was a couple of years younger than Will, and single. He had a small commercial salmon troller of his own, but he also crewed on the larger boats from time to time. Jonah tried to remember if Lou had any special link to the artifacts, but he couldn't recall. The question hadn't seemed important in the past.

It was getting late for phone calls, but Jonah didn't want to wait until morning. He caught Lou at home watching television. He didn't seem surprised that Jonah wanted to talk to him. In fact, it seemed to Jonah like he had been expecting him to call. He agreed to come by Jonah's place and said he'd be there in about ten minutes.

Next, Jonah called Mike. Jonah knew that Mike and Will had been friends since they were kids. They had both started out salmon fishing from skiffs and had slowly worked their way up into larger boats. Mike was fiercely independent and very vocal about his dislike for the increasingly strict fishing regulations that he believed threatened his ability to make a good living. But Jonah couldn't remember his stand on keeping versus selling the screen.

Mike's wife answered the telephone. When she found out it was Jonah, she sounded upset. "Mike's laying down," she said.

"Would you ask him to come to the phone? It's important."

"Can't I take a message?"

"No, sorry. I need to talk to him."

Reluctantly, she agreed to get Mike. When he came on the line, he didn't sound like someone who had been sleeping; he sounded uneasy. Without mentioning why, Jonah asked if Mike could come by for a talk.

"It's late," he protested.

"I know. Lou is on his way. I'd like to talk to the two of you."

There were a few seconds of silence. "It's about Will, isn't it?"

"Yes. I wouldn't ask you to come over if it wasn't urgent. It's better to talk here than at your house."

"All right. I'm on my way."

A few minutes later, Jonah saw Lou and Mike coming down the street together. Maybe he should have talked to them separately; they could be coordinating their stories. Although why would they need to do that?

They came in and made themselves comfortable in his living room, like they had on previous social occasions. Only this time it was clear that things were different. There was no beer, no banter, just semi-formal politeness.

"We can't tell you anything you probably don't already know," Mike said straight off.

Lou nodded. In contrast to Mike's compact, muscled body, Lou was thin and wiry. Both were serious men, more ambitious than many of their peers. They kept their boats in good condition and were always talking about expanding into other fisheries to make more money.

"Can't or won't?" Jonah asked, his tone flat and firm.

The two men exchanged looks but didn't respond.

"So, you have no idea where Will might have gone." It was a statement, not a question. "But you know how worried

Ellen is and how she has been searching everywhere for him."

"We haven't seen him around today," Mike said, apparently speaking for both of them.

"If I'm going to find Will, I need some information."

"We'd help you if we could." Mike met Jonah's eyes for an instant, then looked away.

"Can we talk off the record, as people who care about Ellen and Will?"

"There's nothing we can tell you," Mike said. He seemed calm, but Jonah noticed Lou restlessly moving his feet, as if he was itching to get up and leave.

"I have my suspicions," Jonah said pointedly. "And it would be better if you came clean now, better for everyone."

Lou and Mike didn't say anything. Lou's knee started bobbing up and down.

"I can't force you to level with me. But if there's any chance Will is in danger, don't you owe it to him to tell me what you know?"

Lou now looked like he was in pain, but Mike remained stoic.

"I mean it when I say that I'm more concerned about Will's safety than anything the three of you might be involved with."

Still nothing.

Jonah sighed. "OK. I guess if that's the way you want to play this, there's nothing I can do. If you change your minds about talking to me, or if you think of some way I can help, let me know."

Lou and Mike stood up at the same time, as if connected by invisible bonds. "Thanks, Jonah," Lou said. "We appreciate what you're trying to do."

Do you, Jonah thought? But he held back his frustration and anger. He sincerely hoped that if something happened to Will because they were unwilling to share what they knew that they would be able to live with the consequences. Because he had a bad feeling about Will's disappearance. And he was determined to get to the bottom of things.

TLEIDOOSHÚ

(SIX)

It was early morning. The sun was not yet visible on the horizon, but the night's gray world was slowly easing into daylight. It was like watching the development of a Polaroid picture—staring at the blank photo as shapes began to emerge, gradually becoming more defined, until color and details burst forth. Of course, watching the sun come up involved more senses than when developing film. The sounds of early morning critters searching for food, the smell of damp earth and pine needles. And the lingering aroma of coffee from his thermos.

Jonah checked to see how much gas he had in his Jeep and was pleased that he would be okay for a while. The Jeep was a recent purchase that had cost far more than he should have paid for a vehicle that would soon rust in the salt air. No one expected any type of motor vehicle to last in Koloshan. Everywhere you looked there were rusted out auto bodies or fenders held in place with rope or duct tape. But the Jeep had appealed to him because it was compact and somewhat sporty while still rugged enough to withstand the punishment of local logging roads and rough terrain. And with the official truck not working, he had to use his Jeep.

His first stop was Will's driveway. He wanted to see what the tire prints from Will's pickup truck looked like. And not only were there some clear prints, but he couldn't have asked for anything easier to track—there must have been a piece of something stuck in a groove, leaving a deep, jagged indentation as the wheel went around. It was too bad he hadn't known about the connection yesterday. Sometimes you only see what you're looking for; not necessarily everything that's right in front of you.

Back at the Center, there were still two cars in the parking lot. Although weather and vehicle traffic had obliterated most of the tracks, he still managed to find an impression of Will's pickup at the exit, although he couldn't tell which way he had turned. Guessing that he'd followed the truck, even though he knew Will had not caught the ferry, Jonah walked down the hill looking for the truck's tire prints. He finally gave up and went back to the Center and got his Jeep. He drove to the road where the truck had turned right toward the ferry and went on foot again to search further.

He felt certain he was going to find more of those distinctive tracks, but he didn't. He ended up jogging back to the intersection where he'd left his Jeep and returned to the Center. This time he tried going in the other direction from the parking lot. Will hadn't gone home after he parted ways from the truck, and if his pickup truck had ended up in a residential area or anywhere nearby, someone would have noticed. And they would have told Ellen. The most logical options remaining were that Will had either driven to the airport or followed the main road out of town to where it connected with a logging road.

There was no sign of Will's truck at the airport, and there was no indication it had been parked there. Jonah was almost relieved; Will hadn't run away. Then again, maybe he should have been hoping for that outcome.

On the road heading to logging territory, he searched several sections of road before he came across one distinct indentation in a tire print that he felt fairly certain was from Will's pickup truck. But after that, tire tracks crossed and crisscrossed each other, destroying the tread marks he was trying to follow. Each time he came to a crossroad, he made a guess as to which way Will had most likely gone. He would drive up the road a short distance, pull over, and get out to look for the tracks. If he didn't find any, he would go back to the crossroad and try another direction. It was a tedious and slow process. Time and again, Jonah lost the trail. Each time he feared he would never pick it up again, yet somehow, he did.

Mile by mile he worked his way farther and farther from the village. At one point, he found a print that suggested Will may have followed a logging road that angled off toward the east. Another truck, a heavy one with big tires had passed that way recently. Maybe a logging truck. It had obliterated the other tracks. Still, if Will had started out in that direction, it seemed worth it to go a little farther.

The sun had made its debut. It was going to be a bright, clear day, the kind of day that made Jonah want to walk far into the woods with nothing but a gun, a thermos of coffee and a couple of candy bars. He liked sitting on a log, enjoying the view while taking a coffee-and-candy break. He knew he drank too much coffee and that his sweet tooth was probably not healthy. But on hunting trips with his father when he was young, they always took along large Hershey bars for what his father called "quick energy." More likely, he'd simply liked chocolate.

The Jeep bumped over the uneven road. If the screen had been taken off island, and Will was involved in the theft as Jonah now suspected, then why had he driven his pickup truck up here? It didn't make sense.

He came to a logged off area. On either side of the road there was nothing to see but a tumble of stumps and tangled piles of uprooted vegetation. Everything was gray-brown— rotting tree limbs, clumps of dirt, withered foliage. Jonah knew the area would look like that for a long time, as though it had been struck by some sort of natural disaster. But eventually the trees and brush would reappear, and the forest would heal itself. At least that's what the proponents of logging argued. The timber industry created jobs and was a profitable business venture. Even many locals defended them by arguing there was plenty of wilderness to accommodate the needs of the community *and* the timber industry. Besides, the logging roads made it easier for local hunters. It was a trade-off that satisfied enough residents to let it happen without much opposition.

He passed through the logged off area into a stand of second growth timber. There was still no sign of Will's truck. The road branched. He stopped the Jeep and got out to examine the road but found nothing to indicate whether Will had passed that way. Eventually he would have to make a more thorough search of the entire area, but for now he decided to head for higher ground. Maybe he would find some tracks farther up.

The road got worse, and Jonah considered turning back. Then he came around a curve and caught a flash of light ahead in the trees. A vehicle perhaps? He pulled over to the side of the road, grabbed his rifle, and got out to have a look on foot.

It was quiet, a few birds chittering in the distance, but no sound of human voices. Jonah moved forward slowly, uncertain what he might find. He bushwhacked his way through thick underbrush surrounding a stand of tall trees to a clearing. And there it was: Will's pickup truck. The front door was open, and the tailgate was down. Why would Will leave it like that? And where was he?

Smashed brush between two trees suggested how the truck had been driven into the clearing from a side road. The ground was damp with runoff from a small stream that wound its way down a gully at the far side of the clearing. Jonah walked around the vehicle, studying the surrounding area for some indication as to where Will had gone. The ground on the driver's side had been disturbed. He knelt to take a closer look. There were two palm prints in the dirt, as if Will had fallen out of his truck and put his hands up to break the fall. From there it looked as though he had crawled toward the woods.

At the edge of the clearing, Jonah came across the scene of another disturbance. This time there was what looked like blood pooled and splattered across the moss and brush. And there was another set of prints—those of a large bear.

Jonah stood very still, listening.

Was it possible that this was the bear the kids had wounded? What if Will had inadvertently come across the animal? But why had he been crawling away from his truck in the first place?

He didn't have far to search after that. Just a few feet beyond the area where the encounter had occurred, he came upon a pile of leaves and brush. A wave of nausea hit him as a rank smell wafted in his direction. He stood there and stared at the pile, dreading the task before him. He knew bears often hid their kill, leaving it out of sight until they were hungry. Jonah had seen bear caches before, and he was certain that was what he was looking at.

It took him a few minutes to calm himself. He knew bears never went too far away from their caches; they hung around to protect their next meal from other predators. If the bear was nearby, Jonah needed to locate it before it located him. Keeping his gun ready to ward off an assault, he quickly scouted the area.

He found no recent signs to indicate that the bear was still nearby. Maybe the villagers had driven it further into the woods. Or maybe this bear was in pain and not behaving like he might have under normal circumstances.

Reluctantly, Jonah returned to the cache. He didn't want to look. As long as he avoided looking, there was hope that he was wrong. He had seen too much death in Vietnam, ugly, violent death. And he had also once seen a person who had been mauled by a bear. If Will had tangled with a bear, it would be a terrible sight.

He didn't want to look, but he had to. He remembered reading about a person who had been attacked by a bear and left alive in a cache. Another hunter had come along and rescued him. That was why he had to check. Even if Will was there under the pile of leaves and sticks, there was the possibility he was still alive. A horrifying thought.

Jonah used a stick to push aside some of the debris. The smell of forest floor and decay rose up from the pile. He probed the clump of leaves. There was something there, something he feared was a human body. He brushed away some of the leaves. The first thing he saw was a partially severed arm with the hand badly mangled. He knelt and touched the skin on the arm. Without looking further, he was certain the person was dead. He swept more brush aside and uncovered what was barely recognizable as a head.

People unfamiliar with bears usually thought that they mauled people by striking at them with massive paws, the way a cat plays with a mouse. But a bear, after a few initial swipes, will take the head of its prey in its mouth and shake it to end the struggle.

Will was missing most of the top of his head and the side of his face, but there was enough left for Jonah to tell who it was. In another few days, after the bear returned or the body had attracted more wildlife, nothing might have been left except bones. And those might have been scattered around.

At least Ellen and his other relatives would have a body to bury.

Jonah stood up and turned away from the cache, taking a deep breath to clear the smell of death from his lungs. Then he made another brief search of the area to make sure the bear wasn't lurking nearby. Finally, he braced himself to face the task of removing Will's body from the cache. Even if he could raise someone on the radio in his Jeep, he didn't want to hang around and wait for help; it was better to stay active.

He hurried back to his Jeep, got a tarp, and laid it on the ground next to the cache, acutely aware that the bear could return at any moment. There were bits and pieces of material and skin fragments everywhere, splattered with dried blood. Jonah forced himself to look at the body, to examine it dispassionately, to think of it as a specimen and not what was left of Will. He needed to be able to describe what he saw for his report. Later, he could return and have a closer look at the site.

Wrestling Will's remains onto the tarp was a gruesome chore, the bear scent filling his nostrils, clinging to everything like a putrid version of L.A. smog. Once he got it contained, he wrapped the tarp around the remains, tied it with rope, and dragged it back to his Jeep.

Jonah was consciously trying not to think of what it must have been like for Will in those last minutes of life, but his mind wouldn't let go of the image. It was like a lingering nightmare that you wanted to end but couldn't control. Nor did he want to think about what it was going to be like to tell Will's family about his death. And . . . there was one more thing he didn't want to think about but would have to eventually face: the wounds at the base of what remained of Will's head that looked suspiciously like they had been caused by something *other* than a bear.

He opened the rear compartment and wrestled the wrapped body inside, struggling to keep it contained within the tarp. Bits and pieces of what was once Will seemed determined to escape, ending up resting against the interior of the Jeep. Suddenly Jonah was angry with himself—for God's sake, the man had been half eaten by a bear and here he was worried about making a mess in the back of his precious Jeep. He slammed down the door and pressed his forehead against the cool surface. Why did Will have to die like that? No matter what he had done, he didn't deserve to die like that. No one did.

Turning away from his Jeep, he tried to focus on what he needed to do next, but his thoughts kept returning to stories he'd heard about bear attacks. Like the guy who had remained conscious during an attack and afterwards described how he had heard his bones crunch as the bear chewed on his shoulder and bit into his head. Saved by a friend, he lost part of his scalp and the full use of an arm, but he'd survived. Then there were the boots found with nothing but toes in them next to a camera that the victim had used to document the attack. Nature was appealing in so many ways, but it was neither kind nor forgiving.

On the journey back to Koloshan, the smell of bear mingled with the smell of death and blood. He rolled down the window and avoided looking at the dark smudges on his shirt and hands. Perhaps, he thought, in the final analysis it didn't matter how you died. A violent death seemed somehow worse though, especially to those left behind, but the result was the same. In some stways, it might have been harder for Will to have died a slow death from cancer or heart disease. Any way you looked at it, dead was dead. Final and forever.

Jonah tried to focus on what he needed to do when he got back to Koloshan, but the grim presence of Will's body seemed to make rational thinking impossible. He drove back to the village on autopilot and went straight inside to take a shower. He left his clothes in a pile on the floor and lingered under the hot, pounding spray, wishing it could wash away the last few hours. But he knew no matter how long he stayed in the shower, Will's body would still be in his Jeep.

After putting on fresh clothes, he forced himself to think about what needed to be done. First, he called to arrange for an airplane. Then he called to make sure there would be someone there to pick up the body at the other end and take it to the morgue. There would be time later for an official identification by a family member. After the body was cleaned up and made presentable. There was no need to put Ellen through that now. He didn't want the last memory of her husband to be the one in his own head.

He also notified the State Troopers, explained the situation, and asked if they could send a team to check out the truck and the cache. He suggested that they might want to have someone in Juneau take a look at the body, too. Since Jonah was the only law enforcement person in the village, death investigations were handled less formally than in the city. But in this instance, when it was not only possible but probable that Will's death wasn't an accident, he wanted more eyes than his to take a good look at the site and the body.

His next call was to Matt. "I need a large container, maybe one of your insulated shipping boxes," he said. "And I need to have you bring it to me here, at my place, as soon as possible. Can you do that?"

"Right away," Matt said. Matt always sensed when something was urgent and didn't waste time on unnecessary questions. It wasn't more than fifteen minutes later when he arrived with a refrigeration carton used to transport fish in the back of his flatbed truck. When Jonah explained the situation, Matt was visibly shaken. "Poor bastard," he said with feeling.

Jonah gave Matt a pair of gloves and they lifted the tarp with the body in it out of his Jeep and lowered it into the carton. They were unable lay him out straight, but Jonah didn't think it mattered much at that point. Matt fussed a bit, obviously uncomfortable with how they were forced to handle the body. "It feels disrespectful," he said.

"I didn't want to bring him back like this—."

"You couldn't leave him there."

"No, and I want to get him on the plane before I tell Ellen."

"She's going to be angry with you for not letting her see him."

"I know."

"If it helps, I think you're doing the right thing."

They lifted the carton into the Jeep. It stuck out the back, making it impossible to close the lid. Jonah secured the rear door with a rope. On the drive to the airstrip, Jonah told Matt where he'd found Will's body.

"You didn't see the bear?"

"No. In some ways I wish I had, but it made it easier that it wasn't around."

"I'll let the men hunting for him know they should search near there."

"Wait until I get a chance to go back and check out the scene, okay? I've asked for assistance from Juneau."

Jonah pulled his Jeep up next to the small structure they used for a terminal. It was a place to get out of the weather while waiting for a plane. A few chairs and protection against the rain, wind, and snow. The landing strip wasn't much either, an open area lined with dense trees. But it was both wide enough and long enough to accommodate the small planes that came in.

The two men got out and stood a few feet from the Jeep, putting some distance between them and Will's remains.

"Do you know what Will was doing up there?" Matt asked.

"No, but I'm afraid it had something to do with the artifacts."

"You don't think—"

"The timing is right. But I hope for Ellen's sake that I'm wrong."

"I do too."

"Another thing that bothers me. I didn't see a gun on the ground or in his car. Who goes up there without a gun?"

"I suppose it depends on why he went there in the first place."

"That limits the possibilities, doesn't it?"

"So, what do you think happened?"

"Off the record, I think he got in a fight with someone. They hit him on the back of the head and left him for dead. The bear finished the job."

"You think he had some of the artifacts and someone took them from him?"

"Maybe. It was probably faster to load the smaller stuff into a second smaller truck while they were getting the screen into the larger vehicle. I do know that the larger and smaller trucks were parked side-by-side in front of the Center. There could also have been another vehicle that I haven't identified. It's hard to know what transpired. Maybe Will ended up with some or all of the smaller artifacts and someone stole them from him. Or maybe Will hadn't realized they were going to clean the Center out. He may have felt good about stealing the screen, but balked at taking things that had been donated by individuals he'd known all his life. What if he tried to stop the other thieves?"

"You're thinking that Will was the 'inside man,' and the others were outsiders."

"It's a scenario that makes sense."

They heard the airplane before they saw it. It appeared suddenly over the tops of the evergreens at the south end of the runway. Then it landed and taxied over to where they were waiting. After loading the body on the airplane, Matt and Jonah stood there watching until the plane disappeared from sight.

"I don't envy you your job right now," Matt said.

"Do you ever?"

"Sometimes. You have the respect of most villagers. You do good work."

Jonah appreciated the compliment but wondered if all that would change when it became obvious that he suspected one of their own was involved in the theft at the Center. Would his status as an "honorary" insider evaporate? Would he become the adversary?

One thing he knew for sure, there would be an unrelenting cloud of fear and anger dividing the community until he found the artifacts and identified Will's killer.

DAX̱ADOOSHÚ

(SEVEN)

Jonah knew he should tell Ellen about Will, but he couldn't face it yet. Instead, he tried to find Lou and Mike. No one seemed to know where they were, but Jonah could guess. They either already knew what had happened to Will or they were out searching for him. It was unlikely but not impossible that they would come across his pickup truck. Just like he had. He needed to talk to Ellen before then. But first, he was going to have a cup of coffee and think things through.

The two-story structure stood on pilings over the water. There had once been a sign that simply said "The Café" stuck in one of the windows, and ever since then, everyone referred to the restaurant as "The Café." Jonah went in and was surprised to find that he was hungry.

It was past the lunch hour rush, but a few customers lingered at the small wood tables scattered around the room. One or two nodded at Jonah as he entered and took a seat at his usual table off to one side, away from other customers.

The owner and cook, Joe, caught sight of him and went to pour a cup of coffee without being asked. Joe was bent with age, like the weathered pilings that supported the building, his voice roughened by years of smoking, the insides of the first two fingers on his right hand the color of dried tobacco leaves.

"You look like hell," Joe said as he put the coffee cup down in front of Jonah.

"I feel about that good," Jonah acknowledged, picking up the coffee and taking a long drink, the dark liquid burning his throat.

"Want something to eat?"

"What's the soup?"

"Clam chowder. I'll even run a clam through it for you."

"Sounds good."

Joe left to get the soup. Jonah sipped his coffee and gazed through the dust-streaked window. A young boy rode past on his bike. Barely able to reach the pedals, his lips were stretched taut in concentration. Two teen-age girls strolled by, their smooth young faces masked with make-up. A truck sped past, a cloud of dust exploding in its wake. Then a pack of dogs appeared, moving restlessly back and forth, sniffing and nosing each other and everything around them. All familiar sights, all part of village life.

"Here it is," Joe said. He put a bowl of chowder in front of Jonah along with a plate of bread and tiny, wrapped pats of butter. Then he got himself a cup of coffee and joined Jonah.

"I hear they haven't found that damn bear yet," Joe said.

"Not yet," Jonah agreed.

"Those kids feel real bad."

It hadn't occurred to Jonah that he would also have to address the guilt the boys would feel once people found out how Will had died. Not that it was their fault; Will shouldn't have been out there in the first place. "These things happen," Jonah said.

"Yeah. Kids. They think they're invincible. And they haven't seen what damage a bear can do to a human."

Jonah's spoon paused in midair. He took a breath and forced himself to keep eating. Joe didn't ask what was wrong, but Jonah knew his sharp eyes hadn't missed a thing.

"You see Lou or Mike around?" Jonah asked.

"Not today.

Jonah picked up a slice of bread. Joe made his own bread,

and it was usually good. Not always though. Sometimes Joe drank a little too much and his cooking suffered. Today's bread was perfect though, a whole wheat rye, hearty and flavorful.

"You looking for them cuz you think they were involved in the theft?" Jonah had known Joe since he first went fishing with his dad, and sometimes felt like Joe could read his mind. Joe also had a pretty good handle on what was happening in Koloshan because almost everyone in the village passed through The Café from time to time.

"What do *you* think, Joe?"

Joe's finger traced the rim of his coffee mug. "I think it's possible. They wouldn't mind making a fast buck. And they aren't exactly thrilled about all this heritage bullshit."

"You think it's bullshit?"

"Dwelling on the past don't make the present any better."

"True enough, but to a lot of villagers, it's the past that gives their existence meaning. Not unlike people from down south holding up their Mayflower lineage, or whatever, as a badge of honor."

"But it doesn't change the present. We live in a different time." He took a few sips of coffee. "You and I know what it was like here before television started creating expectations of a 'better' life to be had out there somewhere."

"You're right. But I wasn't born into the culture. They were. After hearing the stories—I mean, it seems to me like they *should* care. It's a past they can be proud of. It explains why things are the way they are today. It provides a sense of place, of belonging." He stopped, staring into his empty soup bowl. "When I moved in with Dennis, I felt like I'd been given a gift. I've told you that before. His stories are a part of me. But I'm still an outsider."

"Hell, I've been here almost as long as dirt, and I'm still an outsider."

"I didn't realize you felt that way."

"Should have married a local. That gets your foot in the door." He grinned. "You still can, you know."

Jonah brushed off the hint. "It's a good place to live, Joe. I think we agree on that."

"I don't know. Young people today want more than stories, Jonah. They want to have what other people have. And it's hard to get a leg up living in Koloshan."

"Once it's gone, it's gone forever," Jonah said. "I can't imagine how they could do that to the community."

"They probably don't think of it that way. They see the Center as a waste. I mean, when was the last time you went there? How many locals drop by? How many visitors do they get?"

"That's not the point. I knew what was there, and I knew that I *could* drop by when I wanted to."

"You can't buy things with pride or memories. For some, that's what it boils down to. Just sayin'."

"You taking their side, Joe?"

"I've never been in favor of selling those artifacts. I have one foot in the past and the other in the grave. You know that. But things have been stolen before. Sometimes you get them back, sometimes you don't. All you can do is your best. No one can blame you if you can't find those artifacts. And there may be a few reasons why it would be best if you don't find out who did it."

"I'm going to get them back, Joe."

Joe sighed. "Okay, give yourself ulcers. But don't go expecting me to fix you milk toast for dinner." Joe got up, picked up his coffee mug and went back to work.

Jonah downed the last of his coffee. It was time for him

to get back to work too.

Ellen peeked out the window as he came up the path to her house. His face must have told her there wasn't going to be good news. When she opened the door, she shrank back as though bracing herself for a physical blow.

"Did you find him?" she asked before Jonah could say anything.

"We need to talk, Ellen."

That was all he needed to say. She turned away from him and hunched over, her shoulders shaking. Jonah stepped close, put his arm around her, and led her into the living room. Her little girl was playing on the floor. A smile lit up her full-cheeked face as they entered the room but twisted into puckered lips when she saw her mother's demeanor.

"Who can I call for you?" Jonah asked.

Ellen shook her head as she leaned down and scooped up the little girl. "I'll take her next door. The baby's asleep."

Jonah let her go. A little time alone would allow her to brace herself for the news she already guessed. The details would be disturbing, and he had to ask her some unpleasant questions about Will's possible involvement in the theft. He felt certain that she would want to help him find the person responsible for her husband's death.

When she returned, she seemed composed, but Jonah knew the composure was a façade, one that would quickly fade when the facts sank in. She sat down on the edge of a chair and waited for Jonah to formalize her fears. He felt like she needed to hear the bad news quickly. It wouldn't serve any purpose to prolong the suspense. There weren't words to cushion the facts.

"He's dead, Ellen. I'm sorry."

"What happened?" Her calm question indicated that she

had indeed guessed what he had come to tell her.

"It's complicated."

She waited while he struggled to find the right words.

"He was parked in a clearing up in the woods, off one of the logging roads. He'd been in a fight and was badly injured. Then . . . then he had an encounter with a bear." He didn't want to tell her; but he didn't want her to hear it from someone else either.

"Oh no!" Her eyes wide with disbelief, she repeated "no" several times more.

"He died quickly, I'm sure of that." He wasn't at all sure, but it was a kind lie.

"He was in a fight?"

"That's what I think, but I can't say for sure."

She put her face in her hands and rocked back and forth.

"Ellen, I have to ask you some questions if I'm going to find out what happened."

She looked up, her face streaked with tears.

"When we talked before, I sensed you were worried that Will was mixed up in the theft at the Center. Am I right about that?"

Her hands went up and covered her mouth. "Oh, Jonah, I'm so ashamed." She leaned forward and began rocking back and forth again. "It's my fault. I pushed him too hard. The baby—." She didn't finish the sentence, but Jonah could imagine the discussions she and Will must have had about how they were going to pay the hospital bills, how they were going to survive as a family.

"Ellen, I want to catch the person who did this to Will." He waited until she stopped rocking. "Tell me who you suspect might have been in on it with him."

"What difference does it make now? Will's gone."

"Someone left him there in the woods not knowing or

caring if he was alive or dead. Whoever did it should be held accountable for what they did."

"You said he was in a fight."

"There was some indication that he was struck from behind. I won't know the details until the coroner has had a chance to do an examination." He'd almost added "of the body" but caught himself just in time.

"Could he have been unconscious when the bear attacked him?" Her eyes pleaded with him to say "yes."

"Yes," Jonah said. She didn't need to know that he had crawled from his pickup toward the woods, probably disoriented from the blow to his head, but obviously still alive.

She sighed and leaned back in the chair. "I wish I knew something," she said. "But he didn't tell me anything about planning to rob the Center. He wouldn't have told me anything; he would have wanted to keep me out of it." She started sobbing. "But if he was involved, it was only because . . ." Her voice trailed off.

"Who can I call to come and sit with you?" Jonah asked gently.

"I want to be alone for a while."

"Ellen, we both know Will was a good man. He may have made a mistake, but he didn't deserve to die. And I am so truly sorry for your loss." He stood to leave, then paused. "One last thing." He waited until she looked at him. "It would be best if you didn't mention to others how Will died. Not just yet. Give me a chance to figure out who might have been there with him. Okay?"

She nodded. Jonah wasn't convinced she understood why he was asking her to keep quiet about the cause of death, but he hoped she would heed his request, at least for a while. He hated leaving her there like that, but he understood wanting to be alone with grief. The neighbor who was watching her little girl would undoubtedly check in. And as soon as the news of Will's death hit the village grapevine, she would have family and friends coming by to offer support.

As he walked toward Lou's house, he passed Phil and Randy and an old woman sitting in wooden chairs on the front porch of Phil's house. They were engaged in an animated discussion but paused to wave at Jonah. Under other circumstances he would have joined them for a few minutes, but not today. Phil was a good source of village gossip though. Maybe he should talk to him later. People came by his place to pass the time of day, and he did a lot of walking around. For his health, he said. And sometimes because he had insomnia. But Jonah guessed it was as much to check the pulse of the residents as it was for physical conditioning.

Lou still wasn't home. Neither was Mike. He wanted to talk to them in person rather than call them later, so he drove down to the docks to see if they were there, but they weren't. He also checked at the Dís-schu Tavern, in case they were trying to dull their guilt with alcohol. But no one there had seen them.

Jonah gave up looking for the two men and went by his office. There were no messages. They must not have caught up with the bear yet. Given the number of people out looking for it, he worried about someone coming across Will's truck and the cache before he could get the Troopers there to examine the area. But it would be difficult to warn people to stay away without explaining why. Roping off the area wasn't practical either; it wasn't the way things were done around Koloshan. And if he assigned one or two people to guard the crime scene and the bear came back, it could be dangerous for them.

He sat down at his desk and attempted to make a prioritized list of what he should be doing. Others were searching for the bear. The coroner had to verify cause of death before he could be certain his assumptions were correct. The State Troopers would let him know if and when they got a lead on the missing artifacts. Meanwhile, he needed to find out when someone would arrive to fingerprint Will's pickup and examine the crime scene. But first, he wanted to take one more look around on his own.

His official truck was still there at the jail, but even if he could get it started, it was too unreliable to take up into the hills. Unfortunately, he hadn't had a chance to disinfect his Jeep properly, and it reeked with unpleasant odors. But he didn't want to delay. He would leave the windows down and air things out.

It was a gorgeous day. Instead of visiting a crime scene, Jonah wished he could play hooky and go for a walk in the woods. As much to escape from having to return to the cache as to avoid dealing with the aftermath of his investigation. If he linked Will to the theft while trying to find the missing artifacts, there would be a lot of unhappy people. The divisions within the community would become even more entrenched. On the other hand, if he found Will's killer but didn't recover the artifacts, that could in some ways be worse.

As he headed up the dirt road, he thought of all the villagers who were determined to keep traditions and stories of their heritage alive. Living with Dennis had been like being caught in a slipstream of time. The past was an integral part of the present for Dennis. As it was for Phil and his cronies who spent a part of each day reminiscing. Because of the stories Dennis and Phil had shared with him over the years, he felt a strong connection to Koloshan. In fact, when he was young, he'd often wished that the ancestors they talked about had been *his* ancestors, that the native culture was *his* culture. He felt a closeness of spirit if not of blood. It made him sad when some of the younger villagers seemed not to care about those who had lived there before them, about the way of life that was slowly disappearing.

When he arrived at the clearing, Will's pickup was in the same spot with the driver's door still hanging open. It didn't appear as if anyone else had been there. He pulled on a pair of gloves and carefully searched the front seat and the glove box. There was nothing of interest inside the truck. And definitely no gun.

He studied the palm prints that were still visible in the crusted mud. Why had someone left him alive if it was a question of who ended up with the artifacts? Either they must have thought he wouldn't come after them when he recovered or that he was already dead. Unless there was an entirely different explanation for why Will had driven up there. Could it have been a coincidence he had done so on the night of the theft? Too much of a coincidence, perhaps, but not something that could be completely discounted without more evidence.

Rifle in hand, Jonah headed for the bear cache. He walked around it, looking for signs that it had been disturbed since he removed Will's body. There were no fresh prints of either animals or humans that he could find. Maybe the bear had moved on, trying to evade the hunters who were after him. Perhaps at this very moment, someone had it in their sights. Jonah hoped they caught up with the bear soon so everyone could relax. Not that they would let down their guard right away. It always took a while after a scare before people lost their fear and became complacent again.

Jonah studied the cache without touching anything; he

didn't want to mess up the crime scene for the experts. He could, however, examine the surrounding area. In some ways, he was better suited for that search than anyone they might send from Juneau.

Methodically moving outward from the cache in a series of half-circles, he didn't really expect to find anything. And he didn't—not right away at least.

Then he saw it. The object was coated with blood and half buried in the soft earth: a roughly carved bone amulet. He reached down and picked it up, cradling it in his gloved hand, trying to remember if it had been in the Center. If it was one of the stolen artifacts, it would have been displayed with the other shaman objects. Shamans had hung them around their necks on leather thongs or carried them in deerskin pouches. They were believed to aid the shaman in the execution of spiritual and healing powers.

The woods were silent and cool. Light flickered through the trees and seemed to collect in the dark ovoid eye of the amulet. Jonah stood very still, staring at the flat, two-dimensional design with its lidded eye, the wide mouth filled with pointed teeth, stylized lines and circles extending to the edge of the bone. It was not great art by some standards. Nor did it mean anything to him personally. But if it could speak—

If it could speak, it might tell him the name of a murderer.

PART II

A Slipstream of Time

NAS'GADOOSHÚ

(EIGHT)

Before leaving, Jonah searched the area around the truck more systematically and found an interesting set of footprints nearby. The soles of the shoes were worn, the heel on the left foot more run down than that on the right. They weren't hiking shoes or tennis shoes but leather-soled city shoes. Not something you'd expect to see in the woods.

There were also some bicycle tire tracks near the back of the truck. But he couldn't find any tracks to suggest where they had come from. He followed them up a trail that forked after a few hundred yards. He went to the right first, his eyes moving back and forth across the trail while glancing up and down the foliage on either side. There was no indication that anyone had come this way, so he retraced his steps and tried the other fork. The bicycle had been there, slicing through mud, occasionally seeming to wobble a bit.

Abruptly the trees ended, and he came out onto a spongy muskeg dotted here and there with stunted trees. He'd always liked the greenish brown colors on the barren muskeg terrain, the ground soft underfoot. Later in the summer there would be crow berries blanketing large areas, sweeter than blueberries and easy to pick. He knelt on one knee and studied the muskeg. There were deep indentations made by the bicycle heading to the left. And just a short distance away, he could see an opening in the trees and another logging road.

Logging roads frequently crisscrossed their way up a

hillside, so it wasn't unusual for two roads to be so close together. Jonah wasn't surprised when the bicycle appeared to head back to the village. Unfortunately, the road was awash with tire tracks, making it next to impossible to follow the bike's route. Besides, how often does a murderer ride a bike in the wilderness? Especially a murderer balancing a box of artifacts on its handlebars. Was that even possible?

But what if the murder and the stolen artifacts were not connected? Could someone else have fought with Will and taken off on a bike? If so, where were the bike tire tracks leading *into* the clearing? And if the biker had simply witnessed the altercation and left to avoid getting involved, that still left the problem of one-way tracks. Nor did it explain why the tracks were so close to the truck. And even if the biker had come across the abandoned truck after Will was out of sight, there should have been tracks. Unless the bike belonged to Will and someone had come with him to the clearing. That seemed highly unlikely, but he would have to check with Ellen about the bike. One thing he knew for sure: he needed to find that bicyclist.

Jonah walked back to the clearing. After one last look around, he got in his Jeep and drove to the village. He needed to ask Ellen about the bike and still wanted to talk with Lou and Mike. He tried Lou's house first, but his car wasn't in the driveway, and Lou didn't answer his door. Mike's wife was home but said she didn't know where her husband was or when he would be back. "He doesn't always check in a lot during fishing season," she said. "He goes where the fish are." Jonah didn't challenge her explanation—she either believed what she was saying or was very good at evasion. But the last time he'd checked, Mike's boat was tied to the dock. So was Lou's.

He put off calling Ellen about the bike and went to The Café to get something to eat.

It was busier than usual, late lunch or early dinner for some. Fishermen kept irregular hours, unloading fish and running errands between trips. Jonah headed for his usual table and did a doubletake when he saw Austin Mann there. Had the archeologist chosen his table at random? He wouldn't know unless he joined him.

"It's about time," Mann said when he saw Jonah. "You're not an easy man to catch up with."

"I've been busy." Jonah said, hiding his irritation at the remark. He would have preferred to eat alone, but Mann had apparently been waiting for him to show.

"I know. I've heard." Mann smiled. Jonah thought Mann smiled too much and kept his own face neutral.

A new waitress came over to take his order. Jonah recognized her as the daughter of one of the locals. She had matured a lot during the last year and was obviously proud of her blooming figure. Still, it bothered Jonah to see Mann staring at her snug T-shirt.

"Just a sandwich," he said. "Whatever Joe feels like fixing. And coffee. Black. And a piece of pie."

Mann was just finishing his meal. He asked for more coffee and settled back in his chair. "So," Mann said, "any chance you can take me over to the old village site one of these days?"

"I did get your message, but there's a lot going on right now."

"But you're willing to do it," Mann said, as if asking for a verbal commitment.

"If the council gives you permission." Not exactly eager to do so, but "willing" might cover it. Maybe he could put it off until Mann found someone else.

"I didn't think I needed permission. No one owns the site, do they?"

"It's the appropriate thing to do."

"Okay. I get it. I'll check with them. The road project should be done in another couple of days. I was hoping we could make it after that."

"I'll keep that in mind. But it depends on how things go."

Matt patted his shirt pocket like someone who was once a smoker but no longer carried cigarettes. "That's all I can ask."

"Have you found anything at the road site?" Jonah asked, to be polite and to change the subject.

"Not much, but we're not done yet." Then Mann quickly turned the conversation back to the old village site. "I've been trying to determine how long the village was occupied. I assume at least a couple hundred years."

"I'm not sure." Jonah knew he could ask Dennis, but he didn't offer.

"I'm hoping I'll find something there to help date it."

The waitress brought Jonah's food and a small pot of coffee so he could have as much as he wanted. Jonah picked up the sandwich and started to take a bite.

"Aren't you going to look at what's in it?" Mann asked.

Jonah bit into the homemade bread. It seemed obvious to him that he would find out what kind of sandwich it was when he tasted it.

"Well?"

He chewed a moment before responding: "Meatloaf."

"Good?"

"Yeah." He would have eaten it even if it wasn't to his liking just to spite Mann.

Mann stirred something into his coffee from a packet he took out of his jacket pocket. "Have to watch the old waistline," he said, smiling. He was thin and athletic looking, still young enough not to have to fight too hard to maintain his weight. Jonah could picture him in a jogging suit with a matching sweatband taking his morning constitutional before work. He took a sip and smiled again. "Making any headway on the theft?"

"Some."

"You sure don't waste words, do you?" This time the smile turned into a short laugh.

Jonah swallowed a bite of sandwich and asked, "You don't know anything about it, do you?"

Mann choked on a swig of coffee he had just taken. "Of course not. Why would I?"

"It seems to me that I remember you asking about whether the screen was for sale."

"For sale, yes. But I wouldn't steal it."

"What if someone offered to give you a cut if you let them into the Center?"

"I assume you're joking."

"But you *do* know people who would like to have the screen, right?"

"Yes."

"What if someone who claimed to have title to it asked for your help? Would you have lined them up with an interested buyer?" Jonah had considered the possibility earlier; not too many locals would know how to contact a buyer for the screen. Mann was a logical go-between. But maybe a bit too obvious.

"Someone who 'claimed' to have title? That's what courts are for—to settle ownership disputes."

Jonah concentrated on finishing his sandwich. Mann drank the last of his coffee and pushed his cup aside. "Well, I guess I'd better get back to work." He smiled one last time before saying "I'll be in touch."

The pie was apple, and very tasty. Jonah lingered over his coffee, hoping to get a chance to check in with Joe, but he was being kept busy behind the counter. His conversation with Mann had reminded him that he needed to pick up the list of people who had inquired about the screen. He drank the last of his coffee and drove to the Center. It was getting late, but Stella was in her office staring at a pile of papers.

"Hello, Stella." Jonah went in and sat down in the chair next to her desk. "How are you doing?"

"As good as can be expected, I suppose." She looked on the verge of tears. Her husband had died about two years ago, and the Center had been a big part of her life since then. "Have you made any progress?" She asked the question as if afraid of the answer.

"Some." He didn't want to say more until he had something concrete to report. "I was wondering if you had that list of people who asked about the screen?"

"Oh, yes. Right here somewhere." Usually she was quite efficient, but she had to go through several stacks of paper to locate the list. "Here it is."

"Thanks." There were only five names, including Austin Mann. He didn't recognize any of the others.

"I gave the names and a list of what's missing to the Juneau police and the State Troopers like you asked me to." She handed him a copy of the missing items. He scanned it for the carved bone amulet he had found near the bear's cache and located it about a third of the way down.

"I appreciate that, Stella." He stood up. "I want to leave a note for Mann. Think it's all right if I go into his office and write it there?"

"I'm sure he wouldn't mind. His door is probably open— I don't think he locks it."

Stella was right, Mann's office door was unlocked. It was a large room, sparsely furnished. There was a small desk, a folding table, a waist-high filing cabinet, a bookshelf and a couple of chairs. He didn't know what he was looking for. Maybe a name or a telephone number. Some Koloshan contact. Or the name of a private collector. He didn't really have Mann high on his suspect list, but it was worth a quick search.

With a glance to make sure Stella was still at her desk, he flipped through the folders and papers on Mann's desk. There were some telephone numbers on a pad next to the telephone. Two were for Juneau. Just numbers, no names. The Koloshan numbers were all ones he recognized: The Café, the cold storage plant, and the jail. Not much to go on there. He jotted down the Juneau numbers. Then he went through the desk drawers, checked out the handful of books on the bookshelf, glanced in the nearly empty filing cabinet, and called it good.

After the visit to the Center, he dropped by the jail to call the librarian he knew in Juneau. She was always willing to look up things for him. In this instance, he asked her to check out the two Juneau numbers from Mann's office. The results were disappointing: one was for the University and the other a car repair shop. Two more dead ends.

After checking with Matt to find out if he knew if there was any news about the hunt for the wounded bear, he decided to drive past Lou's one more time. When he saw Lou's car in the driveway, he pulled in behind it and went up to the front door. No one answered when he knocked. After a few minutes, he went around to the back of the house. It was getting dusky, but there were no lights on inside.

He knocked on the back door. Still no one answered.

After a moment's hesitation, he tried the knob. The door was unlocked. He opened it a few inches and called out Lou's name. Even though there was no response, he felt certain there was someone inside. Was Lou avoiding him? Was he in the bedroom with a woman? Jonah was going to feel pretty stupid if he surprised Lou in bed with someone. And he didn't have cause for entering uninvited. But a voice in his head was urging him to do it.

He moved quietly into the house. There was no reason to advertise his presence. If Lou was there alone, he would confront him. If not, he could leave just as quietly.

There was no one in the kitchen. He went into the hall and paused. There were three doors, all closed. He thought he remembered that the first door on the left was the bathroom. The other two were probably bedrooms.

Why was his heart beating so loudly? What did he expect to find behind those doors?

Feeling wary and a bit foolish, he took a few more steps, then paused. If he were back in L.A., he wouldn't be doing this. They would throw the book at him for acting without probable cause. He didn't even have a good reason for being suspicious, for God's sake. So, what the hell was he doing?

He was about to retreat when he heard a sound, like a moan, or the noise a dog makes when dreaming. Still feeling uncertain, he moved toward the door on the right. "Lou?" he called. "You in there?" He stood off to the side, like he had been taught to do in situations where there could be a hostile behind the door, even though he had no reason to suspect that was the case in this instance. It was an automatic move.

"Go away." The voice was muffled, but clearly Lou's.

"Are you okay?"

"Go away, Jonah. Leave me alone."

"Dammit, Lou. I'm coming in." He gave it a few seconds

before cautiously turning the doorknob. He pushed open the door and waited off to the side. When nothing happened, he peeked into the room.

The curtains were pulled and there were no lights on. Jonah could barely make out Lou laying on top of the bed, his back toward Jonah. Feeling like he was being melodramatic, he nevertheless checked behind the door before entering the room. "What's wrong, Lou?"

"I told you to go away."

Jonah went around to the other side of the bed. Lou put his hands over his face, but that didn't hide the blood that was dripping off his chin onto the blanket. Jonah crouched beside the bed and put a hand on Lou's shoulder. "You don't have to tell me what happened if you don't want to, but I'm either going to help you get cleaned up, or I'm taking you to the clinic. You pick it." He went over and turned on the light.

Lou took his hands down from his face. He had been badly beaten. One eye was almost swollen shut. The blood was coming from a cut on his forehead. There were abrasions on both cheeks and on his chin.

"You always were a pushy bastard," Lou said. One side of his mouth was bleeding. He dabbed at it with the corner of the blanket. "Nothing's broken."

"Me or the clinic?"

Lou groaned. "Damn you. I don't want your help." He tried to sit up but couldn't manage on his own. Jonah leveraged him into an upright position. "Shit," Lou said with feeling.

"You *look* like you need help," Jonah observed.

"It was just a fight, that's all."

"I repeat, that's not my concern right now. All I want is to make sure you're okay. Let me check you out to see if I think you need medical attention. I might need to get someone over here to keep an eye on you in case you have a concussion or internal bleeding."

"You don't have to scare me." He waved one arm in a feeble attempt to ward Jonah off, then suddenly gave in. "Oh, get it over with, why don't you." He collapsed back on the pillow, wincing with pain.

Jonah got a pan of warm water from the kitchen, along with a washcloth and towel from the bathroom. He cleaned off Lou's face first, examining each cut carefully. They all appeared to be superficial. "I doubt you need stitches, but these could become infected. You should let Sue take a look. You need more first aid supplies to deal with these than what you have in your medicine cabinet—I looked." Lou let out a yelp as Jonah touched a particularly sensitive spot on his forehead.

"Okay, let's take a look at your chest." Jonah helped Lou off with his shirt. One sleeve was torn but the skin underneath was intact. Jonah ran his hands up and down Lou's ribs, pressing gently. "You'll live," Jonah said when he didn't find anything broken. "Let's get you out of your pants and into bed."

"Why aren't you some beautiful woman?" Lou moaned.

"It's going to hurt like hell tomorrow."

"Tomorrow? You've got to be kidding."

Jonah helped Lou ease himself between the covers. "Want something to drink?"

"I could use a drink, alright. You'll find a bottle in the cupboard next to the stove."

Jonah brought back two glasses, one slightly fuller than the other. He gave the larger one to Lou. "Don't gulp," he advised. Then he pulled up a chair and sat down next to the bed. "Now then . . ."

"I have nothing to say."

"You have a lot to say. The question is *when* you're going to say it."

Lou leaned forward and took a big swallow, coughed, and sank back down on his pillows. "Nothing to say."

"Will is dead, you know."

Lou half rose up, supporting himself on one elbow, the glass almost falling from his hand. "What?" He gasped in pain as he struggled to stay upright.

"Will is dead. And despite what you may hear, his death was probably not an accident."

"Oh my god." Lou went pale.

"He too was in a fight."

Color rushed back into Lou's face. "You don't think that I—" Liquid sloshed back and forth in his glass as his hand shook.

"Did you fight with Will?" Jonah knew Lou's wounds were too fresh for that, but he thought the question might prompt Lou to talk about what had happened to him.

"No, I had no quarrel with Will."

"Do you know who did?"

Lou closed his eyes. "No."

"Was it the same person who attacked you?"

"I don't know anything."

"Lou, listen to me. This is serious. I don't want another death on my hands."

Lou opened his eyes and stared up at Jonah. "Jonah, I hear what you're saying, but I can't tell you anything."

"Is anyone else in danger? Or do you want that on your conscience too?"

"Shit, Jonah. Give me some time to think, will you? I need time." He finished off the liquor and handed his glass to Jonah. Jonah put it on the small table next to the bed, along with what was left of his own drink. Then he sat there, patiently, not saying anything, letting the silence weigh on Lou.

"Christ, Jonah. Are you just going to sit there like a stone?"

"Dennis taught me how to be patient."

"Don't give me that stoic ancestor crap."

"Hey, they're *your* ancestors, not mine. And it isn't all crap."

Lou frowned. "You can't live on memories. People have families to feed *today*. Right here and now. Doesn't that count for something?"

"It counts for a lot, sure. But that isn't the issue. What I need to know is who else I might expect to find beaten to a pulp. Or should I just hang around until they come back to finish you off?"

Lou thought a long time before replying. "Let me think on this, Jonah, okay?"

"Don't wait too long, Lou." Jonah stood up. "I'm here for you. Let me know when you're ready to admit you need help." He started for the door and turned back. 'Oh, and I'll send Sue over to check you out." Sue might not be at the clinic, but she always answered her phone or responded quickly to messages. Koloshan was lucky to have a professional nurse on call.

"Don't bother."

Jonah grinned. "No bother. You said you wanted a woman."

"Damn you, Jonah. You really are a pushy bastard."

GOOSHÚ<u>K</u>

(NINE)

Jonah woke up several times during the night. He wasn't sure what woke him, but each time he lay there waiting for something to happen. When nothing did, he would toss and turn for a while, then drop off into a restless sleep.

He got up early and went through the motions of fixing himself a pot of coffee. Getting out the 15-ounce can, counting the number of scoops, putting the pot on the burner—his usual morning routine, something he did on autopilot before allowing the rest of the world to intrude. But this morning he was unable to keep his mind from swirling with questions that had been temporarily put on hold during the night.

Who was the man in the worn city shoes? Was he the one who beat up Will and left him for dead? Had he also attacked Lou? Or was he looking at two unrelated beatings? Should he be trying to locate a kid who had ridden a bicycle past the truck and maybe saw something that would be helpful? Or was he dealing with a bicycle riding murderer? And where was the screen? Were the smaller artifacts and the screen headed for a single buyer or had they been split up? So many questions, so many different avenues to pursue. There was, however, one decision that would narrow his options: was he going to spend his time looking for the person who had assaulted Will—and perhaps Lou—or focus on trying to find the artifacts? There were others working on both lines of investigation, but he couldn't sit back and wait for them to come up with results. Or not—

It was always hard waiting the seven minutes it took for the coffee to perk to his specifications, but he forced himself to sit there until the time was up before pouring his first cup. Then he leaned back and stared at the steam lifting off the black surface like morning fog, letting his thoughts drift, waiting for them to take shape on their own.

Suddenly he felt hungry. He looked in his refrigerator; it was practically empty—some hunks of cheese, a yogurt past its due date, a few oranges. He went through his cupboards and came up with some stale bread and an old jar of peanut butter. He started to fix himself a sandwich, then set everything aside. Five minutes later he was at The Café.

It wasn't unusual for Jonah to be inside with coffee made when Joe came down from his upstairs apartment. The place wasn't officially open until 7:30, but Joe left the back door open just in case. That didn't stop him from complaining about Jonah's early bird habit though.

The coffee was ready to serve when Joe appeared. "What the hell you doing here at his hour?" he grumbled. Jonah handed him a cup of coffee

"I'm hungry. Thought I'd get some breakfast."

"Not yet, you won't. Not until I've had my coffee."

They sat down at a table near the back so no one could look in the front window and see them. After a few minutes, Joe said, "Couldn't sleep, huh?"

"You know I usually wake up early. Well, sometimes earlier than others."

"Yeah. Me too—when I hear someone rattling around down here, that is." Joe rubbed his unshaven chin with a weathered hand. He had long fingers, like a piano player . . . or a pickpocket. At one time he had been both.

"Someone beat Lou up," Jonah said, a blunt fact, no preliminaries.

Joe put his mug down with a bang and coffee sloshed over the edges. "Damn. Will dead and Lou beat up. What the hell is going on?"

"Wish I knew."

"You think it's outsiders?"

"We can hope."

"Lou ain't talking?"

"Afraid."

"Maybe he should be."

"You haven't heard anything, have you?"

"No, but you can count on me keeping my ears open."

"And your eyes."

"No strangers around the last few days that I've noticed."

"I was wondering about that."

Joe downed his remaining coffee. "Come on over to the counter while I rustle us up some breakfast."

Jonah sat on a stool facing the kitchen and watched while Joe fixed bacon and eggs, hash browns and toast. He made a large order for Jonah, a smaller one for himself. There was homemade jelly for the toast, two kinds—raspberry and blackberry. Jonah chose the raspberry.

While they were eating, they discussed who else might be involved in the theft if, as Jonah now suspected, Will and Lou were mixed up in it. Jonah felt comfortable using Joe as a sounding board. He never worried that Joe would blab to anyone or in any way take advantage of the trust Jonah placed in him. Mike ended up at the top of their list, mainly because he was Lou's buddy and was staying out of sight. Then came a couple of other men. One that they knew desperately wanted a larger fishing boat. Another who had five children who all hoped to go away to college. Both men needed more money than they were able to make in Koloshan.

"It's funny," Joe said. "You can think of these guys as greedy, or you can think of them as simply trying to make better lives for themselves and their kin. But any way you look at it, they aren't people you'd expect to get mixed up in a theft of this kind."

"If I had to guess, someone from the outside is responsible for setting things up, with the help of at least one or two insiders, maybe more. Then something went sideways. Now they're covering their tracks."

A customer knocked on the front door. "I'm coming," Joe yelled. "Sorry, Jonah, but I guess I'm as greedy as the next guy."

Back at the jail, Jonah called the Juneau police to see if they'd learned anything. It took a while for his call to go through. The good news was that the lab guy was scheduled to arrive in Koloshan by plane at 9:00. Jonah had been afraid they would make him wait until Monday and was pleased it was happening so soon. Apparently, they had tried to call Jonah to let him know, but there had been no answer. The bad news was that they hadn't made any progress in tracking the artifacts, and they were fairly certain that the State Troopers hadn't either.

As Jonah hung up, he swore softly. He really needed to get an answering machine. He couldn't expect outsiders to know where to leave a message for him if he wasn't in. Although he was pretty sure he had left Matt's number with Jacobson. To emphasize his new resolve, he made still another note about an answering machine on his calendar and underlined it in red.

He had almost an hour before the lab guy arrived. There wasn't much he could accomplish in that amount of time, so he decided to stop off at the Cold Storage on his way and ask if there was any talk about strangers in the village in the days before the theft.

The steep steps going up the side of the building to Matt's office were worn smooth on the edges. The unpainted wood railing was also worn smooth from all the hands that routinely slid along its surface. Jonah took the steps two at a time, his hand dancing lightly along the railing.

Inside there was a sloping ceiling that forced Jonah to crouch for the first few steps after entering. The yellowed corkboard ceiling was speckled with dark brown splotches. The roof was always sprouting new leaks. One of the corkboard squares had slipped out of alignment and looked about to fall. It had been like that for as long as Jonah could remember.

He passed by Matt's secretary/assistant Kathy's desk with a wave of his hand before seeing that Matt was on the phone in his office. Jonah poured himself a cup of strong coffee from the Mr. Coffee on the table by the entrance to Matt's office and went back to chat with Kathy. She gave Jonah a pleasant, dimpled smile. She was wearing a sweatshirt that said Clark Cold Storage, her brown hair held in place by a red headband. "Hi, stranger. It's been a while."

Never good at making small talk, Jonah said, "Yeah, it has." He liked Kathy but had a hard time talking with her even though he'd known her for years. "How're things going?"

"Oh, busy. It's that time of year. And as soon as the halibut start coming in, things will get really crazy."

"I heard they expect a record catch."

"I hope so." She raised her eyebrows. "Did you come in for the really strong coffee made in a pot that hasn't been cleaned for ages, or do you need something?"

"He still won't let you wash it out?"

"Says cleaning it destroys the oils from the coffee, and . .

."

". . . takes away the full-bodied flavor."

"You know the litany." She pointed to a large thermos on a shelf behind her. "I bring my own."

Jonah took a sip and grimaced. "As a matter of fact, I came by to ask if either you or Matt heard anything about any strangers in town recently."

"You mean other than fishermen." Kathy pursed her full lips and tapped a pencil on the pile of papers on her desk. "It's about the theft, isn't it?"

He nodded.

"Sorry." She shook her head.

Matt called to him from the other room. "What's going on out there? You bothering the help?"

Kathy rolled her eyes. Jonah went into Matt's office and sat down on a faded, vinyl couch, its surface covered with cigarette burns and creased with wear. The couch had withstood a lot of abuse over the years. It would probably outlast all of them.

"You look even grimmer than usual," Matt commented. "I take it you haven't made any progress on locating the artifacts."

"Not much." He finished off his coffee and sat the cup on the floor. "I'm trying the dragnet approach now, see if I can find any outsiders to question."

"I'm way ahead of you on that."

"Oh?"

"Yeah. I've been asking around. No one seems to have noticed any new faces in the village." Matt picked up the chipped mug with his name on it, dumped its leftover contents into the waste basket next to his desk, and stepped over to pour himself a fresh cup. "It's a nasty business. Wish I had something for you."

"Just because they stayed out of sight doesn't mean they weren't here."

"It seems to me that even if the thief or thieves are local, they'd have needed outside help to pull off that heist."

"We're thinking along the same lines," Jonah said. "I'm going to try to trace it from the other end, from potential buyers. But that may take time."

Matt pulled out a cigarette and began searching through the piles of papers on his desk for a match. When he couldn't find one, he tossed the unlit cigarette on top of the heap. "One thing that keeps coming up in my mind is Mann. I'm not suggesting he's the ringleader, but he has an office in the Center. And he's in the business so to speak. Maybe he told some local where to go to sell the screen, for instance."

"I've talked to him. He denies any involvement, of course. But he's on my list. There've been other inquiries about the screen though; no one's been exactly secret about their interest in it."

"Do you get a good vibe off Mann? There's something I don't like about him."

"I'm with you on that. The man makes me uncomfortable."

Matt picked up the cigarette again and reached into his pockets. "It's Kathy," he whispered. "I think she's been throwing out my matches."

For as long as he could remember, Kathy had complained about the smoke and nagged Matt about it being an unhealthy habit. But a lot of villagers smoked. There was no way she was going to win a battle against smoking in Koloshan.

"You don't have a match on you, do you?"

"Sorry." Even if he'd had one in his pocket, he would have hesitated to hand it over with Kathy nearby.

Matt fingered the cigarette. "Guess I'll have to walk to the store." He looked thoughtfully at Jonah. "You know, Mann's not too popular with the locals, standing there like a vulture waiting for a body to show up on the roadwork project. Which reminds me, did you agree to take him to the old village site?"

"*If* the council gives him approval. *Eventually*, that is."

"It's funny," Matt said. "I have no ancestral ties to Koloshan. And in some ways, despite all the years I've spent here, I'm still considered an 'outsider.' But I don't like the idea of someone poking around at the old village site or digging up old graves. It's like tempting fate." He stood up. "Before I get too maudlin, maybe I'd better go get some matches. Probably suffering from nicotine withdrawal."

Jonah walked with Matt as far as the store. He figured by the time Matt got back to his office, the cigarettes might have disappeared too.

From the store, it only took a few minutes to walk to the jail to pick up his Jeep. He'd sprayed the interior with Lysol and left the windows open to air it out. But the taint of death from transporting Will's body was still discernible, at least to him. He hoped the fingerprint guy wouldn't be bothered by it.

It hadn't rained since the night of the theft; dust billowed up as he drove down the main street. In Koloshan it was either dust or mud. When it was dry, the dust seeped into the Jeep through vents and gaps in the frame, sometimes seeming to penetrate the metal exterior itself, covering everything with a layer of gray-brown grime. But the mud was worse. Unlike the dust, you didn't breathe it, but it left a yellowish clay coating on everything it touched. And it worked its way up sides of buildings like drifting snow.

The airplane was right on time. Only three people got off.

Jonah spotted the fingerprint technician with his brown leather case and went forward to meet him. "Hello, Calvin," he said. "Glad you're here." Calvin was a small man who wore oversized tortoise-shell glasses that never seemed to stay in place. Before they could fall off the end of his sloped nose, he would push them back up with the index finger of his left hand, a motion as habitual as blinking for him.

"Jonah. It's good to see you again. Sorry I'm a bit late. The order didn't reach us until almost quitting time yesterday."

"No problem. I doubt anyone's interfered with the truck." Jonah kept his tone neutral but mentally swore at the bureaucracy that caused such delays.

They got in Jonah's Jeep and headed back up the dusty road.

"You're investigating a theft, I understand," Calvin said. Jonah noticed he was rolling up his window as tightly as possible. Dust was boiling around the Jeep, practically blotting out visibility on either side. It occurred to Jonah that in Calvin's line of work he might be used to the smell of blood and decay and prefer them to breathing in dust particles. Jonah rolled up the window on his side too, his nostrils twitching as he tried to convince himself the smell wasn't that bad.

"There's a death involved too. I don't have the coroner's report yet."

"Related? The theft and the death?"

"Seem to be, but no evidence to link the two yet. I'm hoping you'll find some prints that will help."

"What was stolen?"

"The Raven House screen and all of the artifacts in the Center."

"Oh my God. That's terrible."

"You've got that right."

Calvin brushed at the case on his lap, moving the dust to another location. "Who died?"

"A local man, Arnold Williams, known as Will."

"Don't know him. Family?"

"Yes. Two children."

"Any leads?"

"Not much. As I said, I'm hoping you find something."

"I'll give it my best shot."

They bumped their way up the logging road and into the cool shadows of the tall trees surrounding the clearing. Everything looked the same as it had the last time he'd been there. The driver's door still hanging open. Jonah hoped there were no critters inside. He probably should have closed the door and thrown a tarp over everything. He'd let his feelings get in the way of police work.

Calvin took his time. Jonah had worked with him on several occasions and knew he was thorough. To pass the time, Jonah looked around the area again, keeping his eyes open for the marauding bear. He couldn't believe it was taking this long to catch up with the animal. It was starting to look more and more like he had died on his own in some out-of-the-way place. As if to taunt the hunters after him.

"That's about it," Calvin called. Jonah had been staring at the cache, hoping for the umpteenth time that Will had died quickly.

"Any prints?" he asked as he re-joined Calvin.

"What you could expect . . . a few on both doors, the steering wheel, glove compartment, mirror. A couple nice ones on the tailgate. Can't tell how many different people they belong to yet, but more than one."

"I'd rather not ask his wife for her prints yet. But we'll have to rule her out at some point. And friends of Will's."

"If we're lucky, running them through the system might produce something without the need to rule out friends and family. You never know."

"I have one artifact back at the jail that I found here. I want you to check it for prints too."

"Where did you find it?"

"Over here." They walked in silence to the cache. "This is where Will's body was. The amulet was about . . ." Jonah paced off the distance and pointed to the ground.

Calvin bent over and studied the ground. "Sorry. Nothing here that I can help with." He straightened up. "I may be duplicating the work the Troopers will do, but I want to get some soil samples. I have some bags in my case."

Jonah let him look around while he went back and got Calvin's case. Then he waited patiently while Calvin scooped up and labeled samples. "I think you just wanted to ruin my lunch," he said at one point.

When he was finished, Jonah asked if Calvin would mind driving his Jeep back. "I might as well take Will's truck back to his family." Calvin agreed and Jonah handed him the keys. Then he got in the truck. The keys were still in the ignition, but when he turned the key, nothing happened. The engine wouldn't even turn over. He sat there for a moment, puzzled.

Calvin had already started off in the Jeep but stopped and backed up when he noticed Jonah wasn't following.

Jonah got out and opened the hood of the truck.

"Something wrong?" Calvin said, stepping alongside him.

Something was in fact very wrong. Someone had made certain the truck couldn't be moved on its own. It wasn't done by someone who intended to temporarily delay Will being able to use the truck; they hadn't limited themselves to pulling out a few spark plug cables or removing the fuel pump or disconnecting the battery. Instead, wires and hoses had been indiscriminately ripped out. The question was whether it had been done on the night Will died or since then.

Dammit. He should have checked sooner.

JINKAAT

(TEN)

After dropping Calvin at the airport, Jonah drove his Jeep slowly back to the jail. The fingerprints on the amulet had been too smudged to be helpful. The only hope was tracing one or more prints from Will's truck. And if they belonged to someone local, it would be a lead, but not evidence of a crime.

A motorcyclist sped past, kicking up a flood of dust ahead of his car; he could barely see the road and was forced to slow to a crawl. His windows were so dirty it was like looking through gauze. He really needed to clean them, even though they would only get dirty again.

As he made his way through the tan haze, he made a mental to-do list: talk to Lou again about who beat him up, follow up on the list of people interested in buying the Raven House screen, tell Ellen about Will's truck and ask her about the bike, check with the coroner, call the driver of the co-op truck to see if he'd been contacted again, and look around the village for the city shoe prints. He was no longer worried about which crime he was investigating; he sensed that everything was connected in some way. It was like manipulating the layers of a Rubik's cube until everything lined up.

He also needed to check on the status of the bear hunt. If only those kids hadn't panicked when the bear charged them. But he understood why they had. His own first encounter with a bear was not something he was proud of. In fact, it had almost been a disaster. He was with his father and a local hunter. They had tracked the bear along an old mining road. Jonah remembered thinking that the prints from the hind paws looked almost human, a huge human with toes arranged in a shallow arc. The hind prints measured about ten inches across and sixteen long. The local man had explained how to recognize the distinctive walking gait of the bear, hind foot a little forward of the front foot on the same side. Then they came to what their guide described as a "bear tree" where the bear had scraped off the bark to get at the juicy pulp underneath. Shortly after that they spotted the steaming scat on the trail just ahead of them.

Jonah hadn't been afraid until the moment the bear came into view. Then he froze, unable to do anything other than gawk at the awesome animal facing them, staring them down, standing its ground.

He couldn't recall the local man telling them to stay back while raising his rifle to make the shot that felled the animal. What he did remember was the coughing sound the bear made just before it charged. That and his own fear, his inability to react. What could have been his first bear kill was instead his first encounter with immobilizing terror.

Yes, he understood why the kids had panicked. It took a lot of experience to remain calm and take careful aim before shooting a thousand pounds of muscle that could easily outrun a human.

City folks were usually under the impression that a bear would leave them alone if they left it alone, but villagers knew there were any number of reasons why a bear might get aggressive—especially the big browns found on most of the islands in Southeast Alaska. For instance, everyone knew you shouldn't get between a mother and her cubs, but in the woods, it was easy to do so without realizing what was happening. Or, if you got too close before the bear became aware of your presence, that could trigger an instinctive defensive move. If the animal was in pain, they could react in anger, like the one the boy shot. It was even possible the bear might be motivated by extreme hunger. The kids were right to shoot to ward off an attack; it was just too bad they hadn't finished the job.

Jonah pulled up at the jail and got out. His police truck was still out front, its official insignia obscured by dust. He really ought to see about having someone look at the starter, or whatever it was that was wrong with the damn thing. One more task that needed addressing. But not at the top of the list.

There were no messages. He dialed the coroner's office. It was Sunday, but he hoped to catch someone in. Depending on the caseload, they sometimes worked weekends. When no one answered, he hesitated, then called the coroner at home. He couldn't remember how he had acquired his home number, and he hated to abuse using it, but he needed some answers to help with the investigation.

"I'm still waiting for authorization to perform an autopsy," the man said after Jonah apologized for calling him at home.

"You did see the damage to the back of his head," Jonah said, immediately sorry for asking. Of course a trained physician would have noticed right away.

The man chuckled. "You mean that indentation that could have been made when he fell and hit his head on a rock?"

"Not something that would have been done by a bear?"

"I doubt it, but can't say for certain yet."

"There weren't any rocks or any sharp objects between his truck and where his body was found." Jonah said, hoping to encourage him to perhaps concede a little more information.

"That's for *your* report, not mine. I deal in describing what there is to see on the body. *When* I get it on the autopsy calendar. Sorry, that's the best I can do for you."

Paperwork and bureaucracy, almost worse in Alaska than it had been in L.A. Partly because incidents didn't happen as often, so the pace was slower. Officials didn't feel as rushed. But to Jonah it felt like everything happened in slow motion, and it was impossible for him to speed things up.

The top drawer of his desk was open a few inches. The eye from the shaman's amulet peered up at him. He opened the drawer a few more inches and stared back at it. It was almost as if the object was trying to tell him something. Was there any way he could use the artifact to put pressure on Lou or Mike?

He was still sitting there behind his desk when Matt appeared in the doorway. "You're here." Matt almost sounded surprised.

"Just got back." Jonah noticed for the first time that the gray in Matt's light brown hair was becoming more visible.

"Well, I came by to leave you a note. They've spotted the bear and are hoping to catch up with it soon."

"Good. Where?"

"In the foothills off one of the logging roads just south of the east ridge. Sounds like it's not too far from where you found Will."

"Do they need help?"

"No, they're okay that way."

"Good; I have enough to worry about." Jonah closed his desk drawer. He wondered if Matt saw the amulet, but if so, he didn't comment.

"Well, I'd better get back. If there's anything I can do, let me know."

After Matt left, Jonah took the amulet out of the drawer

and put it in his pocket. Then he swung by the grocery store to pick up a few things and went home to have some lunch. All too soon he found himself on the front steps of the Williams' house.

"Hello, Jonah." Only her eyes asked if there was any news. "Come in."

It felt to him like Ellen was as uncomfortable with the visit as he was. Even though they'd known each other for a long time, he was still a police officer investigating her husband's death. And she probably guessed that he didn't have good news.

"I'll come right to the point, Ellen. I haven't heard anything specific from the coroner yet; I'll let you know when I do. The tech guy from Juneau dusted the truck for prints, so I was going to bring it back. But there's a problem. Someone disabled the engine, and I'm not sure how much it's going to take to get it working again."

"Disabled it? What does that mean?"

"They pulled out wires and generally messed up the engine. I have no idea why."

"Your car is your lifeline out there. Who would do that?"

"I don't know." Will wouldn't have been able to leave even if he had been lucid enough to do so. But if he'd stayed in the truck, he might have had a chance to survive.

"It's still up there, then?"

"Yes. I was thinking that maybe one of your brothers might have a look at it. They could tow it down here easy enough. I just wanted to let you know it was all right to move it."

"Thanks." She kept looking down, like she didn't want to engage with him.

"One other thing–," he began. He noticed the near panic on her face. "I was wondering if Will had a bike."

She seemed surprised by the question. "No. I mean, I think he did a while back, but it's long gone." Her eyes darted around before settling on his. "Have you found out anything about the robbery yet?"

There was something off about her demeanor and the question. "You must have a reason for asking." It was a statement he had learned at a seminar once, a way to encourage someone to speak up about an issue on their mind.

She looked away and didn't respond.

"Ellen, if there's something bothering you, you need to tell me."

"I don't know what to do . . ." her voice trailed off.

"Listen to me. There are some dangerous people involved in this theft. They beat up Lou. Badly. And they threatened to harm another guy's wife and kids if he didn't do what they asked." Jonah stopped talking and looked around. "Where are your kids?" He suddenly felt cold.

"With their grandparents. They're okay."

"Ellen, I can't protect you or your family if I don't know what I'm up against."

"Oh, Jonah. He said I needed to keep my mouth shut." Her voice shook and tears welled up and trickled down her face. "I don't know what's going on. Lou won't tell me anything. No one will tell me anything."

"What happened?"

"I got a phone call. This man said Will had taken some money in exchange for certain 'goods' and that he hadn't come through with the goods. And if I don't give the money back, he said I'll regret it."

"Did he say how much money?"

The tears began rushing down her face, landing in splotches on her blouse. "Five hundred thousand dollars. He said he gave Will five hundred thousand dollars, and he wants it back. Where would I get that kind of money?"

"When did he call?"

"About an hour ago. As soon as I hung up, I took the kids over to their grandparents."

"Was it a long-distance call?" Long-distance calls were radio linked to the mainland and sounded somewhat different from local calls. But if the caller was smart, he would have called from a pay phone so it couldn't be easily traced.

"I . . . I don't think so. I was so nervous; all I heard was the part about Will owing someone $500,000."

"Ellen, you did the right thing by getting the kids out of the house. But I don't think this guy actually believes that you have the money. I think he's putting the squeeze on everyone." Jonah paused. "I want to go over your conversation with him, okay? From the beginning. What exactly did he say? And what did you tell him?"

She went through all the details she could remember, slowly, sometimes backtracking, trying to recall as much as possible. But it had been a simple conversation, simple and short. Nothing she remembered helped pinpoint who it might be.

"When you told him you didn't have any money and your husband never came home after the night of the theft, what did he say?"

"That, for my own good, I'd better figure out what happened to it, and he would be in touch."

"And Lou wouldn't tell you anything."

"He said he would take care of it."

Sure, Jonah thought. Like he'd done such a good job of handling things so far. "In the meantime, I think it would be wise if you stayed with your parents for a while. And don't go out alone or with just your kids. Okay?"

She was too shaken to argue. He waited while she packed a few things and drove her the few blocks to her parents' house, repeating the precautions he wanted her to take. Then he headed for Lou's.

He saw Lou peek out the front window at him, furtively, only a narrow strip of face showing. It occurred to him that Lou could leave by the back, but he walked up to the front door anyway. Lou would either talk to him or he wouldn't.

Lou opened the door before he had a chance to knock. "Come on in." The swelling on his face had gone down somewhat, but the bruises were coming into their own, a mottled dark blue Rorschach test. Jonah guessed from the way he held himself that the pain wasn't limited to his face.

"You're looking good," Jonah said.

"Sure."

"Alive is good."

Lou lowered himself onto the couch. His jeans had slit holes in both knees, his flannel shirt faded from years of washings. "What brings you here?" he asked, as if he didn't know.

Jonah sat down across from him and slipped the amulet out of his pocket. He held it up briefly, then tossed it to Lou. Lou caught it in midair, looking startled when he realized what it was. "Cute," he said, moving it back and forth in his hand.

"Recognize it?"

"I might."

"Don't play games, Lou. We both know what it is and where it came from."

"Okay, so I've seen it before." He tossed the amulet back to Jonah. "You got more?" It was clear he was trying to be nonchalant, to make it sound like an offhand question. But

Jonah could tell he was dying to know the answer.

Jonah cradled the amulet in his hand without saying anything.

"I'll bite," Lou said finally. "Where'd you find it?"

Ignoring the question, Jonah said, "It isn't worth much by itself, but with the other artifacts, excluding the screen, I've heard that the price tag might be $500,000 on the black market."

"Where'd you hear that?"

"You already know the answer to that question."

"Ellen," he said. He could hardly deny that she'd talked with him about the demand for money she didn't have.

"Settling for $500,000 when the screen and other artifacts are easily worth $1.5 million is understandable. For a local, that is. The point being that someone has the $500,000. So, here's the question . . ." Jonah's dark eyes locked with Lou's. "Do you?"

"Of course not."

"Then tell me who does."

"How should I know?" Lou turned away, staring at the wall behind Jonah as if there were answers to be found there.

"Look at me, Lou."

Lou reluctantly turned in his direction.

"Did Will have the money?"

"I don't know what you're talking about."

Jonah got up and walked over to Lou. "Dammit, Lou. You're not the only one in danger here. Do you want to see Ellen go through what you did? What about her kids? Do you want them beaten or kidnapped or . . . killed? You know what these people are capable of. So quit pretending like you weren't involved."

For a moment, both men thought Jonah was going to reach down and pull Lou to his feet, maybe even rough him up. Jonah had to force himself to back off. "If anything, anything at all, happens to Ellen or her kids, I'll hold you personally responsible. Personally *and* legally. Do you understand?"

"Jonah . . . I can't . . ."

"I'm not just speaking as an officer of the law. If you sacrifice them to save your fucking hide, you'll have to answer to me. And I can promise you that you'll get what you deserve." Jonah's voice ended loud and threatening, as he intended.

"Hell, Jonah—"

"Do I make myself clear?"

Lou slumped down and put his head in his hands. "Everything's gone to shit, man. Everything. I don't know what to do."

Jonah returned to his seat. "You can start by telling me everything you know about the theft and about Will's death. I can't help you if you won't tell me what happened and who you're mixed up with."

Lou looked up, his eyes pleading for understanding. "I don't know anything about Will's death. Honest to God, I don't."

"But you do know about the theft. So, start there."

"Did you find the rest of the artifacts?"

Jonah considered whether it was best to tell him the truth or not. "Only this." He held up the amulet.

"Will I have to go to jail?"

"Thieves usually do."

"Then why should I tell you anything?"

"Because you don't want to be charged with accessory to murder for one thing."

"But why—?"

"It's called felony-murder. If you're involved in one

crime, you're responsible for any deaths that result from it. I'm going to get to the bottom of this. I want the artifacts back. And I want to make sure Will's killer pays for what he did. If you don't help, you could be going away for a very long time."

They locked eyes again. After an awkward silence, Lou said, "Jonah, give me some time. I need to get my head wrapped around this."

"Lou, if you cooperate, I may be able to get you a reduced sentence."

"Gee, thanks, dad."

Lou's phone rang. Jonah motioned for him to answer it. Even at a distance, Jonah could hear the panicked voice of Mike's wife Laurie on the other end.

JINKAAT KA TLÉIX'

(ELEVEN)

"Give me the phone," Jonah said, snatching it from Lou before he could protest. "Laurie, this is Jonah St. Clair. Start over and slow down. Tell me what's wrong."

"I called Lou," she said, hesitating.

"Laurie, I think I can guess why you're calling. Did something happen to Mike?"

"Jonah, I need to talk to Lou."

"Lou can't help you, but I can. You need to tell me what's going on."

Laurie's usual confident demeanor was replaced by a quavery voice: "I got a call, a threatening call. The man told me I had better persuade Mike to . . . to give them what they're owed . . . or . . ."

"Or what?"

". . . or our kids could . . . disappear." Mike and Laurie had two small children with another on the way. She started making little hiccupping noises.

"Laurie, take a deep breath."

He heard her inhale.

"Now listen to me. Is Mike there?"

After a few loud sniffs, she said, "He went to the store. He should be back any minute."

"Tell him to stay put. I'll be right over."

"I'm going with you," Lou said.

Jonah looked at him. "The two of you have to make some decisions before anyone else gets hurt."

Lou looked away, then mumbled, "It wasn't supposed to

be like this."

Mike was just getting out of the car with a bag full of groceries when Jonah pulled in behind him in the driveway. At first Mike looked surprised, then he put on a big smile. "Jonah. What brings you here?" Then he saw Lou. "Lou . . . what's going on?" The smile faded to shock. "Lou, what the hell happened to you."

"Let's go inside," Jonah said.

"Sure, but . . ." Laurie was suddenly in the doorway, her hands folded over her rounded belly.

"Mike," she called out to him, her voice quavery. Mike started to run toward her, a loaf of bread falling out of the bag. Jonah grabbed the bread, and he and Lou followed Mike and Laurie inside.

The kids were in the living room and started crying when they saw how upset their parents were. It took a few minutes to sort everyone out. Finally, Jonah had Laurie take the kids and the groceries into the kitchen while he, Mike, and Lou stayed in the living room.

"Let's start with what we all know," Jonah said. "Someone beat up Lou and threatened your family, Mike. Perhaps that same someone who demanded that Ellen give them $500,000 because Will didn't *deliver the goods*. And someone attacked Will. Those are the facts. What I think happened is that you three were involved with the theft, but something went wrong."

"I thought a bear got Will," Mike said.

"He had a fight with someone, and that someone left him there, exposed and vulnerable."

"You don't think we had anything to do with Will's death, do you?" Mike said. "Will was our friend."

"If he really was a friend, then why don't you help me figure out who did that to him?"

"It's complicated," Lou said.

"How about giving me the names of your accomplices off the record? Once the dust settles, I'll see what I can work out for you."

Mike and Lou exchanged looks. "Hypothetically," Lou said, "neither Mike nor I can give you any names. Because . . . hypothetically, Will coordinated everything."

"So, hypothetically, you don't have any names, any artifacts, or any money from the sale."

"Hypothetically, that's why these guys are so pissed."

"You must have seen who beat you up, Lou."

"There were two of them. They didn't introduce themselves, but I can describe them."

"Were they the same two guys who drove the co-op truck?"

Mike and Lou looked surprised.

"Yes, I know about the co-op truck. What I don't know is why Will had the money."

"And all the artifacts except for the screen and the corner posts," Mike said. "Hypothetically," he quickly added.

"What was supposed to happen to the artifacts?"

"Still hypothetically, if things took longer than expected, it might have seemed better to transport the smaller artifacts on a boat rather than taking a chance on damaging them trying to quickly cram them haphazardly on the truck with the larger, heavier stuff."

"But the money—"

"The bottom line: we have no idea why Will took off. We were supposed to meet after . . . well, let's just say we were supposed to meet up with him. We looked everywhere we could think of, but he'd vanished."

It had become a habit. Whenever Jonah was trying to

work through a problem, personal or professional, he went to visit his adopted grandfather. He wasn't sure whether he was simply seeking reassurance from the familiar surroundings or if he seriously expected Dennis's oblique wisdom to help him find answers. Like the aha that sometimes happened when awakening from a dream or in the shower—when you didn't realize you were even thinking about something that was troubling you. In any case, he knew Dennis enjoyed his visits, so he made it a practice to frequently drop by.

Midway up the steep hill he passed several large black birds worrying something at the side of the road. They stood their ground as he passed by, swiveling their heads to keep an eye on him. One hopped a few times but didn't take to the air. The ravens in the area were large and brazen. They were even slow to run from barking dogs and seemed to consider themselves superior to humans. Maybe they were.

Dennis had told Jonah countless stories about Yéil, "the" Raven of Tlingit myths. The tales had captured his imagination at the time and still lingered in his mind, not necessarily as facts about the world, but as real as the stories told in the Bible. *In the beginning . . . the world was in darkness. Yéil contrived to be born to the daughter of the chef who owned Daylight because he wanted Daylight for his own. He knew that if he tried hard enough, he would get his grandfather to give him what he wanted.* A creation story with a message about family.

First, Yéil threw a temper tantrum until he got the Moon Box. While playing with it, the box fell open and the moon flew up into the sky. Next, he coaxed his grandfather into giving him the Stars. Finally, he got what he had been after all along: Daylight. Then, when the humans refused to cater to his whims, Yéil flooded them with daylight. They fled, becoming the animals of the forest and the sea.

As a child, Jonah had considered the creation tales of Yéil more fun than those told in the Christian church. Yéil had all the foibles of people—he was greedy and mischievous, he made mistakes, and lost his temper. But he was also clever and wise. Furthermore, the stories about Yéil were filled with animals and adventure, so even though they usually taught a moral, it made the behavioral lesson more palatable than a list of commandments whether written on paper or in stone.

Jonah knocked on the door of Dennis's house, but he didn't wait for a response before entering. He knew Dennis was in; he seldom went out anymore.

The old man was in his usual spot, a recliner pulled up next to the front window so he could see out and use the light from the window for reading. His eyes lit up when he saw Jonah standing there.

"I was afraid you'd be too busy to visit me today."

"I'm never too busy for you, Dennis." He went over and sat down close to him so he wouldn't have to speak in a booming voice to overcome Dennis's hearing deficit that had become worse of late.

"I hear Will is dead." Esther, Dennis's housekeeper and long-time friend always kept him up on current gossip and happenings in the village.

"Yes."

"Mauled by a bear. How awful." Dennis's hair was startling white in contrast to his lined, brown-skinned face. Jonah thought he would have made a good model for a Charley Russel portrait with his chiseled features and dignified bearing. "That was what killed him, wasn't it?"

Jonah was somewhat surprised by the question. Were there rumors going around already about the cause of death?

Or was it Dennis's usual intuitive understanding of people and his ability to see the big picture that was behind the question? Maybe he'd already linked the theft to Will's death.

"Why do you ask?" He wanted to find out if his hunch was right before telling him the whole story, his main reason for dropping by in the first place.

"Will grew up here. He was a fine woodsman, a careful one. I can't imagine him being surprised by a bear, although I know it does sometimes happen, even to the best."

"And . . .?"

"And . . . let's talk about his death first." He gave Jonah a knowing smile.

Jonah laughed. "You expected my visit, didn't you?"

"Not necessarily this soon."

"Well, I just talked to the coroner about the wound on the back of Will's head. I think someone hit him with something and left him for dead. But for some reason, he crawled away from his truck, and the bear found him. The coroner hasn't ruled out the possibility that he fell and hit his head on a rock, but there weren't any rocks in the area."

Dennis looked pleased with himself and sad at the same time.

"Don't mention that to Esther, not yet, okay?"

"It will be interesting to see when the village gossip catches up with the truth."

"In my experience, it doesn't take long."

"Esther will be here soon, is there anything else you can tell me 'off the record'?"

Since television had come to Koloshan, Dennis watched reruns of Columbo, The Rockford Files, and McCloud on his ancient television set with its rabbit ears antenna that constantly needed adjusting. He'd picked up some of the lingo and was always asking Jonah if he'd seen this or that episode. Jonah found it both endearing and a bit sad to think that stories told on TV might one day replace the tales he grew up loving.

"Well, 'off the record,' it appears as though Will was the inside contact for the theft at the Center."

"That seems to be 'the word on the street.'"

"That he was involved or that he organized it?"

"Involved. At least that's what Esther told me."

"What else did she say?"

"That Will, Lou, and Mike all needed money. And in the past, they've been in favor of selling the Raven House screen and some of the other artifacts."

"That hardly qualifies them as thieves," Jonah said. "Those two things would put a third of the villagers on the suspect list."

"Well, from their point of view, assuming they are the thieves, they were only taking what was rightfully theirs."

"Are you defending the theft?"

"Of course not. What they did was wrong. They took something that belonged to everyone to satisfy their own needs. But I'm saying that, given how ownership works in our community, they undoubtedly believe they can justify their claim."

"I agree. And I understand Will's motivation. Medical bills pile up fast. But I'm also worried about what this loss will do to the village if I can't get the screen and other artifacts back."

Dennis looked surprised. "What do you mean? Of course you'll get them back."

"I'm pleased that you have so much faith in me, but I'm not at all sure that I can. Especially not now that Will is dead. He apparently made all the arrangements for the sale. And it looks like he made off with everything but the screen, including the $500,000 payment for the artifacts. Why he would do that is a mystery. But it's all gone. And so far, my investigation seems to begin and end with Will."

The old man reached for the pipe on the small table next to his chair. He picked it up, then set it down again. He wasn't supposed to smoke, but he always wanted to when he was either upset or concentrating on a problem.

"You'll find a thread to pull and unravel the mystery of the missing artifacts; I know you will."

He picked up the pipe again and fingered the carved walnut surface. Jonah watched his slender fingers caress the familiar bear's head with its bulging eyes and exaggerated features. A segment from an iron gun barrel extended from the top of the bear's head about a quarter of an inch. Old gun barrels had been a popular material for pipe bowels among the 19th century Tlingits. The pipe had been in Dennis's family for generations and would someday belong to his grandson Dan.

"Dennis, I'm curious. How important do you think the screen and other artifacts are? I mean, what if they had been destroyed by some natural disaster or fire or whatever? Wouldn't you still be proud of your heritage?"

"I took you to see the screen once—do you remember?"
Jonah nodded.

"We held our celebrations there, in front of the screen. It watched over us."

"But none of the younger villagers remember what it was like then."

"That's the point. They weren't there. They can't know what it was like or even imagine what it was like unless they see the artifacts with their own eyes."

"But how does having a few artifacts stuck in the Center

help them understand the past?"

"Do you remember the story of how the Tlingit got fire?"

As fond as he was of the ancient stories, he'd been hoping Dennis would stay on topic and not drift off into the re-telling of an old legend. "Yes, I remember."

Dennis began repeating the tale, quickly assuming the sing-song voice he used for storytelling, a mesmerizing magician's voice punctuated with expressive dialogue. In this tale the dialogue was primarily between Yéil and an owl. *The problem for Yéil was in getting fire transported from the mountain of its origins to the people. At that time, the wood owl had a longer bill than any other bird, so he was the one most capable of carrying the firebrand to its destination.*

Of course, Yéil's motives weren't entirely pure. He also wanted to reduce the size of the owl's bill because he was jealous of it. In the end, he succeeded in both purposes: he captured fire to his people and maimed the owl. The owl's long bill was burned short and became a beak. Even his wing feathers were burned, and hence his wing spread lessened. But the owl persevered and became a great hero in the eyes of other animals.

"Determination and perseverance are wonderful gifts," Dennis concluded.

Jonah already knew he needed to keep trying to find both the missing items as well as the killer. The question he was wrestling with was the significance of their loss. "But fire is essential to life; artifacts aren't."

"You may be wrong, Jonah. The past always speaks to the present." With that he leaned back and closed his eyes. "Xat shaawakux," he murmured. I'm tired. He often lapsed into Tlingit when he was tired or excited. Jonah didn't always understand the words, but this time he did. He waited until he was certain Dennis was asleep. Then he slipped quietly away.

Outside, as if on cue, a raven flew overhead. "Okay, okay, "Jonah mumbled. "I'll keep trying. But don't expect too much."

He returned to the jail and flipped through the papers on his desk. "There must be better ways to spend a Sunday," he said out loud, staring at the brown bearskin stretched across the wall, its massive head drooping slightly as if concentrating on what he was saying. He continued staring at the bear, tempted to ask it about the message behind Dennis's story. Sometimes the message got obscured by the drama of telling. But there were always tidbits of wisdom intertwined with the narrative that didn't necessarily point to a particular solution for a specific problem but oftentimes laid the behavioral foundation for action.

Had Dennis been suggesting that to succeed even the raven asked for assistance? That hidden agendas often ran parallel to what appeared to be good intentions? That you could not only survive but thrive on bad things that happened to you? That determination and perseverance were necessary but more complicated than one might imagine? Or had he simply been reinforcing the importance of the past and therefore validating the significance of the artifacts to the community?

There was so much to do—the question was what he needed to do *right now*.

Ellen was probably safe enough with her family. One of her brothers still lived at home, as well as her grandmother. It was a crowded household, and a loving one, probably a good place for her to be while mourning the loss of her husband.

Lou and Mike were the wild cards. He knew they had

participated in the theft, but he didn't have enough evidence to arrest them. And finding the screen and other artifacts was more important to him than making an arrest. Furthermore, he was concerned for their safety and for the safety of Mike's family. But there was no way he could watch out for them and continue to investigate.

Dennis was right, he needed some backup, some assistance.

Maybe an owl to do the heavy lifting.

JINKAAT KA DÉIX

(TWELVE)

Jonah picked up the phone and dialed the Juneau police number. He didn't expect Jacobson to be there on a Sunday, but he thought it was possible that someone else would have the authority to assign him help. But, after being transferred from one person to the next, he realized that wasn't going to work. "Then call Jacobson at home," Jonah urged the anonymous officer on the other end of the line.

"I guess I *could* do that." He paused a moment as if hoping Jonah would say, *oh, don't bother.*

Instead, Jonah said, "Call me back as soon as you talk to him."

"Will do. But I can't promise anything."

The story of the owl carrying the firebrand to the people flashed through Jonah's mind. "Try really hard," he said.

Even if he got approval immediately, it was extremely unlikely they would fly anyone in that evening. It was late, and Koloshan was often treated like a poor relation. Juneau was, after all, "the city." The state capital, in fact. Not some isolated village dependent on fishing and government subsidies. He could also call the State Troopers, but they would require more explanation. It would be better if Jacobson agreed to send support. Until then, he would have to make do.

He called Ellen at her parents' home to see if everything was okay. He didn't want to make her more nervous, but he needed her to stay put; he didn't have the bandwidth to protect her if she went home.

"Any news?" she asked, her voice hopeful.

"No, not yet. I just wanted to make sure everything's okay."

After a slight hesitation, she said: "You think they will come back?"

"It's possible. That's why I want you to stay with your family. You have to be strong. And don't hesitate to call me if you see anyone suspicious hanging around, or if you get any more calls."

"Will do. Thanks, Jonah."

Don't thank me yet, Jonah thought. I haven't made much progress.

Next, he called Lou. "I'm going to stand watch on Mike's house tonight. But I'd rather they didn't know. And I'd like you to offer to stay with them. Mike will probably tell you it isn't necessary, but given the threats, I'm sure you can convince him." It was both a safeguard for Mike's family and a way for Jonah to keep an eye on Lou.

"Okay, I can do that."

"And, would you mind spelling me for a couple of hours around midnight?"

"Sure. More if you want."

"Just don't upset the family by mentioning the surveillance. And don't let anyone see you when you join me. I'll be in those trees to the west."

"Got it. No flashlight and bring coffee."

"Great."

"You really think they will make a move on Mike and his family?"

"Unless they've already found the artifacts and the money. Or if they still think you have it all. I can't imagine they are going to write off that much inventory and cash."

Lou was quiet for a moment. "You know, I would give

you names if I could."

"I believe you. As much as I disagree with what you did, I do understand."

"Hypothetically, you mean."

Jonah didn't respond. Everyone in Koloshan knew that Jonah took his role as a police officer seriously and that he didn't let someone off because they were a friend. But they also knew that he would go above and beyond to protect and help the residents of Koloshan. He wasn't about to let Lou and Mike off the hook just because he understood their need for money. On the other hand, he wouldn't take official action without sufficient evidence. And in this instance, he almost hoped he wouldn't find enough evidence to arrest the two, even though they deserved to go to jail for what they had done.

He went home to pack some food and snacks to pass the time and filled up a large thermos with hot coffee. His phone was ringing as he went in. He was almost surprised it was the officer from Juneau calling him back so soon.

"Good news," the man said. "We'll have someone there to support you by mid-day tomorrow."

"That *is* good news," Jonah said, thankful they were sending someone, even if not in time for the first night's surveillance.

In addition to food, he put together another pack with two flashlights, extra ammunition, binoculars, camera, notepad and pen, and a mini first aid kit. He tossed both packs and a sleeping bag in his Jeep. It had been fairly warm during the day, but it got chilly at night. If he was able to catch a few hours' sleep while Lou watched the house, he needed to stay warm.

Mike and Laurie's house occupied two lots at the end of a row of look-alike houses. Mike had added onto their house to accommodate their growing family. A rusted bike with training wheels lay on its side in the tall grass that was their front yard. Mike's old Ford station wagon was in the driveway.

Jonah drove past the row of houses up a side road. The sun had gone down, leaving a dusky shadow over the village. At least it wasn't raining, Jonah said to himself as he hauled his stuff into the wooded area behind Mike's house. There were several trails, probably made by kids and animals, so access wasn't hard. He passed by scattered pop cans and empty snack bags and a sock hanging from a branch next to a bedraggled baseball cap. Maybe he ought to get some kids together and clean up the mess on these back trails. Then again, someone else would come along and leave their garbage behind, so what was the use?

He found a spot with adequate cover where he could see the back of the house as well as most of the front yard. He wasn't sure if he wanted the two men to show up or not. If they did, it would be better if it happened tomorrow night, after the officer from Juneau was there as backup.

It was a relatively warm and dry night. He cleared a space in a tangle of brush and settled in for what could easily be a long and uneventful night. From his lookout, he could see people moving around inside the house. There were no curtains on the windows facing west. Maybe tomorrow he would suggest they hang up curtains or sheets, anything to provide less visibility for potential intruders. On the other hand, it was helpful for him to see inside and know everything was okay.

He'd spent a lot of nights on surveillance duty in L.A., but this felt different. For one thing, it was more personal. He knew the people involved, cared about them, and didn't want to let them down. He was confident of his investigative and policing skills, but at the same time, he felt somewhat unequal to the tasks at hand. He was only one person, yet everyone, including Dennis, expected him to bring the screen and artifacts back and to find out what had happened to Will. One person against organized, high-stake thieves who didn't hesitate to threaten people to get what they wanted. The trust placed in him was flattering, but was it realistic? Maybe if he caught the two men—

A pack of dogs was headed up the hill on the side road where Jonah had left his Jeep. The feral dogs of Koloshan were a strange lot. They usually kept their distance from people, but they didn't necessarily try to avoid them, wandering restlessly in search of what—food? Excitement? Other dogs? Not prone to barking, they paused and sniffed the air as they came alongside the trail leading to Jonah's hideout. After a few minutes, they moved on. A human hiding in the bushes apparently wasn't of any interest to them.

At around 7:30, all the lights went out in the house, except for a blue-white glow in the living room. Jonah envisioned everyone gathered in front of the TV. At 8:35, lights came on in one of the back rooms, a shaft of light illuminating a portion of the side yard. From where he was, Jonah couldn't see into the room, but he pictured Laurie and Mike putting the children to bed. When those lights were extinguished, there was still a small light on in the living room. Probably Lou, waiting until it was his time to spell Jonah.

He was on his second cup of coffee shortly after 11:00 when he saw Mike slip out of the house through the back door, moving quickly out of sight. Damn. Jonah leapt up, pushed past the brush, and hurried after Mike. He saw him start up a path heading away from the village toward the old reservoir, a strange thing to be doing at that hour. Obviously, the man wasn't out for an evening stroll.

There was a full moon overhead, but the visibility was poor under cover of the trees. Mike was using a flashlight, so Jonah was able to stay on the trail at a safe distance behind him, trying not to make any unnecessary noise. When he stopped to listen for a moment, all he heard were Mike's footfalls getting farther away.

Although he was used to being in the woods at night, he wasn't used to being out with only a .38, especially with a wounded bear in the vicinity. As he hurried after Mike, images of Will's fragmented body intruded on his concentration. He remembered Phil once commenting that in an encounter with a Grizzley the only use for a handgun was to shoot yourself before the bear got you. Not very comforting advice.

He didn't think Mike had been carrying a rifle either. A foolhardy gesture? Or was he meeting someone who had insisted he come unarmed?

Suddenly he was aware that he no longer heard Mike up ahead. If his calculations were correct, Mike should have made it to the spot where the old boardwalk began its climb over the hill behind the reservoir. It was a perfect place for a late-night rendezvous, easy to find and away from the village.

Jonah ducked into the woods and moved slowly parallel to the trail in the direction Mike had disappeared, maneuvering as quietly as possible through the sparse understory. In case the person Mike was meeting came on the same trail, he didn't' want to get caught in the open.

There were no voices. Maybe Mike was early. Or maybe whoever he was supposed to meet had spotted Jonah already and unilaterally called off the meeting. As he drew near, he could barely make out Mike pacing near the remains of the boardwalk. He squatted down, wishing he could see more. At least he should be able to hear any conversation in the still of the night. Crouching at brush level, he inched forward, hoping to gain a better vantage point.

He glimpsed Mike's dark form against the shadowy moonlight that filtered through the trees into the small clearing. He was still alone. Behind him the boardwalk yawned into the darkness. Mike stopped pacing and sat down on a stump at the edge of the clearing. If Jonah hadn't seen him walk over to the stump, he might not have noticed him sitting there. Perhaps that was what Mike had in mind while waiting for his late visitor.

After a few minutes, Mike stood up and moved toward the center of the clearing. Jonah saw him hold up his arm and turn it back and forth in the dim light as if he was trying to read his watch. Then he started pacing again, obviously becoming increasingly impatient.

Jonah hunched over and tried to read his own watch, but he couldn't even make out the flashing colons between the numbers. The digital beast had been a present, so he wore it, but he'd never liked it. He preferred the visual orientation of his former analog watch, certain its phosphorescent hands would have been visible even in this dim light.

He shifted to a more comfortable position and tried to prepare himself mentally for a long wait. Since he had no idea when Mike was supposed to meet someone there, he didn't know what to expect. And it was hard to judge the passage of time at night with so few visual cues.

It could have been five minutes or fifteen minutes later when Jonah felt a cramp in his leg. He quickly stretched it out and rotated his foot. Not young anymore, he thought. That kind of thing never used to happen. There had been a time when he could kneel indefinitely, waiting for a deer to expose itself. Now he was more comfortable sitting and less and less often longed for the feeling of the ground under his body on a night spent roughing it in the woods.

He wasn't aware when the thought began to take form. It started as a tiny tingle of discomfort at the back of his mind and gradually became a conscious fear. What a fool he'd been. *They* had been, he and Mike. Should he run back on his own or take Mike with him? If he was right, it was Mike's family at risk; he had to be told.

"Mike," he said softly, standing. "It's me, Jonah."

Mike jerked around to face him as he stepped out into the open. "What the hell are you doing here?" He kept his voice low, as if afraid of being overheard.

"I know you're waiting for someone. I assume either they're late, or . . . could the meeting have been a decoy, an attempt to get you away from home?"

Mike shrank back from Jonah. "What are you saying?"

"Is it possible? What time were they supposed to be here?"

"You think this was a trick?"

"Mike, forget for the moment that I'm a police officer. Just tell me, what time were they supposed to be here."

"Oh god, Jonah. No. No." He started off down the trail at a run, his flashlight bobbing up and down. Jonah followed. He'd always been a fast runner, partly because of his height. Even though Mike was younger, Jonah was in better shape and quickly moved past him, relying on dim spikes of moonlight to guide him as he raced down the trail. It might already be too late. Hopefully Lou hadn't been taken by surprise.

Branches whipped his body, more than one slapping him across his face. The bear was forgotten. His only thought was to get back to the house in time to prevent anything bad from happening to Mike's family.

He burst out of the woods and into the murky darkness of the summer night as though he was running for his life. Mike was no longer on his heels and was probably frantic. But that couldn't be helped.

The first thing he saw was that there were lights on in the house. The entire house was lit up. Damn. Damn. Damn. He put on a burst of speed despite his tired legs and aching lungs and went directly up to the front door, pausing a few seconds to catch his breath and draw his gun. If nothing was wrong, he was going to create one hell of a dramatic entrance.

He almost tripped over Lou's body, his eyes on Laurie in the middle of the living room, tied to a wooden kitchen chair, her thin nightgown stretched taut across the round mound of her stomach. She was making little moaning noises through the gag in her mouth. When she saw him, she began to jerk wildly at her bonds and make muffled noises in the back of her throat.

Lou groaned as he stepped past him. He touched Laurie's shoulder briefly before going to clear the other rooms. First the kitchen. Then down the hall, opening each door in turn while standing to one side, ready to shoot any intruders.

The children were both there, tied and gagged like their mother, frightened and struggling to get loose. Once Jonah was sure there was no one else in the house, he went first to the little girl and removed her gag. She immediately started calling for her mother.

"It's okay, your mother is fine." He heard Mike return and yelled to him: "The kids are safe." He was removing the boy's gag when Mike exploded into the room, breathing hard, his eyes wild.

"Oh, thank God," he said when he saw his children. Jonah left Mike to deal with the jumble of "daddies" and sobs and the rest of the untying.

He returned to the other room. Laurie was pulling at her bonds, her chair wobbling unsteadily as she struggled. "Everyone's fine, Laurie," Jonah assured her. "It was just a warning." He removed her gag.

"Jonah, they came here. I thought they took the children." She was bound up more securely than the children, her chair positioned so she couldn't see down the hall. Suddenly the kids appeared and rushed their mother amidst squeals and shouts. Jonah let Mike finish removing his wife's bonds while he went to tend to Lou.

Lou was moving around, trying to get loose. "It's okay, Lou. Everything's okay." Jonah removed his gag and cut his bonds with his pocketknife, then helped him to his feet. There was blood running down his face from a wound near his hairline.

"Sorry, Jonah," Lou said, his voice fogged with pain. "I didn't hear them until they were right on top of me. What happened? Where were you?"

"They lured Mike away, and I followed. I can't believe I fell for that."

"I should have been watching with you."

"Lots of should haves to go around."

Mike joined them as Laurie took the kids into the kitchen. "She's going to make them some hot chocolate," he said.

"Why don't you make the hot chocolate, Mike. I need to talk to Laurie."

Lou collapsed on the couch. Laurie came in, looking shaken and unsteady. There was an afghan throw over the back of the sofa. Jonah wrapped it around her shoulders after she took a seat, one hand protectively stretched across the stomach that held their third child.

"You okay?" he asked.

"I think we're fine," she said, patting her stomach.

"That's good." He took a deep breath. "I'm sorry to bother you now, but I need to know what happened."

"It was awful. I heard them when they attacked Lou."

"How many were there?"

"Two. Just two. Mike's gun was in the bedroom. I was trying to find it when they came charging in. They grabbed me and dragged me out here and tied me to that chair." Her shoulders started to shake.

"Take it slow," Laurie. "You're okay now. And so are your kids."

"They told me that we had all been warned, and they intended to get what was owed them."

"Then what?"

"The kids are heavy sleepers. I don't think they knew what was happening until . . . I heard Linda scream. Then she stopped screaming."

Those bastards, Jonah thought. Terrorizing a pregnant woman and two small children.

"Did you see their faces?"

"No, they wore masks, knit ski masks."

"What can you tell me about them?"

She closed her eyes as if trying to visualize the two men. When she opened her eyes, she shook her head. "I'm so sorry. I was panicked."

"That's okay, Laurie. Why don't you go back to your children and send Mike out."

Maybe now Mike would be willing to cooperate. *If* he knew anything.

"I suppose you think I'm pretty stupid," Mike said as he sat down on the end of the couch next to Lou's feet.

"Neither of us deserves any medals for smarts on this one. But that's in the past. The question is how to protect you and your family from these two in the future. They're not going to give up, you know."

"I suppose I should say 'thank you for trying,' but that's all I have to say." Mike frowned at him. "You were spying on us, weren't you?"

"Don't be an ass, Mike." Jonah felt anger welling up inside him. "You may have the right to put yourself in danger, but you don't have any right to do this to your family."

"I can take care of my family."

Jonah didn't point out the obvious. Lou was staring at his hands, avoiding eye contact. He and Mike must have talked earlier about what they were willing to share with Jonah, assuming they knew more than they admitted.

"As I told you before, I don't give a shit if you stole those artifacts or are sitting on the $500,000. This is no longer simply a disagreement between clans and individuals about the fate of some artifacts. Outsiders are involved, dangerous outsiders who aren't averse to hurting, even killing, people."

Mike and Lou glanced at each other, avoiding eye contact with Jonah.

"This may be your last chance to help me stop them before somebody else dies."

JINKAAT KA NÁS'K

(THIRTEEN)

His alarm went off at 7:00, a piercing sound like an angry bird. He was tempted to turn it off and go back to sleep. But even though his internal clock screamed for more, he tossed his comforter aside and pushed himself into an upright position. He'd never been one to party all night and go to work the next day feeling fine, but he'd pulled a lot of double shifts in L.A. And in Nam there had been no routine, no guarantee of uninterrupted sleep even for a few hours. Life in Koloshan was making him soft.

He savored his morning jolt of coffee and made extra to take to the jail. Then he called Ellen to make sure she had stayed put and hadn't been threatened again. A child answered the phone and dropped it with a loud clunk and yelled: "Mommy, it's for you." A cacophony of voices and a blaring radio or TV competed for attention in the background.

"Hello?" She sounded tired and tentative.

"It's Jonah. Just checking in. Everything okay?"

"Yes, fine."

"Any more threatening calls?"

"No. Maybe they've given up."

"Let's give it a little more time, okay?" Although it seemed likely that the two men were focused on Mike now rather than Ellen or Lou, having Ellen stay with her family was one less thing for him to worry about.

He wondered if the two men were surprised to find Lou

on the couch at Mike's. Whether they knew he was there or not, they hadn't wasted time trying to get him to talk. Maybe they'd decided that Mike had more to lose, and that gave them more leverage with him than with Lou. Jonah was certain it was only a question of time before the two men either called Mike to see if their actions had softened his resolve or returned to his house for a face-to-face showdown. If they returned, it would most likely be at night under cover of dark.

The piece of the puzzle that had to be forced to fit was why Will had taken off with the money and the artifacts. $500,000, even split three ways, was a lot of money for villagers. Besides, Jonah didn't believe Will would have deserted his family. Of course, he never would have considered that Will would double-cross two long-time friends either. There had to be another explanation.

The only good news was that he would have some backup by evening. You really needed two people for a stakeout— to keep each other awake and to spell each other for breaks. Even with backup, it would be another long night. Maybe a nap would help him stay alert later. He could use a bunk in one of the cells. But first he had a few calls to make.

Someone was in the building with him. He sensed their presence as he struggled to regain consciousness. Even a few years back he wouldn't have let someone sneak up on him like that. He was slipping.

The telephone rang as he swung his legs over the side of the cot. From the other room, he heard Matt's voice answer the phone and say: "He's right here. Just a moment." Matt poked his head around the corner. "You aren't locked up in there, are you?"

Jonah pushed open the jail door, went into the main room,

and picked up the receiver. "Thanks" he mouthed to Matt. "St. Clair," he said. He listened a minute to the person on the other end of the line. "Sounds good. I'll meet the plane." He hung up and turned to Matt. "Reinforcements."

"You need them?"

"Yeah, to keep an eye on a few people."

"If I can help—"

"Thanks, but I need someone who can make an arrest." Besides he didn't want to risk Matt getting hurt. He knew how to use a gun, but running a cold storage plant wasn't a substitute for police or combat training. Jonah had both, and Matt had neither. Matt had managed to miss being drafted for the Korean conflict by taking a few extra quarters to graduate from college, and he'd been too old for the Viet Nam War.

"Well, I just dropped by to tell you they didn't get the bear. They thought they had him cornered yesterday, but they lost him."

"That's one hell of an elusive critter."

"Yeah, there's some talk that he's not really alive, that he's a spirit wandering the land."

"Spirits don't maul people."

"But they wander the land?"

Jonah knew Matt was teasing, but he pretended to give the question some thought. He and Dennis had engaged in similar conversations about the relationship between myths and reality over the years. "People always want explanations for things. It's hardly surprising that those with a reverence for nature feel there's a life force that goes beyond the physical."

"Hey, I didn't mean to sound like I was putting the idea down," he said.

"Just that you don't believe it."

"Do you?"

"Well, no. I don't think there are spirits that take the form of animals and walk the earth. But, at the same time, myths serve a purpose. They fill a void in the unknown. They connect the here-and-now with the past. Like most religions do."

"Thank you, Professor St. Clair."

"I think people who aren't part of a small community have a different relationship with cultural tales."

"True. But the old Norse legends my grandparents used to tell are still vivid memories for me. At the time, I didn't think much about whether they were reality based or not. That didn't matter to me then. They were fascinating stories, and a very memorable part of my childhood."

"We're all caught in a time warp, aren't we? But maybe some communities have more to remember, and more to lose."

They left together. As Matt was about to go on his way, he suddenly turned back to Jonah. "I almost forgot—did you hear about the flap at the road site?"

"No. What happened?"

"Some of the locals are pretty upset about a grave that was unearthed."

"That was what Mann was hired to do, wasn't it? To supervise the excavation and protect anything found."

"But this grave was different. It seems there was a body outside the coffin."

"You mean a slave buried with its owner?"

"Yeah."

"Why is that a big deal? The fact that Native Americans had slaves and that occasionally they were sacrificed at the death of their owner isn't news."

"I know. Supposedly so they would have servants in the

afterworld. But this grave is different. The slave body is missing its head. And Mann said the remains could be as recent as the early 1900s."

"He probably should have kept that little detail to himself. Until he can prove it, at least. I see why that makes him the bad guy in this.

"A number of locals are going out there to confront him."

"How long ago did you hear this?"

"About half an hour."

"Thanks, Matt. I'll stop by and see what's up." Damn, that was the last thing he needed, another reason for people to get all riled up.

He drove along the winding dirt road faster than he knew he should, his tires skidding on the uneven surface, dust swirling upward in a thick brown haze, the color of LA smog on a bad air pollution day. When he arrived at the site, he found a crowd already there ahead of him, including some of the same people who were upset over the theft of the artifacts.

"How can you be so sure?" Jonah heard someone yell as he joined the group.

Mann was standing in front of the crowd, looking confused and belligerent at the same time. "There are several indicators. I've just gone over that." When he saw Jonah, he immediately brightened up. "Hey, did you hear about what we uncovered?"

Everyone turned to look at Jonah. "Yes," he replied.

"I'm going to have the remains transported to the University for testing."

A ripple of protest went through the crowd.

"I'm authorized to make determinations about anything with historic significance unearthed during the project." He was looking at Jonah but speaking to the crowd.

"Maybe you could hold off for a bit, until you have a chance to talk to the council about what you've found," Jonah said.

Mann quickly went on the defensive while the bystanders watched the exchange between the two men with an intensity that felt palpable. "This is something we didn't anticipate, something that might have historical significance."

Someone shouted: "He can't do that, can he, Jonah? That's grave robbing."

"Don't worry," Jonah assured the onlookers. "Everything will be done according to procedure. Why don't you all go home and let me take care of this."

No one seemed eager to leave, unsure whether Jonah had given them an order or a suggestion. After a few minutes of murmuring and foot shuffling, the crowd slowly dispersed. Some drove off, others began walking back toward the village, swallowed up by the dust created by the departures. As soon as they were alone, Mann turned to Jonah. "It's a good thing you showed up when you did. Some of them were getting a little aggressive."

"You can't blame them, can you?"

"What do you mean?"

"How would you like it if you found out your grandfather not only owned slaves but approved of the practice of beheading and burying them with their owners when they died?"

Mann shrugged. "It wouldn't bother me. It's rather like having a pirate in the family, isn't it?"

Jonah decided not to pursue the conversation about culture. Mann knew that the Tlingit were not unique in their ownership of slaves nor in the ritual of sometimes burying slaves with their owners, even beheading them for burial.

But most liked to think of that practice as not only in the past, but as ancient history. Mann's response suggested he hadn't a clue what the label "primitive" meant to the native culture and why they wanted to distance themselves from anything that evoked that label. "Where are the remains?"

"Over there." Mann pointed to a large box. "I've sent for a truck to transport them."

"Can't you do the testing here?"

"In Koloshan?"

"Yes"

Mann frowned. "It would be awkward."

"It might save you a lot of trouble."

"You think there will be trouble if I try to remove the remains?"

"First of all, you may not have the right to do so under your contract. If it's at all unclear, you will get legal pushback. Are you sure you want to deal with that? And keep in mind that the villagers are already upset about the stolen artifacts. They aren't in the mood to be reasonable. You would be doing everyone a favor if you figured out how to do the testing here. Once the age of the remains is determined, you can work with members of the council to assess the best way to handle the situation."

Mann considered for a moment, then relented. "Okay, I don't want trouble; I'll have them take the remains to the Center."

"Thank you. That should lower temperatures a notch or two."

"I appreciate you taking the time to come out here like this. I know how busy you are."

Jonah didn't have to reply because a truck pulled up, and Mann excused himself to direct the loading operation. Jonah hung around to make certain no one interfered before heading back to the village.

He spotted Lou in front of the marina and pulled over to see how he was. "You have Sue check out your head?" he asked. Lou had a butterfly bandage on his forehead.

"Yeah, she thinks I'll live."

"Well, they may show up again tonight. I'd appreciate you staying at Matt's another night. And I'll have backup, so you won't need to spell me."

"I'm already tired of sleeping on a couch."

"Hopefully it won't be for much longer. And don't wander off by yourself today."

"I'll be here. I'm going to do some work on the boat."

The first thing Jonah did when he got to the jail was to call the coroner's office. "Did you do an autopsy on Williams yet?"

"First thing this morning."

"And—?"

"I can tell you a few things."

"I'm listening."

"Sadly, he was still alive and possibly conscious when the bear attacked. There were some discernable defensive wounds. The blow to the base of his skull was caused by some smooth, heavy instrument. It did considerable damage, but it would not have resulted in death. That's it. Unless you want the technical version."

"No, that's what I needed to know. Thanks."

He hung up and sat there with the receiver still in his hand. Had the person who struck Will left immediately? Did they have any idea that there was a bear in the area? Was it a case of negligent homicide? Manslaughter? Attempted murder? Whatever the legal charge, it was a cruel act to leave someone incapacitated like that in the woods. But unless the person knew Will was still alive, why disable his truck?

The next call he made was to the police lab.

"I ran the prints through our files," Calvin said. "No matches there. So, I sent them off. It will probably take a couple of days before I get anything back. I'll call you as soon as I do."

There was no pen on his desk. Where did they always disappear to? He opened the top drawer and rummaged through the papers and other odds and ends until he came up with a dulled pencil. It would have to do. His previous *to-do* list was also gone; probably left it in a pocket. He started making a new one.

Technically, if Will's death wasn't murder, it was no longer an official top priority, although still near the top of the list for him. No matter how a prosecutor looked at it, he wanted to know who struck Will and left him there to die. He would have thought whoever attacked Lou and threatened Mike was responsible, but if Will had absconded with the artifacts and the money, then why were the two men still searching for them? Even if neither of them had attacked Will, they might have some information that would help him unravel the details of the theft and, in turn, enable him to put the rest of the puzzle pieces together.

The airplane wasn't due for a half hour, but Jonah decided to drive out to the airport early and relax with a cup of coffee and mull the facts that he knew. Let his little grey cells search for patterns.

It was a calm, overcast day, not warm, but a typical summer day for the area. He rolled the windows down and leaned back, enjoying the light and warmth of the moment. If he'd had longer to relax, maybe he would have connected some dots, but the flight was right on time. The plane made a smooth landing and taxied over to the terminal shelter.

The first person out was the pilot. He waved at Jonah before turning back to watch his passenger descend. She was a petite young woman with red hair, a duffle bag hanging from one shoulder. When she reached the bottom of the steps, she shook hands with the pilot and walked quickly over to Jonah. As she approached, he noticed the smattering of freckles across a small, straight nose. She flashed a warm smile and said, "You must be Jonah St. Clair. I'm Officer Jenny O'Farrell."

Jonah automatically reached out when she extended a hand, leaning over slightly to compensate for their difference in height. She couldn't have been more than a few inches over five feet tall. Her hand felt tiny in his, but her handshake was firm.

"You're my backup," Jonah said, immediately regretting his skeptical tone and wishing he could take back the comment.

"That's right." She was wearing dark brown corduroy slacks and a brown and gray sweater that camouflaged her shape without hiding the fact that she was female. As she bent over to retrieve the duffle bag she had put down to shake hands, Jonah instinctively reached for it. "I can manage," she said, firmly but not defensively.

They started back toward the Jeep. Jonah's mind was racing. She couldn't stay with him as he'd planned, so where was he going to put her up? It would have to be the Lodge. There was no budget for that sort of thing, but he could pay for it himself. Damn Jacobson. He'd done this on purpose.

"How long have you been on the force?" Jonah asked.

"About three years."

"Like it?"

"I like the work a lot."

Jonah sensed there was a double meaning in the response,

but he couldn't quite put his finger on the message. "Have you been told much about this assignment?"

"Some people have been threatened, and you need someone to accompany you on a stakeout. That's all I know."

"You bring a gun?"

"Yes." She glanced over at him with an impish grin. "And yes, I know how to use it."

"I'm hoping you won't need it, but the two men we'll be watching for have already beaten up one man and threatened the families of two others. Some show of force may be needed in order to make an arrest."

"I may be small, but I'm strong," she said. "And I'm a good shot."

That made him smile. He liked the fact that she was straightforward and sounded confident. After all, what he needed was a second set of eyes, not a linebacker.

When they arrived at the Lodge, he explained that she would be staying there. "I'll have to run you back and forth to get you though, because I don't have a spare vehicle at the moment."

"No official car?"

"A pickup truck. But something's wrong with it."

"I'm pretty good with motors. I had several brothers who were always taking engines apart and putting them back together. They let me help. Maybe I could have a look."

"Sure. I would appreciate that."

They went inside and Jonah arranged for her room, explaining who she was and that they weren't sure how long she would be staying. Maybe one night, maybe a few more. Then he waited while she went to drop off her stuff. It only took her a few minutes before she returned.

She had never been to Koloshan, so as they drove to the

village, he pointed out a few landmarks before turning up through the residential area past Mike's house. "That's the one we'll be watching."

"Looks like you have a pretty good view from the woods over there."

"That's where I spent last night."

"Sorry I wasn't here to spell you." She glanced at her watch. "If there's time before we start, I could take a look at that pickup of yours. What's the problem?"

"Well, for a while it was slow to start, sluggish once I got it going. Now I can't get it running at all."

"I'd be happy to take a look."

"Sounds good. I have a couple things to do."

"I will need a work shirt though; I didn't bring anything like that. And a few tools."

"No problem." They stopped by his house to pick up what she needed. Then he drove her to the jail. "I'll be inside if you need me." He felt guilty leaving her like that, but she was the one who'd made the offer, and he didn't know anything about cars or trucks except how to drive them.

He'd managed to check off a few things on his to-do list when he heard an engine rev up. He went outside and saw her standing proudly beside the truck, a smudge on her forehead, a wrench in her hand, and a triumphant smile lighting up her face. "Thought I couldn't do it, didn't you?"

"I had my doubts. Not about you," he added quickly. "But I had no idea how bad it might be."

"If you took better care of it, you wouldn't have these kinds of problems," she said, beckoning him over to look at the engine. She pointed: "Air filter was filthy. You must drive this thing on really dusty roads." She paused, glanced around, and laughed. "Obviously. Anyway, I've cleaned it off with a brush. It will be OK for a while. But you need to replace it soon. You ever get this thing in for regular service?"

He shook his head. "Not a lot of Jiffy Lubes in town."

"I made a few adjustments, but it wouldn't hurt to have this thing tuned up by a professional. You might also consider changing the oil occasionally." She laughed again, this time at him. "Is there a place inside where I can clean up?"

He waited while she washed up. When she was done, she asked: "Now what?"

"You hungry?"

"I'm always hungry."

"Then I guess I owe you a meal at the very least."

They walked to The Café. On the way, she asked questions about what had been stolen from the Center and pressed him for details about his suspicions. He didn't want to say much about his conviction that Lou and Mike were involved in the theft, so he emphasized their friendship with Will as the probable reason they were being targeted by the two men suspected of taking the screen and corner posts.

As they went inside, he was aware that everyone was sneaking looks at them. Jonah almost wished he was ten years younger and they were on a date. By village standards, it was impolite to stare at someone, but they couldn't help themselves; she definitely didn't blend into the surroundings. Not with that hair. And not being accompanied by their only police officer, a single male. Jonah wondered how long it would take before village gossip figured out that she was a Juneau police officer. He wasn't going to enlighten them . . . at least not yet.

Joe was behind the counter when they came in. He raised his eyebrows in question, but Jonah ignored the look as he steered her toward his usual table.

"I'll get some sandwiches for later," Jonah said. "You'd better eat as much as you want now though. It could be a long night."

Jenny studied the stained handwritten menu. "What's good?"

"Just about anything—if Joe's in the mood to cook."

"Okay, then I'll have the fish and chips with a salad and a piece of pie." She set the menu aside.

"Ice cream on the pie?"

"Sounds good" She didn't seem to realize Jonah had been teasing her. "Tell me more about these two men you're after."

Joe waved his teenaged part-time waiter away and personally came over to take their order. "Joe, this is Jenny O'Farrell." He glanced around, then lowered his voice and added, "She's a police officer from Juneau here to help out with my investigation." Joe's face didn't show what Jonah knew to be disappointment. A confirmed bachelor himself, he was always hoping Jonah would meet someone.

"Hope you enjoy your stay with us," Joe said loud enough for the nearest customers to hear. Joe was a quick study. "Now, what can I get you to eat?"

After Joe went to fill their order, Jenny leaned toward him and in a hushed voice asked, "Why tell him so softly that I'm a police officer? And why did he loudly make a point of me *visiting*?"

"As to your first question, I would rather the entire village didn't know why you're here. But Joe and I are friends. He knows about the investigation, and he's very familiar with the gossip grapevine in Koloshan."

"Should we hold hands?" she said.

"I don't want to mislead; just keep them guessing."

"Got it. No hand holding."

"You like to tease, don't you?"

"Sorry. I'm often too outspoken." For the first time she looked uncertain.

"That's a good thing. But I doubt I'm known for my sense of humor."

"You take life seriously? That's OK. It *is* serious."

"Maybe too seriously."

Their food arrived, and they both dug in. It was definitely one of Joe's good days. The food was excellent, and Jonah was amazed at how much she ate. Joe's portions were always large, and he had gone all out. While they were lingering over coffee, Jonah asked, "How'd you end up getting this assignment?"

"I was told you needed someone with surveillance experience."

"Did they warn you it could be dangerous?"

"*All* police work is potentially dangerous."

"But you weren't told any details."

"No. But I would have wanted to come even if they had."

"Well, my plan is to have one of us watching the house at all times. I'll sleep there when you're on watch. You can go to my place to nap while I'm watching."

"That isn't necessary. All I'll need is a blanket, or whatever you're using."

"You're sure?"

"I like camping; I can sleep on the ground." She grinned. "And pee in the woods."

"Did I mention we have a rogue bear that we're trying to find?"

"No, but I always carry bear spray."

"Does nothing scare you, Jenny O'Farrell?"

"Failure," she said. Then quickly added: "Oops, that slipped out. But I'm afraid it's true."

"It's not something I'm fond of, but so far with this investigation, I've not had much success."
"Maybe tonight we'll turn things around."

JINKAAT KA DAAX'OON

(FOURTEEN)

It was another warm night. A pale moon dominated the evening sky. Stars flickered on and off. A dark bird spread its wings and soared upward as a light breeze chased itself through the trees. It was a night for stargazers and lovers. But for Jonah and Jenny, it was a night for vigilance and stealth.

They couldn't talk much for fear of their voices carrying in the motionless air, but just being together under the night sky produced a certain kind of intimacy, a cocoon of isolation from the rest of the world, like being in a dark theatre watching life at a distance.

Jonah felt comfortable with Jenny, although he had some concerns about how well she could handle herself in a physical confrontation with the thieves. Hopefully it wouldn't come to that. Two officers with guns and the element of surprise should be enough to subdue the two men without a fight.

Jenny took the first shift. While she watched the house, Jonah lay there in the sleeping bag. At one point, he studied her outline against the night sky. She seemed young and fragile to him, in spite of her jauntiness and air of confidence. Being with her made him realize just how much he missed by not being in a relationship. Living in Koloshan limited the dating pool and made it next to impossible to have a casual relationship without everyone in the village speculating about whether it would end in marriage. It wasn't that he was against marriage, but he liked being independent and was happy living alone with no one to answer to. Still, if the right person came along—

A car sped down the street, the engine noise unnaturally loud against the backdrop of nature's subtle night sounds. Jonah closed his eyes and tried to sleep, but thoughts of Mike and Lou intruded. Neither man was pleased with the stakeout, but for different reasons. Lou didn't want to stay at Mike's again. He said he felt like he was intruding on their family life. And Mike argued that he should be able to take care of his family on his own. By Koloshan standards, they were tough men, not afraid of a fight, men used to standing up for themselves. But from Jonah's perspective, they had given up the right to be left to their own devices after they put others in jeopardy.

Earlier, he had explained the situation to Jenny, making it clear that at this point it was all guesswork; he didn't have any solid evidence. Together, the two of them speculated about scenarios that explained what might have happened if Will was the one who ended up with the smaller artifacts and the payment money. One possibility was that the three local men plotted together to keep the smaller artifacts and sell them separately, assuming the person behind the theft wouldn't come after them for fear of exposing their own involvement. What if Will had been designated to meet with the buyer, and he or she double-crossed them, took the artifacts and the money, and left Will to die? That seemed more likely than Will going entirely rogue.

But there were other possibilities. For instance, what if the two outsiders involved in the heist had kept the artifacts and the payment money for themselves and were pretending the three locals had run off with it in order to throw off whomever had hired them in the first place? If that was the case, they were putting on a damn good show, and that didn't explain what had happened to Will, since the two outsiders supposedly left with the screen on the ferry before he drove up into the woods.

Other scenarios they considered involved unknown players, either outsiders or locals. When so much money was involved, greedy people could be incredibly creative. Maybe they would get some leads from fingerprints or from the two men when they caught them. *If* they caught them.

It was unfortunate that Lou and Mike were still refusing to talk openly about the heist. They were apparently banking on Jonah not being able to gather strong enough evidence to tie them to the theft. For them, catching the two men was a double-edged sword. It might end the threat of physical harm, but it could also mean jail time.

Jonah dropped off to sleep, awakening when he heard Jenny pour herself some coffee out of the thermos. He lay there thinking about what would happen if he didn't find the screen and the rest of the artifacts. He would definitely lose credibility with the community, and it would be a failure that some might find hard to forgive.

About 1:00 a.m. Jonah got up and shared a sandwich with Jenny. Then he suggested she take a break, stretch her legs, or get some sleep. She didn't want to sleep, but she did do some stretching exercises before resuming her watcher's position.

The night passed slowly, like stakeouts usually did. Seconds as long as minutes, minutes as long as hours. Time almost but not quite standing still. Jonah napped again, waking up at 5:00 a.m. and unable to go back to sleep. He joined Jenny, and together they watched the slumbering house as the sun gradually forced itself upon the world. They drank the last of the now lukewarm coffee and ate a few dry cookies.

At 6:30 a.m. they called it a night. It was too early for the Lodge to be serving meals, so Jonah offered to make breakfast. While he cooked, Jenny sat at the table holding a hot cup of coffee in her hands, occasionally taking a sip.

"Same thing tonight?" she asked.

"Yeah, and we may get another officer to help out. At least that's what they said originally."

"Good. That means you can get some real rest."

"I still want to be there, but you two can trade off."

"Don't trust anyone, huh?"

"This is important to me."

"I take my assignments seriously." She sounded matter-of-fact, not self-justifying.

"It's knowing all the players. That makes it personal."

She nodded. Under the harsh track lighting, he noticed for the first time that she had gold flecks in her dark brown eyes. "I won't argue. You're every bit as stubborn as my father."

Jonah felt a stab of annoyance. Was that how she saw him? As fatherly? He was only about ten years older than her, although there was definitely a chasm between their perspectives on life. She was still walking the Yellow Brick Road to enlightenment, optimistic about what the future might bring. Hers was a world in which one simply had to work hard and persevere and good things would happen. He'd felt that way once. But now, he accepted that the wizard behind the curtain was an ordinary human with no special powers. Living was for him all about managing emotional scars from the past and seeking happiness in the moment.

He stirred the fried potatoes in the pan, perhaps more vigorously than necessary.

"That smells wonderful."

He put two slices of bread in the toaster and got out the

eggs. "How do you want your eggs?"

"Over easy."

She sat there quietly while he concentrated on cooking. He felt comfortable with her silence. That was something it usually took time to achieve.

When breakfast was ready, they both ate with enthusiasm. Jonah put out a jar of Esther's blueberry jam, and Jenny liked it so much she ate three pieces of toast.

"Where are you from?" He hadn't thought to ask.

"Oregon. What about you?"

"Originally California, but I spent time fishing out of Koloshan with my father when I was young. Then I stayed with a friend's grandfather for a couple of years after my mother passed away."

"I heard that you spent time with the LAPD."

"Six years."

"Did you like it?"

"It was a valuable experience, but I can't say I *liked* it. Then I did a tour in Nam before coming back here."

She gave him a raised eyebrow at the mention of Nam, and he held up a hand to stop her from asking more about his time there. "I've been here ever since."

"And do you plan on staying here?"

"It's home."

"So, no desire to move up the ladder?"

"I like it here. What about you? Are you ambitious?"

She laughed. "It depends on what you mean by that. I can't picture myself in an office job, and promotions often take you there. What I think I would like to do is start some programs for young kids. Keep them from turning to drugs or alcohol for answers. That sort of thing."

"Sounds admirable."

"I don't know about that, but I would like to find some

way to make a difference."

When he first joined the LAPD, he had wanted to make a difference. He believed his role was to protect the community while enforcing laws and responding to emergencies, and he assumed he would be part of a team with similar attitudes. Instead, he frequently encountered cynicism, self-interest, and sometimes brutality. It didn't take long to become distrustful, wary of the brotherhood, and somewhat warped by his own experience with criminals. It was different in Koloshan. In more ways than he could name. He didn't mind dealing with petty crime or being the only one responsible for maintaining order in the community, and he valued the respect showed him by villagers. He also enjoyed coaching kids on the basketball court and engaging in conversations with locals. If at times it was frustrating to have to deal with bureaucracy from a powerless position, that was the price he had to pay.

"With a name like O'Ferrall, I assume you're Irish. Ever been to Ireland? I suppose everyone asks you that."

"Yes, people ask. And, no, I haven't been. But some day. It's funny, I never think of myself as Irish, but with red hair and the 'O' surname, people always assume I am. Irish and all that goes with it—shamrocks and Irish coffee."

"Leprechauns and pots of gold."

"Guinness."

"St. Patrick's Day."

"Riverdance."

"James Joyce."

"James Joyce—have you read James Joyce?" she asked.

"Gave it a try in college. But as Irish authors go, I'm more of a Jonathan Swift or Bram Stoker fan."

"I admit to having a fascination with vampires. It's strange how tales about vampires and werewolves have become part of the American culture."

"It's all about the stories we tell. Like your associations with being Irish or the stories handed down by the Tlingit from one generation to the next."

"Living in Koloshan, do you feel connected to the Tlingit culture?"

"I feel like it's at least a part of me. Not in the same way as if my ancestors were from here. But whatever Koloshan is now and becomes in the future is part of my identity."

"That's why catching these thieves is personal."

"Yes."

They talked and drank coffee, both seemingly reluctant to end their time together. But finally, they had to get on with their day.

Jonah gave her the keys to his official truck. Now that it was running smoothly, she could drive herself out to the Lodge. Then he went to the jail to see if there were any messages and to make a few calls. He was pleased to find out that the other officer was arriving around 5:00, in plenty of time to take a shift in the stakeout. It did cross his mind that Jacobson might have still another surprise in store for him, but it didn't really matter. An additional set of eyes was what they needed. And if the new officer was a woman, she could share Jenny's room at the Lodge.

The telephone rang while he was trying to decide on his agenda for the day. It was Mary Jo at the school. She asked if he could drop by before her first class. There was something she wanted to show him.

He met her outside the main entrance. She was wearing a flattering summer dress that accentuated her Nordic stature and fair complexion. He couldn't help comparing her to Jenny. They were both appealing, but in entirely different ways. Still, it was a moot issue; he didn't intend on pursuing a relationship with either woman.

Without a word, Mary Jo handed him something. It was a Tlingit spoon made of a curved mountain sheep horn with an ornate carved handle. Jonah instantly recognized it as one of the missing artifacts. "Where did you get this?"

"Some of the kids brought it to me late yesterday. I tried to reach you but couldn't."

"Why did they bring it to you?"

"Because they know I'm interested in native artwork."

"Did they realize it's from the Center?"

"I don't think they made the connection."

Jonah looked down at the horn spoon. "Who gave it to you?"

"Jayme Latham and Gavin White."

"Jayme and Gavin?" Jonah knew the boys; they were both native—surely they realized the significance of the piece. "Where did they get it?"

"You can talk to them first period if you want. They're in study hall then. They can tell you all the details." She glanced at her watch. "I need to run—"

"Thanks, Mary Jo. I appreciate this." This could be the breakthrough he'd been hoping for. He went inside to the principal's office and told the secretary that he needed to talk to the two boys.

"They aren't in any trouble, are they?" she asked, sounding sincerely concerned.

"No, I just need to talk to them about something they found."

She paused a moment as if hoping he'd say more, but when he didn't, she left to get the boys. In just a few minutes she returned with them in tow. They looked apprehensive, and a bit puzzled. Mary Jo must not have prepared them for Jonah's visit. That was smart of her.

Jonah took them into the gym to talk. He remained standing, facing them, using his height as a power strategy. "Recognize this?" He held out the horn spoon.

"It's the spoon we gave to Miss Johansson."

The boys exchanged worried glances.

"It's okay," Jonah said. "You aren't in any trouble. I just want to know where you got it."

"You tell him," Gavin said to Jayme. They were both seventh graders, but Jayme knew Jonah better because of his interest in becoming a basketball player. He was short but agile; Jonah had done some coaching with him and thought he had promise.

"Well . . . we were up in the woods near Eagle Peak, following the big stream that runs down the hill toward the village. It was just lying there on the ground."

Eagle Peak was a rock formation on the east ridge, not too far from where Jonah had discovered Will's body. Perhaps if Jonah had gone upstream instead of down the day he had tracked the city-shoe footprints, he might have found the horn spoon himself.

"How close to the Peak were you?"

"About . . ." Jayme turned to Gavin. "What would you say, about two miles?"

"That seems right."

"And you found it lying on the ground, not covered up or anything?"

"Right out in the open."

"Did you look around to see if you could find anything else?"

"You mean more spoons, stuff like that?"

"Yes."

"A little; not much. We didn't really think there would be more. We figured someone dropped it."

They probably figured right, but not in the way they were thinking. "What were you doing up there?"

Both boys immediately looked down. Jonah had apparently asked something they didn't want to answer. He left the question hanging, waiting patiently for the boys to look at him.

"Do we have to say?" Gavin finally asked, still unwilling to meet Jonah's eyes.

"It has nothing to do with the spoon," Jayme said, bravely meeting Jonah's gaze.

"I need to know what you were doing there."

"Do you have to tell our parents?"

"I can't promise anything until you tell me why you were there."

"You know my dad," Jayme said. "He thinks I'm still just a little kid. He didn't want me to go along when they were tracking the wounded bear." He motioned toward Gavin. "His parents said he couldn't go either."

"So . . .?" Jonah prompted.

"Well, everyone's been out there looking, and . . ." He stopped and glanced down again.

"And you thought you might get lucky," Jonah finished for him.

"Something like that."

"You understand that what you did was dangerous, don't you?"

The two boys nodded, still avoiding eye contact with Jonah.

"Wounded bears can be unpredictable."

"Dick Hill got to go, and he's only in the sixth grade," Gavin said with surprising force.

Finding that bear had become a major activity for villagers; Jonah understood why the two boys wanted to be part of it. But even if they were proficient with guns, it was too unsafe for them on their own.

"What if I talk to your fathers . . .," he began.

"No, please don't," both boys said in unison.

". . . and suggest that they take you along on the bear hunt."

"You'd do that?" Both boys set aside their guilt and stared up at Jonah.

"Only if you promise not to go out alone again. Agreed?"

Both boys nodded excitedly. Then Jayme asked: "Are you going to tell our parents what we did?"

"I see no reason for that." The two instantly relaxed, already looking ahead to being included in the search for the rogue bear.

"I do have one more question though." He struggled to find the right words and finally settled for being direct. "Did you realize the spoon was one of the artifacts stolen from the Center?"

Both boys looked stunned. "I didn't think of that," Jayme said. "Did you, Gavin?"

Gavin shook his head. "We should have, shouldn't we?"

"You know about the theft."

The boys nodded.

"Well, for now, do you think you can avoid telling anyone about the spoon?" To make sure they kept mum, he added, "Otherwise, I can't encourage your fathers to include you on the hunt. Nor can I guarantee that I won't have to tell them what you were doing when you found the spoon." Jonah looked from one boy to the other. "Do I make myself clear?"

They both nodded again.

When Jonah said they could go, they rushed off as fast as their worn tennis shoes could carry them. As Jonah reflected on their conversation, it made him sad to realize how removed the two boys were from the emotional impact of the loss of the artifacts to the community. In spite of being born and raised in Koloshan, they already had one foot outside of the culture. Maybe the artifacts *were* better off in a museum somewhere.

But Will would have been better off alive.

PART III

Consequences

JINKAAT K̲A KEIJÍN

(FIFTEEN)

Jonah discovered the camp by accident. He had been looking for the footprints of the two boys, doing a zigzag search along the stream in the Eagle Peak area where they said they'd found the Tlingit spoon. It was a fairly warm day, the sun a bright shaft of light occasionally piercing the cover of the heavy evergreen tree limbs. The air was motionless and soft, resting from spring storms.

The camp was in a small clearing a short distance from the stream and surrounded by trees and scraggly bushes. It wasn't that far from where he'd found Will's body. If you were trying to stay out of sight but not too far from water and a road, this would have been a good place for the thieves to set up camp. Obviously, it had been used by a number of people at one time or another. There was even a makeshift lean-to where gear could be stashed to keep dry if it rained.

Jonah circled the clearing twice, fanning farther away from it each time. It wasn't until he was fairly certain there was no one around that he went back to examine the campsite more carefully. There were two sets of footprints, crossing back and forth upon themselves. Two sets of tennis shoe imprints with standard soles and no unusual wear marks. Judging from the size and depth of the imprints, the men were about average height and weight. Most hikers and hunters in the area wore boots, so there was a good possibility the prints belonged to the two men from the robbery.

He noted that the campfire near the center of the clearing had been much larger than necessary for either heat or protection. No attempt had been made to bury the coals as a fire precaution, and they had left a few cans with charred labels strewn around the edges of the campfire. They either liked stew, didn't care what they ate as long as it was nourishing, or lacked the imagination and know-how to create a better campfire meal.

On either side of the campfire, weeds and rocks were cleared away, suggesting that two people had spent the night there in the open. It wasn't a particularly good place for a campsite if you were hiding out; anyone or anything could come at you from any direction, including a wounded bear. They must not have known about the bear, or else they were too inexperienced to realize how much they were putting themselves at risk.

Near what could have been the "pillow" end for one of the cleared spaces was an impression about the size and shape of a handgun. Did they think a handgun was a match for a bear or any other animal that happened by? Or were they only anticipating a possible attack by humans?

Jonah went over the campsite one last time, disappointed not to find more to give him some clue as to the identity of the two men who had been there. Their footprints indicated they had headed west after breaking camp. Jonah followed their trail for about a half mile. It ended in another small clearing near a logging road. A car had been parked there. There was nothing special about the tire tracks to set them apart from any others in the area. They were worn, but with no distinguishing features.

Assuming the campers were the two outsiders involved in the theft and that they were still in the area searching for the artifacts and the money, would they return to the same camp site? If smart, they would probably move to another location. Staying on the move was usually the best way to avoid getting caught. Although if they had come by Mike's last night and discovered it was being watched, they may have given up and left altogether.

Following the stream, he continued up the hill. About two miles short of Eagle's Peak, exactly as the boys had described, he came across an area that had been disturbed by what looked like a search. Brush trampled, bushes bent, branches snapped off. The prints were not the same as those at the campsite. They were smaller, fairly shallow, like those made by two light-weight boys.

The stream widened at that point, circling lazily over spotted rocks. He searched on both sides of the stream but didn't find anything. No more artifacts. No prints that hadn't been obscured by the footprints of the two boys. Nothing to tell him how the spoon had come to be there. The most likely scenario was that someone had dropped it while searching for a place to hide the artifacts. Or, maybe that's what it was supposed to look like, a time-eating distraction while the thieves made off with their plunder.

He still couldn't understand why Will had come up there in the first place. He found it hard to accept the idea that Will had intended to double-cross his buddies and keep the artifacts and money for himself. And although he knew Mike and Lou weren't telling him everything, he believed them when they claimed they didn't know what had happened to Will the night of the theft. His hope was that he would find outsiders responsible for Will's death, outsiders who could perhaps take most of the heat for the theft too. Especially if he could convince Lou and Mike to cooperate in nailing them.

Jonah continued on toward Eagle Peak. As he climbed, he

came upon a number of narrow trails, trails used by both people and animals. Recent overlapping footprints suggested that the villagers had searched up and down those trails looking for the wounded bear. He didn't see any bear sign, but he did come across fresh deer scat.

His stomach rumbled; he was hungry. He should have brought something along to eat. But then he couldn't stay much longer anyway. He wanted to get back before school got out so he could ask Gavin and Jayme if they had seen anyone near that campsite. He also needed to pick up the other officer at the airstrip. And at some point, he needed to talk to the fathers of the two boys and suggest that they take their sons out on the bear hunt.

It was a long hike back the way he had come, so he took a shortcut through the woods on a series of game trails. It occurred to him that if you were going to hide something in the woods, you might use a less-traveled trail for doing so. But he didn't really expect to find anything. If the artifacts had been hidden with care, a random search was at best a crapshoot, but more likely an impossibility given the vast expanse of wilderness.

When he got back to the jail, there was a message on his desk to confirm the other officer was arriving at 5:30. That would give him plenty of time to get done what needed to get done, grab something to eat, and coordinate plans for the evening. He would also have to be sure to thank Jacobson for sending him support. Maybe he could use this opportunity to mend their otherwise bumpy relationship.

None of his calls took long. The bear was still out there eluding hunters. The fathers of Jayme and Gavin told him they'd already been thinking about taking their sons out with them on the bear hunt for a few hours after school since several other kids were coming along. Jacobson didn't answer his phone, so he'd left him a thank you voice message. Jonah also gave Mike and Lou a call. Neither had heard anything more from the two men. They were resigned to another evening of sleepless anticipation.

Jenny called while he was fixing some sandwiches and snacks for the all-night vigil. He told her he would pick her up on the way to the airport. "Rest up," he said. "It could be another long night."

The boys were waiting for him as he'd requested. They apparently thought he was going to ask them to take him to the spot where they'd found the horn spoon and seemed disappointed to learn that he'd already been there. "Are you sure you found the right place?" Jayme asked.

"I'm sure. What I want to know is whether you saw a campsite in the area."

"No," Jayme said, and Gavin shook his head in agreement.

"And you didn't see anyone? Or think you heard anyone on the trail?"

"No one," Jayme said, and Gavin agreed.

At 5:15 he went by to pick up Jenny. She was waiting for him in front of the Lodge; her bright red shirt looked surprisingly good with her red hair. Jonah's spirits lifted as she smiled at him when she got in the car.

"Anything new?" she asked.

He filled her in on what he had learned.

"Sounds like we could see some action tonight."

"Unless they made us. Or unless they found what they came for and are gone for good."

They drove the rest of the way to the airport in silence, windows rolled up against the swirling dust.

While waiting for the airplane, they wandered along the edge of the narrow strip of meadow next to the landing field.

Sunlight skittered cheerfully across the small stream that bordered the area. It was a pleasant snapshot in time. Jonah was relaxed and a bit sad when they heard the plane in the distance.

"Any idea who's coming?" Jenny asked.

"No. All I was told is the arrival time."

When the plane landed and a slim man started down the steps, Jenny gasped, "Oh no. It's not—" She cut herself off in mid-sentence.

"It's not . . .?" Jonah asked

"I shouldn't have said that. Sorry." The freckles across her nose were lost in the red blush that had traveled up from her neck.

Jonah studied the man as he came toward them. He was sharp featured, his head topped with hair that seemed to stick straight up from the back of his head like a spiked bird crest. He moved like he was in "fast forward," his movements jerky and quick.

"Officer Chumley here," he said as he approached. His bony hand found Jonah's and began vigorously pumping.

"Jonah St. Clair," Jonah said, quickly extricating his hand.

Chumley turned to Jenny. "Officer O'Farrell," he acknowledged. Jenny didn't offer her hand; simply nodded.

"Well," Jonah said, ignoring the thought that this was another of Jacobson's jokes. He wished he could take the thank-you message back. "Let's get going."

Once in the car, Chumley began talking. He talked about the trip from Juneau, his impressions of Koloshan from the air, and how eager he was to work with two such fine officers. He told Jonah that it was his first field assignment and that he was thrilled to be of use.

"What do you normally do?" Jonah asked, not at all sure

he wanted to know.

"I work in records. I organize and maintain files and information."

"I see. And why were you sent on this assignment?"

"I've always wanted a field assignment. This is my chance to prove myself. That's what I was told. If I do a good job for you, I'll get another opportunity at a street job."

"Then we'll have to make certain you do a good job, won't we?" Jenny said in a too-sweet tone. Jonah didn't comment, but he promised himself that no matter how badly Chumley screwed up, he was going to get a glowing report, a report intended to get him out of records and into Jacobson's hair.

Chumley chattered all through their meal at The Café, oblivious to the frowning scrutiny he got from Joe and the voluntary silence of his dinner mates. At one point Jonah got up to get some more coffee and Joe whispered to him: "Who the hell is that?"

"CIA," Jonah whispered back. "Don't blow his cover."

By the end of their meal, Jonah could tell that Chumley was really getting on Jenny's nerves, perhaps even more than he was on Jonah's. It must be disappointing to her to be put in the same category with the man, although Jonah guessed it was for entirely different reasons. But no matter how finger-on-chalkboard irritating he was, tonight they would have to get along; the stakes were too high.

"Okay" Jonah said, breaking into Chumley's monologue mid-sentence. "Here's what we are going to do." He went over the plan in elaborate detail, emphasizing that neither Chumley nor Jenny was to take any action without him. He would stay there all night, while they would take turns going to Jonah's to rest.

"I could handle a shift by myself," Chumley said.

"These men are dangerous," Jonah said. "You are here as eyes and ears, not for engagement. Do you understand?"

"But what if . . ."

Jonah cut him off. "There is no 'what if.' If I'm asleep when the men show up, you are to wake me immediately. If you take any action without my knowledge, I will personally see that you never work in the field again." He knew he sounded harsh and that it was an empty threat, but he doubted that anything less would sink in. Even so, he wasn't sure he could trust Chumley. Glancing at Jenny, he was confident she felt the same.

"If you do as you're told, I'll make certain that Jacobson gets a good report." Out of the corner of his eye he saw Jenny suppress a smile. She was a sharp woman and a good sport.

Jonah gave Jenny the first shift since she had been able to sleep during the day. Chumley was at Jonah's resting up for the next shift at 2:00. Since it was possible that the two men might already be in the area when Chumley was scheduled to join them, he was supposed to approach their hideout from the west through the trees. Tired from the night before, and confident that Jenny was a good lookout, Jonah closed his eyes, let his mind relax, and drifted off.

He awoke with a start. Jenny was shaking him. "Jonah," she whispered. "Quick. A man just came out of the house."

It took him a few seconds to register what was happening. Adrenaline started pumping through his system. It was like stepping on the gas and going from 5 mph to seventy almost instantly. He motioned for Jenny to stay put and took off down the hill after the rapidly disappearing figure.

The night was dark with few stars overhead and the moon mostly hidden behind slow-moving gray-black clouds. He could hear the muffled sound of footfalls on dirt and sensed rather than saw movement ahead. The man was running, but staying on the main road rather than trying to evade pursuit.

Jonah was closing in on him, his gun ready. Suddenly, he recognized who he was chasing. It was Lou. What the hell was going on? Lou knew the score; he was supposed to stay put at Mike's. Jonah dropped back, adjusting his speed to Lou's. They were headed in the direction of Lou's house. Was this nothing more than a trip to pick up something he'd forgotten? Or a late night run to de-stress? If so, why hadn't he warned Jonah? And why was he in such a hurry?

Lou disappeared around the corner, and Jonah sprinted to catch up. Lou's house was all lit up. Was this another decoy like the message that had lured Mike away the other night? Should he turn around and hotfoot it back to Mike's? Could Jenny handle things on her own if she had to?

It was a tough decision. Silently giving thanks that it was Jenny and not Chumley back at the stakeout, Jonah hurried up to Lou's front door. He found Lou standing in the middle of his living room, swearing loudly. The place was a mess. Everything had been torn up and spray paint covered the walls in messy streaks. When Lou caught sight of Jonah he yelled, "See what happens when I take your advice?"

"It wasn't my advice that got you into this mess," Jonah said calmly. "How did you find out about this?"

"A call from my uncle. He knew I was staying with Mike and was surprised when he saw all the lights on." They quickly went through the rest of the house. Drawers had been emptied, their contents scattered on the floor, but the walls in the other rooms had not be spray painted.

"OK, Lou. Lock up and let's get going."

"Going? I'm not going back there."

"This could be an attempt to get you back here, to get you

alone. I can't let you stay."

"Am I under arrest?"

"Lou, I need to go back to Mike's. It's your choice. But you know I'm on your side. I don't want to see you hurt."

Jonah turned to leave, hoping that Lou would follow. After a brief hesitation, he did, cursing when he realized the lock on his door was broken. He mumbled something about how there was nothing left to destroy anyway and dutifully hurried after Jonah.

If everything was all right inside at Mike's when they got back, Lou was supposed to signal Jonah from the kitchen window. If there was no signal, Jonah was going in.

They separated at the corner. Jonah's heart pounding as he rushed back toward their stakeout post. He hoped to God he hadn't made another bad judgment call.

JINKAAT K̲A TLEIDOOSHÚ

(SIXTEEN)

The vision of Lou's house all lit up and ravaged inside pushed him to run as fast as he could on the dark road. What if . . .? Why hadn't he turned back when he realized it was Lou running from Mike's house? Even if it had been someone else, why hadn't he checked with Mike before leaving his post?

He careened around the corner, sliding in gravel, almost losing his balance. When Mike's house came into view, Jonah stopped, his breathing loud in the empty night. The house was dark, except for a single light in the back. Just like it had been earlier.

Lou caught up with him and Jonah watched as he went inside. When nothing changed, Jonah headed back to the stakeout, pausing at the edge of the woods to look around and listen, concentrating on slowing his breathing and regaining his composure. When he didn't see or hear anyone nearby, he made his way as quietly as possible back to where Jenny was hopefully waiting. When he saw her right where he had left her, the tension washed away. "Anything happen while I was gone?" he asked, kneeling next to her. He might have been returning from a bathroom break or a casual stroll in the night air.

"Who was it? What happened?" Unlike Jonah, she wasn't trying to hide her concern. It was always harder to be the one left behind, wondering if something bad was happening and what you should be doing about it.

Before he could answer, he saw movement in the kitchen

window. Lou was letting him know that everything was all right.

"It was Lou," he said softly. "Someone trashed his house. His uncle got suspicious because all the lights were on and he knew Lou wasn't supposed to be there."

"Poor Lou. Was it bad?"

"Bad."

"Were they looking for something? Or was it still another warning?"

"My guess is that it was a little of both."

"That means they are in the area. Do you think they were watching Lou's house, waiting for him to return?"

"If they were, they saw the two of us rush inside. I didn't know what the situation was, so I didn't take a look around before charging in. That could have been a mistake; hard to know at this point." But to him, it felt like he was losing his edge, making one reckless move after another.

"Do you think that means they won't show up *here* tonight?"

"It depends. I guess we'll have to wait and see."

After watching the house together for about a half hour, Jonah suggested she take off. "I can handle it until Chumley arrives. I'm wide awake."

"I would rather stay."

"I may need you tomorrow."

"I understand, but I'd still rather stay. Just a little longer; I'm wide awake too."

They continued their vigil together. Everything was quiet. Like nature had been tucked in for the night. Occasionally they would hear something in the brush, muted and indistinct, perhaps an animal prowling for food or trying to avoid becoming a meal for a larger predator. But there were no human sounds. No cars. No flashing lights.

Jonah was the first to hear the footsteps. Jenny responded a millisecond later. They exchanged a look and quickly moved away from each other, fading into the shadows.

The footsteps grew louder. No locals who used the trails at night would be that noisy. Remembering the amateur campfire near Eagle's Peak, Jonah wondered if the two men were scouting Mike's house.

There were flashes of light, bobbing back-and-forth, up-and-down. Then a figure came into view, and Jenny immediately stepped forward. "Put that flashlight away," she whispered loudly.

"Oh, there you are." Chumley's voice pierced the night's calm.

Jonah saw Jenny reach out and grab Chumley's flashlight.

"What are you doing?" he asked as darkness enveloped them. "I can't see."

Jonah stepped next to them and said: "Keep your voice down." He didn't add that he had warned Chumley against using a flashlight unless it was absolutely necessary to get his bearings, and then it should be pointed downward, shielded with one hand, and turned off after a few seconds. "You're early."

"I couldn't sleep. It's so . . . so quiet here." He'd lowered his voice, but it still seemed to reverberate through the forest, bouncing from tree to tree like a whistling wind.

Jonah wondered if Chumley lived in an apartment with thin walls that echoed the lives of other tenants, perhaps on a busy street or next to an all-night store. In LA, those noises had become background music for Jonah, although he never grew to like the constant din. Chumley, however, apparently considered a city's lullaby of night sounds essential for sleep.

"Do you want me to leave?" Jenny whispered. He sensed

she was reluctant to leave him with Chumley, but he didn't want her to stay up all night. There were some tasks she could do for him during the day if she was up to it.

"Why don't you get some rest. Take the pickup to the Lodge. I'll get in touch tomorrow."

The rest of the night Jonah managed to catch fitful snatches of sleep while Chumley watched the house. At first Chumley was as excited as a young boy playing cops and robbers, but eventually the novelty wore off. He became peevish and restless, complaining about the damp night air, the tedium, the unforgiving hardness of the ground, and the fact that he had been hoping to see some action. Even when Jonah was awake, he found it easier to pretend he was sleeping.

When the first rays of light filtered into their hiding place, Jonah called it quits. They walked back to his place, Chumley grumbling about how his knees hurt from kneeling so much.

"I appreciate your help," Jonah said. At the compliment, Chumley visibly preened. "Lou's house was ransacked last night. It's just a matter of time until something else happens."

"You didn't tell me that a suspect's house was broken into."

"I just did." Jonah hoped the sarcasm he felt hadn't leaked into his tone.

"I mean, why didn't you tell me last night? That means the perps are still around."

"If I didn't think they were, we wouldn't be watching Mike's house. And I didn't want to have a conversation about it—voices carry."

Suddenly Chumley sounded excited. "There's still the possibility we'll see some action?"

"First, you go get some sleep."

"I'm too keyed up to sleep."

"Whatever. But you need to be vigilant this evening. That means you need to rest sometime."

Like he had done the morning before for Jenny, Jonah made breakfast—this time for Chumley. When they were finished, Jonah told Chumley that he was going to take a nap. Chumley was free to do whatever he wanted.

"I suppose I could go see the sights."

"Yes, you do that." Jonah went into his room and closed the door. He slipped out of his pants and shirt and climbed into bed. At the last minute, he remembered to set his alarm. A few hours of sleep and he would have to be ready to face the day.

The telephone ringing woke him up. He glanced at the clock as he climbed out of bed. In just ten minutes his alarm would have gone off anyway.

A shaft of dust particles ran from the window to the floor in the sunlight as he crossed the room to the telephone. It was a beautiful day; time he was up and about.

"St. Clair," he said into the receiver.

"Ah, St. Clair, this is Elwood Edison, from the Juneau museum."

"Mr. Edison, good morning." Elwood?

"I thought you might be interested to know that there is a museum in Seattle that is rumored to have made a very valuable purchase recently, a native artifact, I'm told."

"Oh?" Now *that* bit of information was worth getting up early for.

"Just rumor, you understand. Nothing official."

"But you think it might be our screen."

"The thought has crossed my mind. Not that this

particular museum would intentionally purchase a stolen item. But they could have been duped."

Jonah listened while Dr. Edison filled him in on the details. The location and layout of the museum in question. Personality sketches of those in charge. Acquisition procedures. All things it would be helpful to know when he approached the museum about their purchase.

"This will save me a lot of time," Jonah said. "I can't tell you how much I appreciate the information."

"Glad to be of service." Dr. Edison hesitated. "There is one little thing—"

"Yes?"

"When you check on the screen, I would rather you didn't mention where your lead came from."

"I understand. It's a small world."

"Very small."

Jonah put down the telephone and stood there thinking about what Dr. Edison had told him—he wasn't able to think of him as "Elwood." It was hard to imagine that no one at the museum in question suspected any issue with provenance. On the other hand, there were some clever criminals out there, skilled in the artistry of the con. And given enough incentive, even the most ethical person can sometimes talk themselves into suppressing internal doubts and shutting down the little voice in your head warning you to beware.

A few minutes later he was sitting at the kitchen table, impatiently waiting for the coffee to perk, writing down notes about what needed to be done. This could be the break he'd been hoping for; he had to act on it right away.

Unwilling to wait longer, he poured a cup of partially perked coffee. It was a dark tan, the color of their dirt roads after a long dry spell. At least it was hot. And it smelled good. He loved the smell of coffee.

The first call he made was to check on flights to Seattle. If he could make the Juneau departure, he should be in Seattle in time to talk to one of the two key people on his list. He didn't want to call ahead for an appointment though; he thought it might be best to surprise them. That would make it easier to assess whether they were complicit in the theft or innocent purchasers.

Next, he put through a call to Clark Cold Storage. Matt answered on the first ring.

"I'm going to Seattle, hopefully be back by Thursday. And I have a favor to ask," Jonah said.

"Go for it."

"I hate to put this on you."

"That's why it will be a favor." Matt laughed.

"I just want you to be available if Jenny needs anything. Is it okay if I give her your number?"

"No problem."

"Thanks, Matt. I owe you one."

"Actually, you owe me more than one. You're running up quite a tab."

His last call was to Jenny. He knew the instant she answered that she had been asleep. "Sorry to wake you," he said.

"That's alright."

"I have to go to Seattle, and I won't be back until tomorrow. That means you're on your own tonight. More or less."

"Less than more," she countered.

"I'll leave a note for Chumley to make it clear that you're in charge."

"Write it in permanent ink."

"If you need anything while I'm gone, Matt at the Cold

Storage is the one to call. I've told him that I'm giving you his number, just in case. And Jenny, I want you to know that I'm sorry to do this to you. But something important has come up."

"I'm just glad you feel you can trust me with this."

"I know you can do what needs to be done, but I don't want you to take any chances. I'll let Mike and Lou know. You can count on them for support. I doubt they will be sleeping soundly."

"What about Chumley?"

"Try not to shoot him."

He hung up, packed a bag, called Lou to tell him what to expect, and wrote a note for Chumley. His instructions to Chumley were explicit, but he was still worried about how the man might respond in his absence. No doubt Jenny would stay up all night to keep him from doing something stupid. It was a bad time for him to be leaving them on their own. But he didn't have any choice.

He barely made it to Juneau in time for his flight to Seattle. Exhausted from the last few days, he managed to fall asleep before the plane even took off, waking up in time to see the descent into Sea-Tac Airport. They came from a clear blue sky into a dense, murky smog that hung heavy in the air. There was something about it that made Jonah feel as if he blinked hard enough, his vision would clear. He blinked. Twice. But the smog remained. It wasn't until he got a taxi and left the airport behind that the sun came through and he could see Seattle in the distance. Taking a cab was expensive, but he wanted to get to his destination as quickly as possible.

He arrived a few minutes to four. The building didn't look that large from the main entrance, but it was on a slope, so the view from the front was deceptive. Based on the description Dr. Edison had given him, there were two more floors beneath the entrance level, one even with the ground level at the back of the building and the other a basement. He went directly to the stairs and down to the first floor where there was a row of offices facing a shadow-filled brick plaza.

Dr. Edison had given him two names and had assured him that both were honest men who cared deeply about their museum collections. Jonah found his first choice closeted in a tiny room piled high with papers and littered with art objects. Posters announcing past museum shows lined the walls. The door was open, so Jonah stuck his head in and said, "Mr. Sandifer?"

The man looked up from whatever he was working on, but it seemed to take him several seconds to shift his focus. Finally, he said, "Yes?"

"I'm Jonah St. Clair. I wonder if I might ask you a few questions." Jonah stepped inside the small room.

"I'm rather busy right now—" Sandifer looked around as if to suggest the state of his office proved the truth of his statement.

"I'll only take a few minutes of your time." There was a chair in front of Sandifer's desk. Jonah didn't wait for an invitation to sit. The two men took a moment to assess each other. Sandifer was in his fifties, slightly built with narrow shoulders and the hint of an expanding stomach under his wool vest. He looked every inch the stereotype of the aging, absent-minded scholar. Jonah had no idea what Sandifer concluded about the tall, casually dressed man who had barged into his office, but he had intentionally not yet identified himself as a police office.

In spite of the abrupt and clearly unwelcome intrusion,

Sandifer politely asked, "What can I do for you?"

"You can tell me about the Raven House screen the museum just acquired." He had decided in advance to spring the accusation on whomever he talked to, hoping to catch them off guard.

Sandifer's face registered surprise. Definitely not a good poker player. Jonah knew instantly he was in the right place.

"What screen?" Sandifer finally managed to say.

"Let's not play games, Mr. Sandifer. I know the museum has the screen."

Sandifer took a pair of glasses out of his shirt pocket and put them on. His eyes appeared more intense behind the thick glass, like he was actually "seeing" Jonah for the first time. "What's your interest in the screen you mentioned?"

Jonah noted there was no admission.

Before Jonah could speak, Sandifer added, "Mind you, I'm not saying we have this screen you're referring to." Was he mistaking Jonah for an interested buyer? Or did he not want to talk about a major acquisition until they had made a public announcement? Or . . . did he know it had been stolen and was prepared to lie about it? Dr. Edison could be wrong about the man's honesty and ethics.

Jonah didn't want a confrontation. But he needed to quickly accomplish two things: to verify whether the museum had the Raven House screen, and if they did, to get the name of the person who sold it to them. If Sandifer wasn't going to willingly discuss the matter, Jonah was prepared to assert pressure to get him to cooperate. He stood up, put his hands on the desk and leaned toward the man. "Are you going to show me the screen, or do I have to get a court order?"

"Court order?" Sandifer stared blankly up at Jonah. "We have definitely not acquired a screen without checking its provenance. We don't buy stolen items." Sandifer swallowed hard and pushed his chair back, away from Jonah's intimidating presence. "I repeat, we do not buy anything without checking its chain of ownership."

Jonah stood up straight but did not sit down. "Is it worth the museum's reputation to hide a valuable piece of stolen native art? I don't want to make this a public fight, but I will. And you might want to think about how this will look in the press: 'Prestigious museum involved in theft of native artifacts from a remote native Alaskan village.' Reporters love stories about underdogs. And this one has it all—intrigue, greed, corruption and the arrogance of wealth and privilege. I doubt your donors will be pleased to see that in print."

Sandifer pulled at his collar as if he needed more air. "I really think you are mistaken, but I assure you that the museum will cooperate with any legal inquiry, *if* there is evidence to suggest it's necessary."

Jonah had always been good at detecting lies, and behind Sandifer's protestations, he sensed he was telling the truth. Jonah almost felt guilty for his aggressive threats to shake the truth out of the man. "We don't need to escalate this yet. I'm here to verify if you have the screen in question. If you do, that's another conversation."

"Who are you?" The fact that he hadn't thought to ask that question right off might be an indication that he didn't take Jonah seriously at first.

"I represent the owners of the screen, the *legal* owners, the Koloshan Native Arts Center." Jonah was vague about his role; let the man think he was a lawyer speaking on behalf of the Center.

"Koloshan?" He sounded like he recognized the name. "I'll have to talk with a few people before I can comment on your, ah, accusation."

Jonah felt anger building inside of him. "I don't think you understand. You see, if I'm right about the screen, you unfortunately dealt with criminals on this. There were some mistakes made during the theft. People have been attacked and families threatened." He lowered his voice for dramatic emphasis. "And there was a murder."

"A murder?" Sandifer's voice quavered. His world was a collection of past lives and events; apparently the word "murder" jarred him into the present.

"That's why I can't wait around while you argue over provenance. I have to have names. And I need them now." It was time to play his official role. He took out his police identification and laid it on the desk facing Sandifer. "I hope you're aware that your involvement in the theft makes you an accomplice to murder. It's called the felony-murder rule. You're as guilty as the guy who committed the act." He stared the man down for a moment, then continued in a softer tone: "But before we spend any more time discussing this, perhaps we should verify whether we are talking about the same Raven House screen."

Sandifer looked panicked. "Theft. Murder," he echoed. "I don't know anything about any of this. We have a large and valuable collection; we don't need to get involved in anything illegal like you are suggesting."

"Not intentionally, I'm sure." See, Jonah said to himself, I can be reasonable. "But you have to make a choice—cooperation now or engage in a public legal fight."

Jonah's ID was still on Sandifer's desk. Sandifer looked down at it and asked, "Do you even have jurisdiction here?"

Jonah sidestepped the question: "If you want to make each step of this process difficult for me, I'm sure I can do the same for you."

"I can't make any decisions without talking to someone for confirmation."

"You're talking to me. And given your position here, I think you have the authority to show me the screen. If it's the one I'm looking for, then I'll want to know the name of the person who sold it to you. If it isn't, I'll apologize for taking up your time and leave you in peace."

Sandifer didn't take long to decide. "Alright. But I want to make one thing clear—we did everything by the book. You have my word on that."

"If it's Koloshan's Raven House screen, maybe you should consider a new edition."

JINKAAT KA DAX.ADOOSHÚ

(SEVENTEEN)

Jonah sat down and leaned back in the uncomfortable wood chair in front of Sandifer's desk and waited for him to explain.

"I have every reason to believe it is a legitimate sale. We bought it from a reputable dealer, and he had papers to show its provenance."

Jonah thought they might have ignored any red flags if they really wanted the screen, but he didn't say that out loud. If it turned out to be the Koloshan screen, a court would have to decide any issues related to the sale. But for now, knowing the screen was safe and tracking the thieves was his priority. "The name?" he prompted.

Sandifer opened the top drawer of his desk and poked through some papers before coming up with a card that he handed to Jonah. "Here's his card."

"Bill Daniels, art consultant," Jonah read out loud. The name had not been on the list of interested buyers Stella had compiled. "Have you dealt with him before?"

"No."

"Did you check out his credentials?"

"I knew about him by reputation. And I of course made it clear that everything had to be in order."

"And was it?"

"Yes. As I told you before—"

"Save it," Jonah interrupted.

Sandifer looked offended. "I agreed to help because I want to prove to you that we do not acquire items illegally.

And you mentioned that someone was . . . murdered.”

“A local resident who may have been involved in the theft is dead. And threats have been made against others in the village. What you also need to be aware of is that the entire native community is impacted by the loss of the screen and other artifacts that represent their cultural heritage. For them it was their personal museum.”

“I can understand.” He seemed sincerely sympathetic.

“Sorry if I’ve come on too strong. I do appreciate the information.” Actually, he wasn’t sorry in the least. He looked at the card. “The transfer papers listed the name or names of the sellers, correct?”

“Yes. As I recall, the seller’s name was Arnold Williams.”

Jonah wasn’t surprised, but very disappointed. Poor Ellen. If the ownership was contested, Will’s name would be dragged through the courts in the battle over the screen.

“Have you authenticated the screen? And the corner posts that came with it?”

“Yes. Design and age were considered. And original location.”

“Original location? How did you determine that?”

“There are photographs of the screen and corner posts taken in the early 1900s.”

“Once you knew the original location, and given all of the disputes over stolen artifacts of late, didn’t you consider contacting Koloshan?”

“Determining ownership of native artifacts is very difficult, as I’m sure you know. It involves investigation of acquisition at a time when there weren’t always good records kept— It can become very complicated. Notifying people potentially involved in the chain of provenance almost inevitably generates unfounded claims. And we were satisfied that Daniels had title to the screen."

"Did he try to sell you any other artifacts?"

"No, just the screen." Sandifer cocked his head to one side. "But he did mention he might have more smaller items available soon."

Did Daniels think he could get more money if he broke up the artifact collection? Or had there been two separate deals? Jonah stood. "I'd like to see the screen now. I'm 99 percent certain it's the one I'm looking for, but I need to make absolutely certain."

For a moment, Jonah thought Sandifer was going to refuse, but after a barely audible sigh, he got up and told Jonah to follow him.

They went through a door at the back of the building and down narrow cement steps between beige painted walls that made Jonah feel slightly claustrophobic. "There's an outside entrance, but this is quicker," Sandifer said.

At the bottom, there was a locked wooden door that opened into a huge storeroom filled from floor to ceiling with row after row of labeled artifacts and specimens. Jonah vaguely remembered reading once that most museums stored over 95 percent of their collections due to lack of display space.

In the northwest corner of the basement, they came to another locked door. Sandifer took out a large ring of keys and went through them until he found the right one.

"Double security, huh?" Jonah said.

"We keep some pieces in climate-controlled spaces." He opened the door, stepped inside, and switched on a light. There, right in the middle of the room was the screen, held in place by a stand that looked like it had been made for the purpose. The corner posts were lying on the floor along the wall.

Jonah stopped in the doorway and stared. Isolated from its culture, the screen reminded him of an animal in a cage at the zoo. An unnatural setting for a beautiful work of art. He felt like screaming that the screen belonged in Koloshan, not here locked away in the dark basement of some ugly building in an uncaring city. It belonged among the people who understood its history and cherished its heritage.

"Is this the screen?" Sandifer was obviously hoping the answer would be "no."

"This is it," Jonah said softly, reverently. He stepped forward and ran his fingers over the wood, smoothed with age and use, dusky from wood smoke. At least the screen was no longer "lost"—he ought to feel grateful for that. But at the same time, he experienced a wave of profound sadness at the thought of the lengthy court battle they would most likely face in order to get the screen and corner posts returned.

"Are you certain?"

Jonah turned to look directly at Sandifer. "I first saw the screen when I was ten. It was in a longhouse then. More recently, it's been the centerpiece of the native artifacts in the Koloshan Arts Center. Yes, I'm absolutely certain.

"Lawyers and courts will have to sort this out. For now, if I were you, I wouldn't make any announcements about its acquisition. The money you paid for the screen is missing, along with all of the other artifacts from the Center. And, as I said before, there are a number of criminal charges outstanding. You wouldn't want to do anything to prejudice the case. Nor would you want to do anything that would put you or the screen at risk."

"What are you saying?"

"I'm asking you to hold tight until I have a chance to further investigate the theft and the murder. The men involved are unpredictable and dangerous. Can you hold off making any public announcements for a while?"

Sandifer nodded, looking truly shaken by the situation. Jonah felt a twinge of compassion for the man, but it only lasted for a moment.

"Meanwhile, I need your absolute assurance that this screen will remain right here in this secure room. Will you promise me that?"

The man slowly nodded.

Jonah took several flash photographs of the screen to document its discovery and its location. He was glad he'd had the presence of mind to bring along his camera.

As they walked away, he felt like he was abandoning the screen, abandoning Koloshan's past. Unfortunately, there wasn't much he could do on his own. Still, now that he'd actually found the screen, he needed to be damned sure he didn't somehow lose it again.

They headed back the way they had come, past the rows of overflow objects and collections kept hidden away, awaiting their turn to be displayed. He noticed there were quite a few Native American items on the shelves and wondered if he was wrong—maybe the artifacts weren't "missing" but could be found if they searched through the museum's crowded shelves.

"You're quite certain the museum didn't get any other artifacts along with the screen."

"As I said, Daniels hinted at the possibility, but I never saw anything."

"Do you have some sort of fund you can dip into if an 'opportunity' arises, or do you have to go through a committee or run the purchase past board members?"

"There's a fund. But major acquisitions must be approved."

"But it's a formality."

"You might say that."

"I think I have the picture."

Sandifer stopped abruptly, his cheeks flushed with indignation. "No, I'm not sure you do. You make it sound as though I, as a representative of the museum, am dealing in black market art on a regular basis. That isn't the case. It's a competitive market; you have to be able to act quickly if you are to have a chance at acquiring items that suddenly become available."

"Sorry, I didn't mean to be insulting. But your willingness to buy the screen without a serious investigation into why it 'suddenly became available' has triggered some terrible events. It's not up to me to judge your intentions or your process. But your eagerness to write that check put some very good people in danger. Right now, you owe it to yourself and to this museum to do the right thing. And in my opinion, the right thing is to see that the screen and corner posts are returned to the people from whom they were stolen."

Even as he expressed his angry opinion, Jonah was aware that it wasn't all Sandifer's fault. If it hadn't been for Lou, Mike and Will, the theft never would have taken place. And it sounded like Daniels was the original rotten apple in the barrel, not anyone at the museum.

Sandifer didn't immediately respond to Jonah's comment about the "right thing to do."

Softening his tone, Jonah added, "I realize, however, that sorting this out is going to take time, and I appreciate you letting me see the screen." He paused. "One more thing—please don't give Daniels a head's up about my investigation. He may be complicit in the murder. You need to keep him at arm's length until we know what role he played in everything."

Jonah started to leave, then turned back to Sandifer. "And, if you are offered any more Tlingit artifacts, please make it clear that you are interested, and immediately contact me."

"Certainly."

"Thanks for your cooperation." Jonah wanted to say "belated cooperation," but chose to be gracious.

Jonah hurried through the museum to the exit without so much as glancing at the exhibits. He liked museums, enjoyed learning about history through their exhibits, but at this moment, his heartrate accelerated by a feeling of extreme anxiety, he simply wanted to leave. There had been a time in Nam when he and three other soldiers on patrol had been forced to hide out in a series of narrow, low tunnels for several days. Given his height, it had been particularly bad for him, especially since they had to keep moving in order to elude capture. He remembered how his back ached from hunching over and how desperately he wanted to get out into the open air. He had the same desire now. He wasn't sure why, but being in the crowded space below and the dim interior of the display area had triggered a negative response, nothing he couldn't control, but still disquieting. That kind of thing used to happen to him more often, but the triggers had faded with time. In this instance, the reaction had probably been brought on in part by the heavy responsibility he was feeling and the lack of sleep.

Once outside, he paused and focused on breathing slowly and steadily as he planned his next moves. It was too bad he hadn't rented a car at the airport; he needed transportation if he was going to go see Daniels. Or maybe not. He glanced at the card. There was a telephone number but no address. Depending on where his office was, he might be able to take public transportation. The personal and official expenses for this investigation were starting to add up; he needed to avoid any unnecessary spending.

Several blocks away he found an outside phone booth next to a drug store. When he dialed and got a message answering machine, he slammed the received down. Damn. Nothing was ever easy. He might as well get a rental car. If he didn't need it to get to Daniels, he would have it for a fast trip to the airport. He thumbed through the yellow pages until he found the closest car rental place. He estimated that it was about twelve blocks from where he was, walking there would give him time to think.

If Sandifer's information was correct, Will had claimed ownership of the screen and engaged Daniels to sell it to the museum. He wondered if Will had approached Daniels or vice versa, and what kind of documentation Will had used to verify ownership. Or had Daniels finessed that for him? Assuming Daniels was on the up-and-up and was willing to talk, Jonah might be close to resolving some of the key questions related to the heist. On the other hand, if Daniels had a history of being involved in shady transaction, he probably had ways of distancing himself from the people he hired to do the dirty work. Nevertheless, if Daniels found himself on the hook for the theft, Jonah guessed this could become a situation in which there was no honor among thieves and that Daniels might quickly give up the others to save himself.

Jonah was torn as to whether he should try to enlist the help of the local police or talk to Daniels on his own. If he brought the police in, he would have to admit that he had already talked with Sandifer, and they might not like that he hadn't followed protocol and contacted them first. On the other hand, without jurisdiction, he was limited as to what he could do. Legally, that is. And doing everything by the book usually took time, time that he didn't have.

He walked fast, feeling the hardness of the sidewalk through the soles of his shoes. It took the spring out of his step, like wearing old tennis shoes with cushioning flattened by use. Making it even more unpleasant, he was surrounded by people, throngs of them, most not walking at the same urgent pace as he was, obstacles he was forced to navigate. Then there was the noise bouncing at him from all directions, typical city street sounds—cars, people talking, random music, horns, dogs, machines. It had been a long time since he'd been in a big city. But clearly not long enough.

In spite of the bombardment of people and noise, he felt better by the time he reached the car rental place. Physical activity cleared his mind and helped him focus. Inside, there was a long service counter and no other customers, but the only clerk in sight was talking on the telephone. After a quick glance at Jonah, he looked away and continued his telephone conversation. It would have been bad enough if the man had been conducting business while Jonah was standing there waiting, but it didn't sound like a business call. Jonah found himself wanting to reach across the counter and pull the receiver from the man's hands. Instead, he paced back and forth, glaring at the man until he finished his call.

"I want to rent a car, but first, can you lend me a telephone directory and let me make a couple of quick local calls?" Since the clerk had been rude, he didn't need to know that if Daniels' office turned out to be nearby, he wouldn't need a car.

For a minute, Jonah thought the man was going to say *no*, but another customer came in, an attractive young woman. The clerk shoved a directory across the counter and, with a big smile, turned to his new customer. Jonah reached for one of the three unattended phones at the other end of the counter and tried Daniels again, but he still didn't answer. Next, he found two possible home listings in the directory: one for William Daniels and the other for Bill Daniels. He called William first and got a boy who sounded like a pre-teen.

"Is your father William Daniels the art consultant?"

"Yes."

"Can you tell me where I can reach him?"

"At his office."

"He isn't there right now."

"He visits clients a lot."

"What time does he usually get home?"

"Oh, seven or so."

"Thanks."

Having a kid answer had been a stroke of luck. They had no vested interest in being evasive. They didn't yet know how manipulative adults could be over small things. And now he not only knew that Daniels was an art consultant, he knew where he lived and when he usually got home. If he didn't show up at his office soon, Jonah would pay him a surprise evening visit. The rental car would come in handy for that.

When he finally got his car, it was a compact, cramped for his long legs. He felt like he was in a clown car. But it did the trick. He chose a motel at the foot of Queen Anne near where the map in the clown car's glove compartment had indicated Daniels lived. The motel wasn't much to look at, and it was in a congested, noisy area, but it was convenient.

As soon as he was settled in, he put in a call to the mayor of Koloshan who also happened to have status in the tribal council that served as the board for the Native Arts Center.

Although Jonah didn't want it generally known yet that he had located the screen, someone with official status needed to be informed in case they wanted to initiate legal action to make certain the museum didn't move or try to sell the screen. Sandifer might be ethical, but Jonah didn't know who else was involved in the museum's decision-making process. And in his experience, any time there was a lot of money at stake, it was better to act quickly rather than sit back and trust the other players involved.

The mayor was thrilled by the news, although when Jonah explained what he was doing at his end, the mayor quickly grasped the issues involved. He promised to hold off announcing the discovery until Jonah had a chance to gather more evidence. But he would definitely consult a lawyer right away.

Jonah's next priority was finding a place to get a meal. When he asked the front desk, he was given so many choices he didn't even try to keep them straight. Instead, he headed toward the heart of lower Queen Anne, keeping an eye out for a place that looked comfortable and not too crowded. He ended up on a side street in a cafe that served him a forgettable hamburger and greasy fries. But they took the edge off his hunger. He stopped at a small bakery and bought a half dozen cookies before going back to the motel and calling Daniels again.

Still no answer.

At 6:15 he got in his rental car and managed to find Daniels' home without too much trouble. It was an impressive house, a large two-story affair in a style Jonah felt he ought to recognize. It sat back and up from the street. The embankment bordering the sidewalk had been carefully landscaped with plants and rockery. The garage was level with the sidewalk and there was cement reinforcement on both sides of the driveway. The garage door was open. There was no car inside. Assuming Daniels drove rather than taking public transportation, Jonah decided to wait a while before approaching the house. He found a parking spot across the street and leaned his seat back so he could relax while keeping an eye out for Daniels. It was 6:45.

As he waited, Jonah thoughts drifted to Jenny and Chumley. They should be about to start their evening surveillance. In some ways he hoped the two men didn't show up tonight. Tomorrow night he would be back. By then, he might have more information; he might even have the names of the two men.

And he'd be home. Away from the crush of bodies and the unrelenting noise. Away from all the artificial lights that obscured the stars, making it feel like the day wouldn't let go.

JINKAAT K̲A NAS'GADOOSHÚ

(EIGHTEEN)

A silver Continental appeared around the corner, slowed, signaled, and pulled into the garage. The man who got out was a perfect match for the car, sleek and metallic, with wavy silver-fox hair and an immaculate dark gray suit. Jonah had no doubt this was Daniels. He looked like a man who sniffed wine corks in restaurants and felt comfortable having a waiter place a napkin in his lap. But what he didn't look like was someone who would know how to hire small-time crooks.

Before Daniels started up the steps to his house, Jonah was out of his car and across the street. "Excuse me," Jonah said. "You're Mr. Daniels, aren't you?"

The man looked him up and down. "Why do you ask?"

"I tried to reach you at your office number," Jonah began. "If this is business—"

Jonah couldn't help but think that if he had been wearing a tailor-made suit it might not have mattered whether he was there about business or not. Jonah slowly removed his ID and enjoyed the look of surprise in Daniels' eyes when he realized Jonah was a police officer.

"I don't understand why you want to talk to me. I've never been to this place, Kol-oh-shan."

"You did, however, purchase a valuable native screen and two corner posts from there recently."

"I think you must be mistaken." He moved to his left, as if to go around Jonah, but Jonah quickly matched his move, blocking his escape. He was acutely aware of how his size

215

and demeanor must feel threatening to the older, smaller man.

"There's been a murder," Jonah said abruptly. He let the words sink in, savoring the hint of alarm that crossed the man's face. "You're not only involved in the illegal acquisition of stolen property, but also in a criminal conspiracy that has resulted in a death. You can answer my questions informally, now, or we can go about this the hard way. It's up to you."

He could tell Daniels was trying to gauge the extent of Jonah's authority and determination. What Jonah wanted him to understand was that although he might be a policeman from some backwater village in Alaska, he wasn't about to be bullied or bluffed.

"A scandal won't do you any good," Jonah added. "The people I represent are going to get their stolen goods back, and I am going to catch the murderer. The only thing you should be thinking about right now is whether or not you're going to jail."

"Let's walk," Daniels said.

They started down the quiet residential sidewalk, side by side. "To save time," Jonah said, "you should know that I've talked with Sandifer at the museum, and I've seen the screen."

"Oh?" It was a noncommittal acknowledgement.

"You can argue with the lawyers about whether or not you had legal title to sell it. But you answer to me about the death of one of your accomplices and the threats that have been and are still being made against several innocent village families."

"What do you mean by my *accomplices*? I haven't threatened anyone."

"You hired someone to transport the stolen goods . . ."

"I wasn't involved in any theft."

"With all due respect, Mr. Daniels, at a very minimum, you put out some feelers about the Raven House screen and that became the catalyst for the theft."

"Well . . ."

"Don't bullshit me. Right now, we're talking off the record. But only because I'm trying to prevent further bloodshed. Part of your shipment and a half-million dollars have gone missing. And whoever you hired to do your dirty work has no scruples about what they are willing to do to get everything back. I don't have time to play games when people's lives are in danger. Give me the names of your 'contacts,' and I'll go after them, not you. At least for now."

"I don't like your attitude."

"I'm sure you don't. And I don't like the way you do business. But like it or not, your only choice at this point is to decide which crimes you're going to be charged with. You want to add murder, be my guest."

It felt surreal to Jonah, walking past expensive homes with manicured lawns while discussing criminal acts with a man who epitomized the privileged community. Jonah wondered if any of his neighbors were peeking out of windows, watching the two of them sauntering down the sidewalk, speculating on who Daniels was talking to.

"I wouldn't have *any contacts* in the art world for long if I was too free with their names." He seemed to be struggling with how to respond, but Jonah sensed he was weakening.

"Let me remind you one more time: priceless artifacts stolen from a tiny native community, one man dead, another attacked and badly beaten, and two native families harassed and threatened. All because you wanted to make a few bucks. The press is going to love this story. You and your family's days in that nice home back there could be numbered.”

“Are you threatening me?”

“Consider it a prediction about what might happen if you refuse to cooperate. This story will absolutely make the news. You have one chance to shape how you will be portrayed—cooperative witness or co-conspirator. And if your confederates, partners, accomplices—however you want to refer to them—commit more crimes before you give up their names, that will add obstruction of justice to the charges against you.”

“I don’t think you have jurisdiction here.”

“No. Not officially. That’s why you have a chance, right now, to get ahead of this story. But I guarantee you, if I can’t make headway on my own, I *will* turn all this over to the local authorities. Their procedures take longer, but they will eventually uncover evidence that will land you right in the middle of this criminal mess.”

Daniels stopped walking and turned toward Jonah, no longer the self-assured professional he’d been moments earlier. “I can give you the name of the person I hired to handle the transaction. But you have to promise to leave me out of this.”

“Of course. All I need is a name.” It was an easy lie. Probably one Daniels didn’t believe anyway.

Daniels took out a small notepad and pen, wrote out a name and two telephone numbers, one local and one for Juneau. “That’s all I have.”

Jonah glanced at the paper, folded it in half, and put it in his pocket. “Thanks.” He started off, then turned back to Daniels. “Oh, and I wouldn’t warn him if I were you.” Jonah patted the pocket with the name and address. “You’ve done the smart thing. Don’t screw it up.”

“Of course not.”

Jonah put that down as a "maybe."

He jogged back to his car, past the homes of the rich, their occupants cushioned from nature by materialistic values. Their heritage a fleeting memory in faded photographs or a diary written in a cramped hand, echoes of the past only faintly heard. How could someone like Daniels be expected to understand how much the Raven House screen and artifacts meant to the village when even some of the Koloshan residents no longer understood their significance. At stake was a priceless symbol of their culture. Unfortunately, the memories that gave the symbol its value were steadily evaporating over time, and every passing day made it harder to appreciate why it was still important.

Driving back to the motel, he kept getting slowed down by traffic. Anxious to get there so he could call the numbers Daniels had given him, he found himself laying on the horn, like an LA driver. When he finally arrived, he went directly to the phone. The local number confirmed what he already guessed: Dick North wasn't around. In fact, the woman's voice on the line sounded angry about that fact.

"If you talk to him, you might mention that his rent is due."

"I'll do that," Jonah said. *After I have him in cuffs—*

"And you can also tell him that Sissy ain't gunna hang around forever." She slammed the receiver down.

Jonah was torn—should he call the Juneau police and give them North's name and number? He didn't know for sure what role North had played in the theft, but he could have been one of the two men who had beaten Lou and threatened the others. If he was already trying to return to Seattle by airplane or ferry, the Juneau police or State Troopers could track him down and hold him for Jonah. But that would give North time to lawyer up or to come up with a story to explain everything away. It might also mean the investigation would be taken out of Jonah's hands. At the same time, he wasn't convinced that Daniels could be counted on not to warn off North. Any delay was a risk. Still, he had more skin in the game than the Juneau police; what he lacked in resources he felt he made up for in determination. He could contact them later, after he'd had a go at North.

Decision made, his thoughts turned to Jenny and Chumley lying in wait for the two men to show up at Mike's. Damn. He should be watching the house with them tonight. Instead, he was all alone in a city motel with its smoke saturated wallpaper and cheaply framed pictures of bright flowers and uninspiring landscapes. He glowered at the pictures, resisting the urge to turn them to face the wall.

At least the bed seemed fine. He could catch up on his sleep. And maybe tomorrow he would find some answers.

He woke up before the wake-up call came, surprised to discover he had slept soundly all night. He took a few minutes to collect his thoughts and put some water and a single-serve pouch in the coffee maker. He punched the button, waited until it made a gurgling sound to make sure it was working, then placed a call to the Lodge in Koloshan.

Jenny didn't answer. He dialed his home number in case one or both of them were there. Still no answer. Next, he called Matt.

"Hello," Matt said. "You sound like you are a long way away."

"I feel like I am."

"Well, as far as I know, you didn't miss anything here. Jenny didn't call me, and the bear is still on the loose. You coming back soon?"

"As soon as I can hop a plane."

After hanging up, he tried his home number and then the Lodge again. Still no answer. Maybe they ended their shifts and went out to breakfast. He set his worries aside, got dressed, and headed for the airport. He could try calling again when he got there.

The drive to the airport was hectic—lots of traffic, exhaust fumes, and cars zipping in and out between lanes. Then it took him forever to return his car. He had ten minutes to find a phone before boarding his flight.

They were calling his flight when someone finally answered his home phone on the fourth ring.

"Hello?" She sounded uncertain. He should have made it clear that it was okay to answer his phone when he wasn't there.

"Jenny, this is Jonah. How did it go last night?"

"Fine. More or less."

"Is everything okay? Are you okay?" There was something about the way she said 'more or less'—

"Chumley fell and possibly broke his ankle." She blurted out the news as if relieved to vent.

"He fell?"

"He wasn't chasing anyone or anything—it's a long story."

"I have to catch the plane," Jonah said. "Did anyone show at Mike's?"

"No one."

"My flight is about to leave. I'll call again from Juneau if I get a chance; otherwise, I'll check in as soon as I get back to Koloshan."

He hung up and raced for the plane, falling in line behind a few other stragglers. He had asked for an aisle seat, but someone was in it, a woman with a baby. "Oh, I hope you don't mind," she said. "I have to get up and down so often with Nettie."

Jonah eyed the cramped middle seat. What the hell; he'd survived the clown car, he could manage for a few hours. He climbed in past her and tried to find a comfortable position.

"My, you're tall, aren't you?" the woman said.

How did she expect him to answer? Uh, huh, and that's why I sign up for an aisle seat, lady . . . so I'll have a place to put my knees.

"You play basketball?"

He was saved from having to answer by the baby. She had apparently taken a dislike to Jonah and started screaming at the top of her pink baby lungs. "There, there, now," her mother crooned. "It's going to be okay."

Several other passengers threw irritated looks in her direction, but the woman was oblivious to everything except her crying babe in arms.

As soon as the flight was airborne, the woman started walking the aisles, trying to get her baby to stop crying. Each time she got the baby settled down and returned to her seat, the baby started crying again. Finally, an exasperated stewardess found her a seat in an empty row at the rear of the plane, and Jonah was finally able to stretch out his legs and relax. The rest of the trip was uneventful.

They made a smooth landing in Juneau. It felt good to be back in Alaska. Jonah rented a car and drove into town. This case was starting to add up in personal expenses for him. But being so close to some answers was hopefully worth it.

His first stop was the library to look up North's address in the reverse directory using the Juneau telephone number Daniels had given him. It turned stout to be for a downtown hotel only a few blocks away. He left his car where it was and walked to the hotel.

It was an old building, advertised as an historic landmark

to tourists. The lobby was large and dimly lit, furnished with dark furniture that was sufficiently antique looking to impress visitors with its alleged vintage. There were several pictures of people holding up game they'd bagged in one hand, their rifles in the other. Next to the pictures were mounted trophies of various animals. The overall impression was one of faintly remembered grandeur.

The man behind the long wood counter looked up and smiled as he approached. "May I help you?"

"Yes, you can tell me if Dick North is staying here."

"Let me see—" The man consulted a plastic looseleaf notebook. "He isn't checked in at present, but we're holding some luggage and mail for him."

"I see." Jonah got out his identification. "Mind showing it to me?"

"Ah . . ."

"I can get a warrant if I have to."

"Maybe you should." He sounded uncertain.

"I can be discreet. And you'd be helping me with my investigation."

"Well . . ."

"No one has to know."

The clerk wavered. Finally, he said, "I don't see what harm it could do." He motioned for Jonah to follow him. "It's in the back room." He opened a wood flap that separated the guests from the employees for Jonah to slip through. On the way, the clerk picked an envelope out of one of the boxes. The luggage was in a locked cabinet. It only took the man a few minutes to locate a small black suitcase. "Said they didn't plan to stay long."

"They?" Was North more than the broker?

"North and the man with him. Jim Elliot, I believe is his name."

"Can you describe them?"

"Very average, I would say." He frowned. "That's not much help, is it?"

"No, not much." Jonah smiled. "Then, you didn't know anyone was going to be asking after them."

"I don't always remember faces. I'm good at names though. And assessing personalities. If you know what I mean."

"Yes, I think I do."

"There was something disagreeable about the two of them. Pushy. But not like one of your typical lower 48 tourists. More like someone who thinks they're owed."

Jonah was tempted to tell him how right on he was. "Did Elliot leave luggage too?"

"It's right here." He reached up and drew out another suitcase.

"I don't suppose you'd like to go back to the desk for a few minutes."

"I knew they were trouble." He handed Jonah the envelope he had picked up on the way to the room. "This just came." He turned to leave. "I don't know about any of this." He paused at the door. "You have five minutes."

As soon as the door closed, Jonah set to work. He opened North's unlocked suitcase first. All it contained was a few shirts and some underwear; some of which had been worn. Elliot's suitcase offered more of a challenge, but the lock was easily picked. Inside, there was nothing but clothes. The contents of the suitcases weren't worth much; the two men could easily decide to leave them behind.

The envelope was more interesting. It contained a telegram. The paper inside was tissue thin. He didn't have to open the envelope; by holding it up to the light the single line of dark type was clearly visible: "Call me immediately."

Jonah had no doubt he knew the sender even though it wasn't signed. Daniels was linked not only to the contact he admitted to having, but possibly to the two men responsible for the theft and threats.

Daniels may not have listened to Jonah's advice about not warning North, but it was nice to know that Daniels was starting to panic.

JINKAAT K̲A GOOSHÚK

(NINETEEN)

The flight back to Koloshan was short, but it felt endless. A steady drizzle blurred vision and dulled senses. He could barely make out familiar landmarks below, and after a while, he quit trying. Instead, he leaned back and closed his eyes, letting his mind run free, a kaleidoscope of thoughts forming and re-forming. He pictured the Raven House screen as it had been when he first saw it; now captured in a sterile basement. Then there was Daniels' fancy home and obvious scorn for village culture, willing to sell their stolen heritage to the highest bidder. Jenny's red hair and freckles. Chumley, all elbows and mouth. Lou and Mike choosing money over their own family legacy. Jenny's red hair and freckles. Jonah knew he should purge thoughts of her from his mind. She was too young, too vulnerable, too untested by the jolts of the real world for there to be a relationship between them. He needed to focus on the task at hand.

It was true, the museum was in a better position to care for the screen than a small, cultural center run mainly by volunteers. But who were they protecting it for? Future generations of city dwellers? And even if the museum was a "better" home, the village and not the thieves should have made the decision to sell and benefit from the proceeds.

He stretched his neck and concentrated on trying to relax. Suddenly he imagined Daniels standing next to the screen, hawking it to the highest bidder: "It is one of the finest extant pieces of Northwest Coast Indian art and could be the centerpiece of any collection." Had he read that kind of description somewhere?

No matter how he thought about it, Daniels was the bad guy in all this. Especially now that Jonah knew he'd tried to warn his henchmen. Jonah felt somewhat guilty for hanging onto the telegram instead of returning it, leaving while the receptionist was checking someone in, simply waving a thank-you. If the receptionist contacted him, he would apologize profusely and say he had mistakenly kept the envelope. He didn't want to get the man in trouble, but he doubted anyone else knew about the telegram. At this point, it was illegally seized evidence, but if he'd left it behind, it could so easily have disappeared.

Daniels, the reputable art consultant. Daniels, the dignified and wealthy entrepreneur. Daniels, the employer of thieves. Daniels, the direct or indirect cause of Will's death. How far was he prepared to go to protect his reputation and his money?

It *was* possible Daniels sent the telegram because he wanted to warn North not to cause any more trouble. But whether intentional or not, that warning might encourage North to escalate the pressure on Lou, Mike, and his family in order to get paid for the sale. There was no way they would simply write off the $500,000.

He was feeling drowsy. The trip had been physically exhausting and emotionally draining. He was seeing the Raven House screen in his mind when he started to nod off. Suddenly a raven leapt from the screen and flew upward through the clouds toward him, crying for help.

He woke with a start as they began their descent. They landed with a jarring bump and a loud whishing sound as the pilot applied the brakes to stop the small aircraft. The trees along the runway whipped past until the aircraft slowed down and turned to taxi toward the terminal shelter. Jonah caught a glimpse of the familiar mountains that bordered Koloshan to the east. It was good to be home.

As he took the steps to the ground two at a time, Jonah was surprised to see Jenny standing there, waiting. He'd meant to call her from Juneau but had been in a rush to make the return flight. He'd left the Jeep in the lot and didn't need a ride. So, what was she doing there?

"Everything okay?" he asked anxiously.

She smiled. "I needed a walk. It isn't that far from the Lodge. But I could use a ride back."

His Jeep was right where he'd left it, brown streaks angling from front to back, but the windows had been wiped clean. "You do this?" he asked.

"I hope you don't mind; I had a few minutes to kill."

"Any time."

He turned the key in the ignition and listened to the motor for a moment. "It sounds different," he said. "Very smooth."

"I may have tuned it up."

"You're a full-service officer. Thank you. Now, why don't you tell me the reason you needed a walk."

"Sorry, I was going to give you time to tell me about your trip before I started complaining about Chumley."

"That doesn't sound good."

"It's nothing too bad. But I need to explain what happened before you talk with him." She took a deep breath. "I suppose it was largely my fault. To be honest, I didn't really want him there at the stakeout. I was wide awake, and he kept grousing about how cold it was and how boring it was to just sit there and wait, on and on. The bugs, the damp, the creepy sounds in the woods." She rolled her eyes and shook her head. Sunlight glinted red-gold as it touched her hair.

"I can hear him now." And he could.

"Well, I told him to go back to your place, but in spite of complaining about how miserable he was, he didn't want to go and miss out on the 'fun.'"

"About what time was this?"

"A little after 3:00 a.m. I took the first shift. He came at midnight. I'd managed to convince him that things were most likely to happen after midnight. Anyway, after he got there, I tried to get some sleep, but I kept waking up. That's when I decided to finish out the shift on my own. Anyway, it was a cloudy, dark night, and Chumley isn't used to being out in the woods at any time of day or night. He only left because I insisted. And I warned him not to let anyone see him using a flashlight. He wasn't twenty feet away when he tripped on something and fell."

"I don't suppose he was stoic about the incident."

"No, if anyone was in the area, they heard him scream. I shushed him as quickly as I could. Then I couldn't decide what to do. He said he couldn't walk without assistance. I didn't want to leave, but I couldn't just let him lay there until dawn. Finally, I convinced him to keep an eye on the house while I went for help."

"That made sense."

"He was not pleased about my decision though. I ran back to your place and called the woman from the clinic, Sue. You had her number written on a pad next to the telephone."

"Sue was a good choice. That's who I would have called."

"When I explained the situation, she met me at your place within minutes, and I took her back to our stakeout spot. He was almost hysterical when we got there. For a instant, I thought the two men had showed up and he had been unable to alert anyone. But no, he was just upset about his injury and the fact that he was *suffering from pain and exposure.* Sue wasn't fazed by his rant. She calmed him down, checked out his ankle, then pulled him to his feet and helped him down the path to her car."

"So, Sue took Chumley and you stayed behind. Anything happen after that?"

"Nothing. If they were in the area, it's quite possible they heard all the commotion and ran off. Although given the time, it seems more likely that they never came in the first place."

"Where is Chumley now?"

"I tried to get him to go back to Juneau, but he insisted on staying until you returned. I think he wants to give you his side of the story."

"You can't blame him for that."

"No, but if his ankle is really hurt, he should be getting an x-ray."

"What did Sue think?"

"That it was a sprain. But he doesn't believe her."

"Well, I'll make sure he leaves. After all, he wouldn't want to risk any permanent damage to his ankle, would he? And I couldn't have that on my conscience."

Jenny smiled. "I would love to be there for your talk with him, but I think it best if I'm not."

After dropping Jenny off, he drove home, pulled into his driveway, and paused a moment to take in the familiar surroundings before getting out of the Jeep. It felt good to be back, even after such a short time away. When he got to the porch, he could hear the television was on, turned up loud. Chumley was propped up on the couch with a glass of milk and a plate of cookies on the table next to him. "St. Clair," he said cheerfully, as if greeting an old friend. "I'm glad you're back."

Jonah went over and turned off the television, noting that Chumley had been watching an old sitcom rerun. There wasn't much on in the afternoon. "I hear you hurt your ankle," he said, taking a chair across from Chumley.

"I suppose Jenny told you what happened." Chumley sounded as if he was prepared to disagree with her interpretation of events.

"She said Sue had a look at your injury."

"The nurse wrapped it for me." He pointed to his ankle. "She doesn't think it's broken, but I think it might be."

"Well, you can have it x-rayed in Juneau. I'll arrange a flight for this afternoon."

"I don't want to go back yet."

"Sorry, but we can't take any chances. You don't want to make your ankle injury worse, do you?"

"No, but I have a feeling that something is going to happen tonight."

"I appreciate your concern, but Jenny and I can handle it. You need to take care of yourself."

"But . . ."

"I'll be sure to tell Jacobson what a good job you did. And falling in the woods in the dark wasn't your fault." He could perhaps blame it on woods spirits. Jonah was willing to say whatever it took to convince Chumley to leave willingly.

"I've been thinking. What you need is someone on the inside of the house as well as someone outside."

"Mike and Lou will be inside."

"I mean a police officer."

"I know what you meant."

"Hear me out, please."

"If your ankle is broken, I have to send you back."

Chumley frowned. "The nurse said it's a sprain; she may be right."

That admission made Jonah realize just how badly Chumley wanted to stay.

"They won't stay up all night, but I can. If the perpetrators manage to get inside, I'll be there to protect the potential victims."

Why did he have to talk like an excerpt from a police report? "It's not a bad idea," Jonah conceded, "but you need to get a second opinion on that ankle."

"I'll have the nurse take a second look. It's feeling much better."

Chumley's thin face was pinched with concern. Jonah felt like he would be kicking a puppy to say "no." And Chumley would probably fall asleep sitting in a chair at Mike's anyway.

"Oh, alright." Jonah wasn't entirely sure why he agreed. Although if he sent Chumley back too soon, it would make it feel like Jacobson had won.

He met Jenny at The Café for lunch. "Well?" she asked the minute he sat down.

"Well, I think I'll have the fish and chips."

"You know what I mean. Are you sending him back?"

"Think about how the report will read: *In spite of injuries suffered while in the line of duty, Officer Chumley insisted on fulfilling his duties and remained on the job.*"

"You're joking, right?"

"No."

"You're letting him stay?"

"He'll be our inside man tonight."

"And you're going to give him a positive review?"

"Not as good as yours, but good enough to irritate Jacobson."

"You seem so honest and straight arrow. But there's a softie or a meanie somewhere deep down in you."

"Look at it this way. Chumley may take my advice seriously if he can do so without losing face."

"I hope you're right."

They lingered over their meal, then ordered two pieces of Joe's blueberry pie for dessert. Jenny suddenly started to laugh. "I just hope I can keep a straight face if Jacobson questions me about Chumley's performance."

Jenny had parked Jonah's official truck out front. It hadn't looked so clean since it was brand new. The villagers must be wondering what had happened. Or maybe they thought Jonah ordered his "new" assistants to wash and wax it. No one who knew him well would think that, but everyone would definitely notice. There were no other spotless vehicles in the village. What he couldn't understand was how Jenny managed to keep it looking so good while driving around on the dusty roads.

Back at the jail, he paused before going inside. The crack in the window seemed to have grown in length, and there were hairline cracks branching out from the main break, like tiny electric pulses from a flash of lightning. He would have to order a replacement soon or board it up again.

There were no messages on the door, but there was a note on his desk next to the telephone. "Call Matt." He picked up the phone and dialed the familiar number.

"You're back," Matt said.

"And glad to be here."

"Don't much care for city life anymore?"

"Seattle is almost as bad as LA. So, what's up?"

"I could have left a message, but I thought it would be easier to update you in person. First, there's still no progress on the bear hunt. Just about the time we're all convinced he went off somewhere to die, there's a sighting. I can't remember when a bear has been so clever at keeping away from his pursuers.

"Meanwhile, everyone's upset about Mann. He's been a

little too free with his conclusions about the slave's grave. There's also a lot of grumbling about the screen and other stuff that was taken. Accusations have been flying about. A few threats have been made too."

"Great."

"Sorry to be the bearer of bad news. This is a lot of shit to handle all at once."

"You probably heard that Chumley sprained his ankle."

"Sue may have mentioned something about that." Matt sounded amused.

"Whatever happened to patient confidentiality?"

"I think he managed to push all of her buttons at once. Not that she said a lot, but enough that I got the picture. He on the next plane out?"

"A long story for a later time."

"Really?" After a brief pause, Matt asked: "How about the theft—any leads?"

"That an official question?"

"Just between you and me."

"Then, yes. I've located the screen. A museum in Seattle purchased it."

"Ouch. A legal fight in our future?"

"We'll have to see. But the museum could be out some serious money, so unless they have insurance to cover this kind of circumstance, my guess is that they will fight it."

"If there is anything I can do?"

"Not at the moment." It was good knowing Matt was always there for him.

He barely had the receiver back on the cradle when the telephone rang. Somehow he knew it wasn't going to be good news.

TLEI<u>K</u>ÁA

(TWENTY)

"St. Clair here," Jonah said into the receiver.

The voice at the other end was so loud Jonah had to hold the phone away from his ear. "Goddammit, St. Clair, those remains were valuable." Mann's tone was as angry as his words. "I don't know why I let you talk me into keeping them here."

"Did something happen?"

"Of course something happened! That's what I'm trying to tell you—the remains are gone." His voice went from full volume accusation to sad rebuke.

"Gone?"

"Gone. Removed. *Pilfered.* Vanished. STOLEN."

"You mean someone broke in and took the remains of the slave grave?"

"Isn't that what I just said? Someone stole them."

"When did this happen?"

"Sometime this afternoon."

"Was anything else taken?"

"The skeleton was the only thing worth taking."

"Are you at the Center now?"

"Yes. Are you coming over to have a look?" The statement was more demand than question.

"I'll be right there."

After he hung up, Jonah sat there a moment, staring at the telephone. Matt had warned him that the villagers were upset with Mann. Still, he was surprised that someone would actually steal the remains. Then again, they probably didn't think of it as theft. From their point of view, it was more a question of *preventing* a theft. Or an act of reclaiming what was theirs by right. Or a cover-up. He wasn't going to take sides, but he definitely needed to do something to keep things from escalating.

As he pulled into the parking lot, it seemed strange to think of the Center as an empty building. In his mind, he still saw the space filled with artifacts. If they didn't get them back, what would they use the building for?

The narrow path that wended its way alongside the building and down the hill ran past the small room Mann had been using as an office. Even from a distance Jonah could see that the window had been shattered. He needed to take a closer look from the outside, but first he wanted to talk to Mann.

As he went inside, he avoided looking at the empty display cases and the blank wall where the screen used to be. Stella was at her desk. He wasn't sure what she was doing these days, but she was probably still on the payroll and felt an obligation to at least be present. She opened her mouth to say something, but before she could speak, Mann appeared in the doorway to his office and said, "You're here."

Jonah nodded at Stella. Her eyes followed him, but she didn't say anything as he joined Mann in his office.

"I came right over," he said, even though it was obvious that he had.

"Look at this mess." Mann sounded both aggrieved and sad. Whoever had broken in hadn't been satisfied to simply take what they had come for. Everything in the room had been destroyed. Papers ripped up. Furniture smashed. It had been a hostile act of vandalism as well as a theft.

Mann stood in the middle of the room, giving Jonah time

to take it all in. There was no way to avoid stepping on papers and debris as he walked around the once tidy office. He felt sorry for Mann; after all, he'd just been doing his job. From his perspective, the goal was to help the villagers save the past, not to violate their rights. And he had made a big concession by keeping the remains in Koloshan while he was examining them.

"Do you think they will mess with the site too?" Mann asked "Can you catch them and make them return the remains?"

"Those are two separate issues. I'll definitely ask someone to keep an eye on the site. And I'll try to find out who did this. What I'm afraid of is that they may have disposed of the remains. There was a lot of anger in this room."

"I don't understand."

Of course you don't, Jonah thought. Whether Mann fell into the category of white people who considered natives inferior or quaint wasn't the issue. The slave remains were a symbol of that type of stereotyping. Unfortunately, Jonah had underestimated the anger some might feel about the discovery reinforcing the image of natives as *primitive*. Could he explain any of this to Mann? Should he even try?

When Jonah didn't immediately respond, Mann said: "Why? Why do you think they did this?"

"Maybe we'll find out when I catch up with them." He put his hand briefly on Mann's shoulder then left him standing there in the middle of what remained of his many months of hard work.

There was still time before the stakeout to ask around about the break-in. The question was where to start. Without consciously making the decision, he found himself driving toward Dennis's.

The old man was in his usual place at the window. He waved at Jonah as he came up the walk. Esther met him at the door. "It's good to see you. Dennis just finished a late lunch. Would you like some coffee?" He glanced down at her ruffled white apron with red and yellow flowers embroidered along the edges.

"I would love a cup of coffee."

He went in and sat down across from Dennis. Before he got settled in, Esther was there with coffee and some homemade cookies. Steam from the coffee moved silently toward the big window, leaving a trail of fogged glass.

"Things have become complicated, haven't they?" Dennis said.

"You mean life in general?" Jonah took a bite of a cookie, savoring the crumbly sweetness.

"You're here because of the missing slave's remains, aren't you?"

"I'm here to see you."

The old man smiled. "Of course, Jonah. Of course."

"But if you happen to know something about the theft of the remains and the vandalism of Mann's office, I wouldn't mind hearing about it."

"Are you speaking as a police officer or as a friend?"

Jonah considered the question. "I'm not sure I can separate the two in this instance." Was it ever possible to be both at the same time?

"We become what we do."

"Is that a bad thing?"

The old man laughed. "It depends on what you do."

"Okay, you made your point. But even if they wanted to take the remains back, they didn't have to destroy everything in his office and break a window, did they?"

"Humiliation often results in anger."

"Do you think they destroyed the remains?"

Dennis looked shocked. "Of course not. Why would they do that?"

"If they don't want anyone outside of Koloshan to learn about what was found, why wouldn't they dispose of them?"

"People have to accept both the good and the bad of any culture as part of their heritage. The legacy of slavery is unfortunately a part of our past."

"So why take it out on Mann?"

"They shouldn't have done that. It was an unnecessary act of violence."

"I agree."

"Outsiders place great importance on their possessions."

"Everyone is becoming more materialistic these days, Dennis." There was no longer any such thing as tribal ownership of property. The donations to the Center had been an anomaly. "I admit that I was hoping you might suggest who I should talk to about this."

Most of the village gossip reached Dennis through Esther; it was this pipeline that he was asking him to share. Or to betray, depending on whether he was being seen as an officer of the law or as a friend. Of course he could have asked Esther directly, but that seemed too official. Dennis was almost family, actually more family to him than anyone else in his life.

"It hasn't been easy for Mike's nephews, you know. A lot of people think Mike and Lou were responsible for the theft of the screen."

Jonah resisted the impulse to ask his question a second time. Perhaps in his own way, Dennis had given him an answer. "You mean Conn and Freddie?"

Dennis nodded

Conn and Freddie weren't troublemakers, although they

did tend to drink a little too much from time to time and get a bit rowdy. Stealing the remains in an attempt to prevent negative publicity was something he could imagine them doing. But did they possess sufficient rage to destroy the contents of Mann's office?

"So, the rumor is that Mike and Lou were involved in the theft?" He wondered if people also knew about the threats to Mike's family, Lou's beating, and the fact that he was keeping watch on Mike's house at night.

"Everyone knows Will believed he had family claim to the screen. And Lou and Mike were outspoken about how the money from the sale of the screen could be of use to the community."

"What about Will? Do they think Will was involved too?"

"It was Will's grandmother who gave the screen to the Center. Over his objections."

Poor Ellen. As Will's wife, even if the villagers didn't think she was directly involved in the theft, she would be a target for gossip and associated with their loss. The return of the screen would take some of the pressure off of the families involved, but rumors would linger no matter what he managed to prove.

He finished his coffee, said his goodbyes, and went to look for Conn and Freddie. They weren't home, but it didn't take long to find them. They were at the Dís-schu Tavern, well on their way to getting drunk. Everyone in the bar was apparently buying them rounds.

Jonah navigated through empty tables to the crowd standing around near the windows overlooking the water. There were about a dozen people in the room, most of them with Conn and Freddie, all of them familiar faces. They fell silent as he walked toward them.

"Hello, Conn, Freddie," Jonah said. Conn was still sober

enough to look worried, but Freddie called to the waitress to bring their friend Jonah a drink. She raised her eyebrows in question and he waved her off.

"Would you mind stepping outside?" He sensed that every eye in the room was on them. There was no doubt the rumor Dennis had heard was accurate. Freddie was a year out of high school, several years younger than Conn. Both had spent the last year working for a logging company. Not troublemakers, but not saints either. Jonah thought he remembered Esther saying not too long ago something about Freddie being engaged.

"We can talk here," Conn said, glancing at his drinking buddies for support.

"No, let's step outside."

"Talk here," a few voices echoed.

Conn was a short, muscular young man, a former high school wrestling champ, confident of his ability to handle himself. "Naw, I don't feel like going outside," he said as he took a long swig from his half empty glass.

Without another word, Jonah gripped Conn by the arm and pulled him toward the entrance. "Come on," Jonah said. There were hoots of encouragement for Conn to resist, but no one physically tried to intervene. A flicker of anger in Conn's eyes quickly gave way to acquiescence. Jonah glanced over his shoulder: "You too, Freddie."

"Where're we going?" Freddie asked, downing the last of his drink before hurrying after them, swaying a bit like a sailor on an undulating ship's deck. Every eye in the room stayed glued to them until the trio reached the entrance. Then talk resumed, and the crisis passed without incident.

Once outside, Jonah directed them to his Jeep. Freddie put his empty glass to his mouth, looked surprised there was nothing in it, and tossed it aside as he got into the vehicle.

"It will be more private at the jail," Jonah explained as he started the engine.

"Are we under arrest for something? Don't you have to read us our rights?"

"It's just an informal conversation." After which I may be forced to arrest you, he added to himself.

They drove the short distance in silence, except for an occasional belch from Freddie that echoed in the enclosed space. Jonah wasn't sure how he was going to handle things. If it were up to him alone, he would make the two men pay restitution, return the remains, and call it good. But they had committed what the law would consider a serious crime against property. If he arrested them, it would be up to the local magistrate to decide their fate. She was fair-minded, but she wasn't native; she might render a harsher ruling than the villagers would consider fair.

Once inside the jail, both Conn and Freddie acted almost sober. He hoped they realized that even if they had committed the break-in with the best of intentions, it was a crime nonetheless.

Jonah motioned to a couple of chairs. "Sit down and tell me about it," he ordered. They obediently sat. Neither asked what he was referring to, but neither said anything either. "I can hold you until you're willing to talk." He couldn't actually, but they probably didn't know that.

"Is this off the record?" Conn asked. That seemed to have become a popular phrase to fit a variety of circumstances.

"How can it be?"

"You can't be on their side."

"I'm on the side of the law."

"The law hasn't done much for us lately, has it?"

Conn's bitter response stung. "I'm trying, Conn. And I do sympathize with why you did it. But you shouldn't have taken your frustration out on his office. You destroyed everything in it."

Conn looked at the floor. "I knew that was a mistake. But once we got in there and looked around, well, everything got a little crazy."

"I understand."

"Do you, Jonah?" Conn looked him right in the eyes, a personal challenge to his loyalties given his non-native status.

"Yes, I think I do. But I can't look the other way on this one. You did too much damage. Mann has rights too."

Conn turned to Freddie. "He's got us, bro." Freddie nodded. "Okay, what's next?"

Jonah looked at his desk. His eyes came to rest on the knife he used as a letter opener, a present from Dennis the first year he had lived with him. It had a killer whale design carved into the wood handle. The gift had been Dennis's way of introducing him to the functional side of Tlingit art. He felt close to the culture, but he didn't really know what it was like to live it.

"I'll see if I can get Mann not to press charges."

Conn looked surprised. "You'll do that for us?"

"I can try, but I can't promise anything. Mann was rightfully pretty upset."

The two men nodded.

You'll have to give him back the remains. You still have them, don't you?"

"What if we don't? What if we destroyed them?"

"Did you?"

"What if we did?"

"Then Mann may be less willing to drop the charges against you."

"Tell him they're gone and see what he says." It was the

first time Freddie had spoken.

"I won't lie to him."

"What if we swear that we tossed them in the sound?"

"Is that what happened?"

They both nodded yes.

"It doesn't make any difference, you know. We are who we are no matter how the rest of the world sees us."

They were both still a bit tipsy, but he felt they were sober enough to weigh his words and decide what they wanted to do.

"You may have to make a choice between pride and going to jail. You understand that, don't you?"

"No one in the village wants him to have the remains. That's why we did it."

"They won't stay in his possession. He only has authority to examine whatever is found during the road project and make sure any artifacts and remains are preserved."

"But he wants to tell the world. To act like he's something special for exposing our little secret. That isn't right."

"I see your point. I'll talk to him and see what he says, but I think he will insist on the remains being returned. He won't believe you tossed them."

"You could convince him."

"I still need to investigate more. Sorry."

If he kept Conn and Freddie in jail, he would be responsible for looking after them, and he had too many other things to do, so he let them go. They weren't going to make a run for it; there was nowhere for them to run.

After they left, he sat there a moment studying the knife handle before picking up the telephone and calling the Center.

Mann wasted no time getting to the jail. When he arrived, he sat in the same chair Conn had occupied just minutes before. It crossed Jonah's mind that all three men were victims, just in different ways. Conn and Freddie had committed a criminal act motivated by a perceived need to defend their heritage against negative labels. Mann's office had been violated; he was an obvious victim. But in some ways, he had put himself in that position by using another group's past to further his own future.

"You said you have news about the theft."

"Yes, I know who broke into your office."

"That was fast."

"It's a small village."

"Do you have the remains?" Mann inched forward to the edge of the chair.

"No, I don't. Sorry."

"Oh, no." He slumped back. "They destroyed them, didn't they?"

"What I want to talk about with you is *why* they did it." He hoped Mann hadn't noticed he hadn't actually said the remains had been destroyed.

"What do you mean? You caught them. Now prosecute them. What else is there to talk about?"

"It isn't that simple, and you know it."

"They completely demolished my office."

"Put yourself in their position."

"Walk a mile in their moccasins, you mean."

"I don't see you as a spiteful man," Jonah said, ignoring Mann's tasteless remark. "And you've been aware of the turmoil caused in the community by your discovery."

"What's that got to do with the break-in?"

"This was not an ordinary criminal act. The purpose wasn't to steal something for personal gain, but to keep you from using the remains to discredit the image of the native community."

"That is not my intention."

"I'm not questioning your integrity; or your intentions. I'm asking you to try to see the situation from their point of view."

"If all they wanted was to keep me from analyzing and reporting on the remains, then why did they rip everything apart?"

"They may have been drinking and got carried away."

"That's an understatement." Man sat up and crossed his arms. "So, what's the point of this little talk?"

"I want you to agree not to press charges."

"What? Are you kidding me?"

"In exchange, they will pay damages and do whatever community service you feel is adequate to punish them for their, ah, zealousness."

"You don't know what you're asking."

"Yes, I do. These are two young men who have never been in trouble before. Rightfully or wrongfully, they thought they were doing the village a favor. I don't see that it will serve any purpose to put them in jail."

Mann stood up and ran the fingers of his right hand through his hair. "Oh, for god's sake." He paced back and forth in front of Jonah's desk for several minutes before saying, "I'm a reasonable man, St. Clair, but that's asking a lot. I have obligations as spelled out in my contract for this project."

"It would be a goodwill gesture on your part. Think of the points you would make with the locals."

Mann stopped and looked thoughtfully at Jonah. "I realize that you're caught in the middle of this. Still—" He began pacing again. "I suppose it won't serve any purpose to prosecute them. The damage is already done."

"It's unlikely similar circumstances will present

themselves in the future."

Mann sat down again and thought about it. Then, with seemingly great reluctance, he said, "Okay, I'll agree on one condition."

"What's that?"

"I need to go to Juneau tomorrow. But when I return, you have to take me out to the old village. The council approved my visit. So, at least I'll have something to show for my time here."

Jonah suppressed a smile, surprised but relieved with Mann's terms.

"Oh, one more thing. I want the window in my office replaced."

"Will do." Maybe he could have the jail office window replaced at the same time.

"And I could use some help at the site."

"That can probably be arranged." It would be a good thing for Conn and Freddie to do to make amends. Mann didn't have to know they were the ones who had broken into his office.

Mann seemed to be trying to come up with a few other things to add to his list of demands, but finally stood up and extended his hand across the desk. "Let's shake on that."

TLEIK̲ÁA K̲A TLÉIX'

(TWENTY-ONE)

"Are you out of your mind, Jonah?" Mike was looking at him as if he truly believed he *was* out of his mind. "That guy's a . . . a jackass."

"He's a police officer."

"He's a dumb shit," Lou said.

Jonah was thankful he'd left Chumley in the car while he told Mike and Lou the plan for the evening. Although maybe they would have moderated their responses if Chumley had been standing right there. Or maybe not.

"Look at it this way, if no one shows tonight, he will be on his way back to Juneau. All you have to do is let him sit inside someplace where he can watch the door. That's it."

"I still think it's crazy," Mike said.

"Humor me."

"You'd better hope he doesn't shoot someone, like someone other than the two who are after Mike and me."

"Don't worry—he's a bad shot."

Mike rolled his eyes at the sarcasm, while Lou just shook his head.

"Don't put him next to my couch," Lou said.

"How about a chair in the hall?"

Mike and Lou dragged a recliner into the hall while Jonah went out to wave Chumley in.

Chumley hobbled up the path to the house, using a crutch they had borrowed from the clinic. He was wearing a white cap that looked brand new, pulled to one side in what Jonah assumed was an attempt to look fashionable. Instead, it looked like a cap that was about to fall off at any moment. Jonah stood aside as Chumley clumped up the stairs and made his way inside. The chair they'd set up for him was next to a guest bathroom and far enough away from the bedrooms to give the family privacy.

Jonah handed Chumley the pack he'd brought. It was filled with snacks, a bottle of water, and a thermos of coffee. "This should get you through the evening." For the benefit of Mike and Lou, he added, "And remember, you scream if anyone tries to break in; you don't shoot. Got that?"

"Got it."

Jenny was waiting for him at their usual stakeout spot. "How'd it go?" she asked

"Mike wasn't wild about the idea of having Chumley in his house. Lou wasn't either. But it should be okay. Now all we have to do is hope no one shows."

"Is that a joke?"

"Not a very good one, huh?"

Actually, he very much wanted North and Elliot to show. He didn't know how much longer Jacobson would let him keep Jenny, and he wasn't sure he could keep Lou and Mike in line much longer either.

"You aren't seriously worried about Chumley, are you? I mean, in some ways it's a good idea having someone on the inside to keep watch."

"As long as he doesn't shoot the wrong person."

"He's a lot of things, but I don't think he's trigger happy . . . do you?"

"Not really. Annoying, incompetent, and pathetic, but not trigger happy."

"That's reassuring."

They lapsed into their silent watch-the-house mode and had a cup of coffee while it was still hot. It promised to be another dark night. The moon's pale light peeking from behind clouds that blocked most of the moon and the stars. Because they were familiar with the area, they didn't need much light to feel confident that they could maneuver quickly if necessary. At least they didn't have to worry about Chumley stumbling around in the woods. And with the two of them there, the long hours of waiting seemed less onerous.

As he sat there watching the quiet house, he wondered if these night vigils were still necessary. It was possible that North had contacted Daniels and been warned off. The two men could already be back in the Lower 48. In that event, there was no reason for Jenny and him to be spending hours on the unforgiving ground, drinking tepid coffee and unable to carry on a conversation for fear of calling attention to their presence.

Unfortunately, he had no way of knowing whether North and Elliot had left the area. He hadn't heard from the Juneau hotel clerk about the two men coming back for their luggage, or, thankfully, received a complaint about the missing telegram. They might still be lurking nearby, or they might have abandoned their luggage and left. Maybe it was time to turn the search over to the Juneau and Seattle police.

If and when they did catch the two men, he could have their fingerprints checked against those found on Will's truck. A match would help link them to Will's death

The murky twilight time gradually faded. He wasn't conscious of it happening, but suddenly realized it had become very hard to see. It had completely clouded over and hidden the moonlight they'd been relying upon. He had good night vision, but he could barely make out the outline of the house. Mainly he watched for movement. Sometimes it was possible to distinguish movement even with an absence of light.

They watched and waited, taking turns to either stretch their legs or take a short nap. Slowly, very slowly, the minutes became hours, each hour indistinguishable from the one before. When they could stand it no longer, they would shield the flashlight beam with their bodies and look at his watch. In spite of the flashing colons, there were several times they were both convinced that his watch had stopped.

Jonah wondered how Chumley was faring on his own. His guess was the man was sound asleep.

It was Jenny who first noticed the tiny pinpoint of light in Mike's house. "Jonah," she whispered. "Jonah, come here and look."

He had been on the verge of sleep but her words pulsed through his brain and made him instantly alert.

"A light," Jenny added. "But I can't make out what it is."

Jonah joined her and immediately caught sight of the glow of a small light in one of the rooms. "Looks like a flashlight."

"Is that Chumley's subtle way of signaling us?"

"That wasn't what we agreed on, but with Chumley, how can we know for sure? I have to check it out."

"I'm going with you."

"No, you should stay here."

"I'm going with you," she repeated.

As they started down the slope toward the house, the light went out. There was something about the situation that made Jonah uneasy. Could someone have sneaked in without them seeing and without Chumley hearing anything?

When they reached the house, he put one hand on Jenny's arm and whispered "I'll go around front. You cover the back." He was glad she had insisted on coming with him. He couldn't cover front and back on his own.

There was no light on the front porch, and no one moving around inside that he could hear. He hesitated, then moved up to the front door. He turned the handle slowly. It was locked. If someone had broken in through the front door, would they have taken time to re-lock it? That seemed unlikely. Unless they were trying to prevent a quick escape by those already inside.

He was about to start around back when there was a crash from inside. It was followed by the sound of voices and people moving about. Jonah reached the back of the house in time to see Jenny slip inside. He raced after her, wishing he had directed her to the front and he had taken the back.

The lights came on as he entered the house. The first thing he saw was Chumley sprawled on the floor with Mike standing over him with a gun in his hand.

"Don't shoot," Chumley screamed.

"What the hell—?" Mike looked too startled to do anything but stand there staring at Chumley.

Lou stumbled into the room. His hair was a tangled mass and he was blinking hard against the light. "What's going on?" he echoed in a thick, sleep-filled voice, a gun dangling from his hand.

Jenny was nowhere in sight. Jonah moved past the three men and went to clear the rest of the house. Lights were going on, one after the other, mumbled voices sounding alarmed. "Jenny?" he called.

"Here, Jonah." She came out of what he assumed was one of the bedrooms. "I've got one more room to check. All the others are clear."

He let her go. They had to be thorough. And he had a sinking feeling that the problem began and ended with Chumley.

Jenny reappeared, Laurie right on her heels. "What's

going on, Jonah?" She had on a filmy pink flowered nightgown, her high, round belly clearly visible against the folds of material.

They went back to the kitchen. Chumley was still on the floor, leaning against the wall, his feet stuck straight out. Lou stood to one side, looking not quite awake. Mike was gone and the back door ajar.

"Where's Mike?" Jonah asked Chumley.

"He went outside."

"And you let him?" Jonah didn't wait for an answer but sprinted out the door. "Stay here, Lou, Jenny."

"Mike!" His voice faded into the darkness. "Mike!"

A figure loomed at the corner of the house. Jonah tensed and flattened himself against the wall, waiting for the gunshot, but the figure ducked out of sight.

Jonah inched along the wall toward the corner of the house. He knew he was vulnerable; there was no cover near the house. He sensed someone was there even though he couldn't hear any movement. Was it Mike? Or one of the two men they were hoping to catch?

He pulled out his gun and moved closer to the corner. "Mike?" he called, this time softly.

"Jonah?"

"You okay?"

The two men met at the corner. "Find anyone?" Jonah asked.

"No, nothing.

"Want to check one more time?"

"Okay. You go that way." They started off in opposite directions. Moments later they met back at the opposite corner of the house.

"Anything?"

"Nothing."

Jenny had pulled the curtains closed so no one outside could see in. Chumley was still on the floor. Laurie was standing next to Jenny, her eyes wide with fear. When she saw Mike, she rushed into his arms. "It's okay, Laurie. Everything's okay."

Mike looked over Laurie's shoulder at Jenny. "The kids are fine," she assured him.

Lou came in. He was dressed and had his gun tucked in his waistband. "Is this a posse or a party?" he asked.

"Neither. You can put the gun away." Jonah turned to Chumley. "Tell us what happened, Chumley." It was difficult to keep the irritation out of his voice.

"I . . . I don't know exactly," Chumley began. His voice trembled, and he looked frightened. Was he afraid of Jonah because he had screwed up again, or was it something else?

"Here." Jonah bent down. "Let me help you up." He pulled Chumley to his feet. Jenny got him a chair and the man collapsed as if his knees were too weak to support his weight.

"We saw a light," Jenny said. "Did you see one too?"

"A light?" Chumley looked truly puzzled.

"In here. I think it came from over there." They all turned to look in the direction she pointed. "Oh, no," she said. "You didn't . . ."

Chumley hung his head.

Jonah didn't know whether to throttle Chumley or to laugh. If the stakes hadn't been so high, he probably would have laughed.

"I don't get it," Mike said.

"You raided our refrigerator?" Laurie's voice was tinged with disbelief and rage.

"I . . . I was hungry."

They all stood there staring at Chumley. He had turned

their night into a nightmare because he was hungry. Then Jenny snickered. She caught Lou's eye, and he started to laugh. It was infectious. Soon they were all laughing, all except Chumley, that is. It was partly relief that what could have been a tragedy turned out instead to be a farce.

When they stopped laughing, Mike said: "Actually, this isn't funny. You gave us a real scare." He glared at Chumley. "You realize that, don't you?"

"I'm sorry. Really sorry."

Jonah was mad at himself for agreeing to let Chumley stay. But he also felt sympathy for the man. "Let's call it a night," Jonah said to Chumley. "Jenny, why don't you run him to my place."

"And you?" she asked.

"I'll finish out the shift. Although I don't anticipate anything will happen."

For once Chumley judged the situation correctly and didn't push back on Jonah's decision. Jenny handed him his crutch and lead him out the front. At the door, he turned back briefly and opened his mouth, but no words came out. Shoulders slumped, he limped away.

"I almost feel sorry for him," Laurie said after he was gone.

"Don't waste your sympathy on him," Mike said. He put his arm around his wife and drew her close. "Let's go back to bed, hon."

"I apologize. I shouldn't have let him stand watch here."

Lou slapped Jonah on the back and grinned. "Look on the bright side—it's a night to remember."

The rest of the night was less memorable. Jonah went back to his post. Not too long after that, Jenny rejoined him. "You didn't need to come back."

"I wanted to."

"Chumley okay?"

"He's devastated."

"Well, maybe it's for the best."

"You mean because you think it will make him realize he's not suited for field work?"

"That's what *you* think, isn't it?"

"I think he desperately wants to fit in somewhere and doesn't know how to make that happen."

"I get that. But in this line of work, he puts the lives of others in danger. He can't be allowed to do that."

"So, are you going to tell Jacobson the truth?"

Jonah hesitated.

"What if I end up being his partner? How will you feel then?"

Jonah didn't respond immediately. Then he said, "You know Jacobson won't listen to me, don't you? He will twist whatever I say to make me look like the bad guy. But under the circumstances, I can't give Chumley a glowing recommendation like I'd originally planned."

"Given what happened, I think there's an option you should consider—talk to Chumley. Help him understand the situation. See if you can get him to accept the idea that he may be better suited to something other than field work. You'll be doing everyone a favor, including him. If he screws up in Juneau and Jacobson has to discipline him, it will not be pleasant. Chumley isn't a bad person; he just hasn't found his niche yet."

Given how Jenny felt about the man, that was a generous response. But she was right: Chumley was a miserable excuse for a policeman, and it would be a kindness to convince him that he might be better off doing something different for a living.

"Alright, Jenny. I'll talk to him."

Tomorrow. He would talk to Chumley tomorrow when he sent him back to Juneau.

TLEIK̲ÁA K̲A DÉIX

(TWENTY-TWO)

Jonah walked silently along the trail, looking ahead and side to side, only occasionally glancing down. It was the way he'd been taught. A quick glance was supposed to alert you to dangers immediately underfoot, but it was also important to be aware of what was happening around you.

A breeze high overhead moved the treetops and rippled its way down to the forest floor where small birds were busy searching for breakfast. He had always liked being in the woods in the early morning hours. There was the damp smell of earth and leaves and the feeling of life being renewed as light slowly penetrated the thick overstory. Once the sun was up, the forest somehow seemed more substantial, less spiritual.

He left the trail and cut through the brush. In a narrow clearing he came upon fresh deer droppings, still steaming slightly. The tracks nearby showed splayed hoofs, a sign of old age. Jonah like to think that a lot of deer in the area lived long lives. He enjoyed hunting and liked deer meat, but it seemed fitting that at least some animals enjoyed their full cycles of life.

As he drew near the campsite he had discovered recently, he proceeded cautiously. Out of habit, he always tried to walk as quietly as possible when in the woods. In this instance, however, it was essential to stay as invisible and silent as he could in case the two men had returned.

He circled the area once, then approached the campsite through the woods from the northeast. Two birds raced each other through the trees, skimming under heavy boughs, pausing briefly to scold unseen enemies, apparently unconcerned with Jonah's presence. Gradually the sound of their flight faded and the forest was quiet again.

When he finally reached the clearing, there was no one there. A few fresh animal tracks could be seen in the dirt near the campfire, obscuring any footprints, but everything looked the same as the last time he had been there.

Where were North and Elliot? Had they already left the state? Or had they simply moved to another campsite? As far as he could tell, they weren't in the village. They hadn't returned to the hotel in Juneau. They hadn't boarded the midnight ferry either by car or foot. No private airplane had been seen at the airport. It was possible they had paid someone to take them someplace by private boat. Or maybe they had stolen a boat the owners seldom used and no one had noticed it missing yet. It was also possible, though it seemed unlikely, that they'd made their way to some remote part of the island and been picked up by a boat or a seaplane. He could continue asking around, but things like that would be difficult to trace.

It seemed to Jonah that there was still a chance that the two men were in the area. There were lots of places to hide in the wilderness. They could be moving from place to place, like the elusive bear. Perhaps they'd intended to make their move last night and had been dissuaded by all the activity at Mike's. If so, maybe they would try again this evening.

He branched out, sticking to trails, keeping a sharp eye for some sign of recent prints. He worked his way east in the general direction of the spot where he had found Will's body. It was a random search, but he felt he had to try something. Sometimes trails would peter out without warning, and he would have to bushwack his way through thick underbrush until he found another. Sometimes a path would wander off in a direction he didn't want to go. He saw lots of prints, some old and some fresh, but none were the ones he was looking for.

Then he saw a fresh print that made him stop, drop to one knee and stare. He ran his fingers over the indentations. The track was unmistakable and very sharp, a large humanoid shaped footprint with a shallow arc of toes with claws extended. Was this the bear that had attacked Will? And, possibly the one the community was trying to catch up with? If so, it had been in the area very recently.

He pulled his rifle out of the sling and held it in trail arms position, buttstock tucked under his armpit and the barrel pointed upward and slightly forward. He increased his stride and pace, following the tracks. Occasionally he found further signs—a tuft of hair stuck to a bush, broken branches, an occasional footprint.

As he came around a bend he could see a steep hillside through the trees. The trail seemed to be curving and running parallel to the base of the hill. He spotted another partial print, a round heel pad from a front foot in some soft dirt next to an overturned log. It looked like the bear had stopped to find something to eat. He was about to continue along the trail when he noticed a tangle of brush up against a steep slope off to his right that didn't look natural. It stood out from the foliage nearby, too thick, too uniform in height. He started toward it but hesitated when he heard a noise behind him. Had the bear heard Jonah and circled around? Was he being stalked?

Raising his rifle, he swung slowly around, his muscles tense. Through the trees he thought he saw movement. Whatever it was, it was angling to his left. Jonah backed up to give himself more space between him and whatever it was out there. If it was a bear, he might only have one chance to get off a shot when it charged. Aim was everything.

He kept his rifle ready and waited, telling himself to remain calm. His heartbeat had definitely increased; he inhaled deeply to steady himself. Bears had been known to keep coming after being shot in the heart or between the eyes, carried along by momentum, bodies continuing their instinctive attack even after the brain ceased to give it orders.

When the bushes moved again, as if jostled gently by something passing by, he had second thoughts. A large, heavy animal wasn't that stealthy when surrounded by thick underbrush. Perhaps this was the deer he had seen sign of earlier.

Another bush wiggled, a little more to his left. Whatever it was, it wasn't in any hurry to show itself.

Jonah waited. His rifle at ready.

Moments later a man stepped out from behind a tree. He too had his rifle raised. For a second, they blinked in surprise at each other. Then both men relaxed and lowered their rifles.

"Jonah, I sure didn't expect to see you here."

"Lou, what are *you* doing here?"

"I just had to get out. I feel like I've been cooped up for ages. Thought I might as well have a look around for that bear while I was at it."

"He passed this way not too long ago."

"I know. I was following his trail. Saw that he'd trampled brush in this area. After that I lost him."

"He's a wily one."

"You said it. I can't believe they haven't taken him out yet."

Jonah looked around. "I wonder what interested him around here?"

"What's that over there?" Lou asked, pointing to the strange stand of brush Jonah had noticed.

"I was wondering that myself."

As they got closer, it became apparent that the barrier was man-made. Someone had gone to great pains to weave branches and brush together so it would stay in place, while to a casual observer passing by, it could pass for natural undergrowth. The ground in front of it was scuffed and pitted.

"An animal?" Lou asked.

"There are some ATV tracks going in that direction—back toward the main road." Jonah followed them about twenty feet before Lou called him back. He had pulled some of the barrier brush aside.

"I see something; can't tell exactly what though."

Jonah joined him and they pulled more brush away. There were some lumber stakes in the ground, lined up like fence posts. Behind them was an opening.

"Looks like a small cave," Lou said.

Jonah glanced over his shoulder before pulling out the middle stake so they could get closer to see inside. "I've got a flashlight." He pulled it out and shone it around the entrance. The cave wasn't much, a narrow hollow with about four feet or so of headroom. As he knelt in the entrance, the smell of body waste enveloped him.

"Is that what I think it is?" Lou asked.

Jonah shined his light into the hole and was shocked to see two bodies, shoes facing out. Squatting down, Jonah duck-walked forward. When he got close enough, he grabbed a set of legs. "Give me a hand," he said as he inched backwards, pulling the first body out a way while Lou pulled up more stakes so they could get it into the open.

The man was bound and gagged. Jonah removed the gag while feeling for a pulse. "He's alive."

"Holy shit."

This time Lou went in to pull out the second man. "I think this one's alive too."

When Lou brought out the second man, Jonah checked for signs of life. "He's got a weak pulse, but you're right, he's alive."

They each took one man and untied them. "Holy shit," Lou said again.

"You know him?" Jonah had a strong hunch that the man he was looking at was Dick North. He had a mole on his forehead, just like the co-op driver had described.

"Sort of."

The man Jonah thought might be North suddenly opened his eyes. He moved his mouth, but no sound came out. Jonah got out a bottle of water and poured a capful into the man's mouth. He coughed but swallowed.

"My guy is unconscious," Lou said.

"We have to get them out of here."

"I agree. With the bear on the loose, we can't leave them here."

Jonah considered the logistics of transporting the two back to the village. The two men obviously weren't going to be able to walk on their own. "Think you could find your way back here if you went for help?"

"I think so, but that would take a while. Not sure I could get through by radio even from my car. And I think this guy needs medical attention, sooner rather than later."

"Think you could carry him?"

"He's no heavier than a large buck." Lou reached down and grabbed the man around the hips. The man let out a moan as Lou hoisted him in the air and slung him over his shoulder.

Jonah performed the same maneuver with his burden, hoping the man didn't have any internal injuries. Hauling them back instead of going for help was a judgement call. But action seemed better than waiting around for assistance.

Both men hung limp, arms dangling, as Lou and Jonah trudged single file along the trail, Lou in the lead. From that angle Jonah couldn't tell whether the man Lou was carrying was dead or alive. He wondered if they would know if one or both died en route. In any event, it was going to be a very long hike carrying so much weight. A long, smelly hike. Both men had soiled themselves.

"Do you know who you're carrying?" Jonah called to Lou? He wished he could see Lou's face so he would know if he was lying.

"What makes you think I would?"

"Your initial response. And it seems to me like there's a good chance these are the two men we've been waiting up for the last few nights."

For a minute, Jonah thought Lou was going to deny he had seen these men before, but he didn't. "When someone beats you up, you don't get a chance to ask for names."

"What about when you pull off a job together?"

Lou didn't respond right away. Finally, he said, "I think these are the same two men. But we didn't exchange business cards."

They walked in silence after that, concentrating on putting one foot in front of the other, trying not to think about the weight of the bodies and how far they had to go. Jonah was glad Lou had shown up when he had. He would have hated to leave one of the men there while he went for help. Especially not with that bear still in the area. Who could have left those two men there to die like that? It would have been kinder to shoot them.

At a fork in the trail, Jonah lost sight of the ATV tracks. Not that it mattered; the driver was long gone. And ATVs were common in Koloshan. It would be hard to identify it. The important thing was to get the two men to medical help.

Lou's truck was closer than Jonah's Jeep, so that's where they headed. By the time they got there, Jonah's knees were starting to feel the strain, and he imagined that Lou was equally relieved to reach his truck without collapsing. Although the man Lou had transported was still unconscious, the one Jonah had carried was making little gurgling noises, moving his lips as if trying to moisten them.

"They need water," Lou said. "All I've got is beer."

Jonah took out his nearly empty water bottle. The conscious man eagerly accepted the capful offered. He then wetted the lips of the unconscious man and managed to force a little water into his mouth. Then he hopped in the back of the truck. "Lou, let's take them to the clinic. I'll ride back here with them, cushion their heads. See if you can avoid potholes, okay?"

The trip to town seemed to take forever. The clinic was closed, so they went to Sue's house. She peeked out the window when Jonah knocked and immediately opened the door. Standing there in her old jeans and fuzzy blue slippers she did not look nearly as prim as usual. "Is someone hurt?"

"Two men. One is slipping in and out of consciousness. The other hasn't come to and has a weak pulse. I'm not sure of the extent of their injuries, but they are obviously suffering from exposure and dehydration."

"I'll be right with you." She left him standing in the doorway. In no time at all she came back dressed in her uniform with a jacket in her hand. Jonah was pleased to note that she hadn't taken time to comb her hair.

She glanced briefly at the men before climbing in beside Lou. Jonah could tell she was already reviewing procedures in her head. Koloshan was lucky to have her. A lot of the villages were solely dependent on airlifts and traveling physicians for their medical needs.

At the clinic she directed Jonah and Lou as to the best way to lift and carry the men inside. After what they'd been through, it seemed almost unnecessary to be so careful at this point, but they did as they were told. Once inside, Sue hurried about getting organized. "Can you stay, Jonah? I might need some help."

"I was planning on it." He turned to Lou. "Why don't you stay for a few minutes too."

"Afraid I'll talk to Mike and we'll both decide to clam up or change our stories?"

"Something like that."

"Don't worry, Jonah. This has gone on long enough. I'm ready to do whatever I can to help clear up this mess."

Jonah put his hand on Lou's shoulder. "And I'll do whatever I can to help you and Mike, you can count on that."

"I know, and I appreciate it."

Jonah hesitated, then said, "Go on, go tell Mike we've got the two guys. I'll come by when I can."

After Lou had gone, Jonah helped Sue remove the men's clothing. The man who was semi-conscious tried to resist but was too weak to do so effectively. "I need to get you cleaned up," Sue told him. "Then get you hydrated." The other man had opened his eyes briefly before lapsing back into unconsciousness. She turned to Jonah. "No visible injuries that I can see." She pointed to the refrigerator in the alcove next to the supply cabinet. "Could you get me a couple of power drinks?"

When he came back, she directed him to give the man he was thinking of as North as much to drink as he would accept. "Prop him up with a couple of pillows from that cupboard so he can swallow easier." Jonah did as he was told, and the man guzzled almost half a bottle before stopping to breathe. He stared at Jonah as if suddenly seeing him for the first time.

"Can you talk?" Jonah asked.

"A little." His voice was raspy and barely audible.

"You Dick North?" Jonah asked.

The man looked surprised, then nodded.

"And is that man Jim Elliot?"

He nodded again and took another long swig.

"Jonah, the man has obviously been through hell," Sue said. "Can't your questions wait?" Elliot had his eyes open, and Sue was helping him take in some fluids.

"I've been looking for you," Jonah told the two men, ignoring Sue.

"Glad . . . you found . . . us," North said. Jonah wondered how happy he was going to be once he realized why Jonah had been looking for them.

"You do realize that the man who carried Elliot from the cave recognized both of you."

"Who . . . ?"

"One of your partners in crime." Jonah waited a moment before adding, "And do you know that one of the men involved in your heist is dead? He wasn't tied up like you two were, but he ran into a bear who was more than happy to make a meal of him."

North's eyes opened wide, as if he hadn't known about what had happened to Will. Maybe the two men weren't responsible for Will's death, after all. Obviously, someone else had to be involved. Someone who had disappeared with the artifacts and the money. Someone who had left North and Elliot to die in that cave.

"Who put you in that cave?" And why? What had they done to earn such a horrible death?

"Wearing a mask . . . didn't see . . . his face."

"Don't tire yourself," Sue warned.

"You must have some idea about who wanted you out of the way bad enough to do that to you."

He shook his head "no."

"Jonah, why don't you let them rest."

"Sorry Sue, but as soon as they can be moved, they're going to jail."

TLEIK̲ÁA K̲A NÁS'K

(TWENTY-THREE)

Jonah looked out the window and saw the large black bird hop three times before taking to the air, its wedge-shaped tail a steadying sail for its broad-beamed hull. Jonah remembered his father telling him that ravens needed to "wind up" for take-off. Like the mechanical car he'd had when he was young. He'd loved that car. With a will of its own, it had raced here and there, stalling in the tall grass, or flipping over if the obstacle was too steep. Then one day he'd left it outside in the rain, and by the time he came across it again, it had rusted. Life was like that. You can't go back and do things differently. There are always consequences for your actions.

Two more ravens landed in the driveway just as Lou pulled up. He was taking Jonah back to where he'd left his Jeep.

"Those damn ravens act like they own the place," Lou said. "I'm surprised more of them aren't run over."

"Some might argue that they *do* own this land."

"Spare me; I've heard the tales."

After the initial exchange they didn't talk much. Jonah knew Lou was worried about what was going to happen to him and Mike because of what they'd done. But now that the two men were in custody, at least they wouldn't have to keep looking over their shoulders anymore.

Jonah had transferred Dick North to the jail earlier. He'd given Sue a key and asked if she would look in on him during the day. Elliot was still at the clinic, but Jonah had moved the cot close to the wall so he could handcuff him to a chair that he had secured to a hefty file cabinet. He was fairly certain Elliot was too weak to try anything, but he wasn't taking any chances. "It's for your safety as well as to make sure he can't escape," Jonah had told Sue when she'd protested. As soon as Elliot recovered enough to be moved, Jonah was going to transfer both men to Juneau.

His Jeep was right where he'd left it, paint intact under a layer of dust. In a few years it would be spotted with rust that would spread like a cancer. Eventually, he would abandon it, like he had his wind-up car when he was a kid.

"Thanks," Jonah said. "North told me they left their car on one of the logging roads near here; he couldn't be too specific. I'm going to look around before I head back."

Either North had given him bad information or their assailant had taken or moved their car; there were none in the vicinity that he could find. The drive back was like being in a sandstorm. If they didn't have rain soon, everything in the village would be the color of dust. Jonah envisioned what the village would look like if featured in National Geographic. Instead of huts made of sand blocks with dingy brown mules nibbling brown blades of dying grass next to dried up ponds, there would be mountains and glaciers in the distance, but the same tan tones would stretch across the Alaskan village from forest to shoreline.

He stopped at his house to pick up Chumley. He had intended to put him on a plane on Friday but had been sidetracked by finding the two men. So today was the day. He wasn't looking forward to the talk that he had promised Jenny he would have with Chumley, but he knew she was right—someone needed to do it, and if not him, then who?

Chumley was in good spirits. He'd slept in, his ankle was better, and apparently memories of what had happened at Mike's had lost some of their sting. "In a few more days, I may be able to walk again without a cane," he announced.

They went to The Café for an early lunch. Jonah thought it would be easier to talk to him there with other people around. After they put in their orders, he took a deep breath and asked, "So, how do you feel about your experience here in Koloshan?"

Chumley immediately looked wary. "What do you mean?"

"Just what I said. I want to know how you feel about how you did on your first field assignment."

"You're thinking about Thursday evening, aren't you?"

"Partly."

"Well, that was unfortunate."

Jonah thought it was an interesting choice of words—*unfortunate.*

"You blame me for what happened," Chumley said in a defensive tone that implied he disagreed.

"I'm not interested in placing blame." Jonah wished Dennis was there to tell a raven tale to enlighten Chumley. But he wasn't. It was up to him to make a point that needed to be made. In plain English. "I want to talk to you about police work. About *you* and police work." He'd be direct; if that failed, then Chumley would have to find out another way that he was unsuited for the job.

Chumley was leaning back in his chair as if preparing to dodge a physical blow.

"Not everyone is suited for field work, you know. But that doesn't mean they aren't valuable in other ways."

"You mean 'me,' don't you?" He sounded wounded but not surprised.

"Yes, I mean 'you.' Sorry."

"I get what you're trying to say."

"I was on the force in LA for six years. It took me that

long to figure out that it wasn't a good fit for me. Sometimes it isn't easy to give up a dream, but you have to do what's best for you and for the force."

"Are you going to write a bad report on me?"

"No, I see no need for that. But I want you to give your future some serious thought. Think about what you're good at; where you can make the best contribution."

Their food came. The two men ate in silence for a few minutes. Then Chumley said, "I know you didn't need to talk to me about this. I'll give it some thought."

Joe came over to the table to say hello and comment on rumors about Lou and Jonah finding two men left in the woods to die. "Are they the thieves?"

"They were probably involved," Jonah said non-committedly. "But so far, no artifacts or money." He was aware that the room had become unusually silent, every ear in the place straining to hear what Jonah was saying. He would give Joe details when they couldn't be overheard. But it was clear, the word was already out about the two men. Otherwise, Joe wouldn't have asked in public.

Chumley and Jenny were both going to hop a float plane back to Juneau that afternoon.

Jonah drove by his place to pick up Chumley's belongings and headed for the Lodge to get Jenny. She was waiting out front on a wood bench under the eaves. She gave them both a big smile, but as soon as Chumley's back was turned, she raised her eyebrows in question. Jonah gave her a thumb's up, even though he wasn't entirely certain his little talk with Chumley had succeeded.

When he returned to the office, he intended to write feedback on both Chumley and Jenny. He had decided to blame Chumley's ankle for his limited contributions to the assignment while praising Jenny for going above and beyond. Although he was convinced that she had an uphill battle to prove her worth to Jacobson, he wanted it on the record that she had done an outstanding job on her Koloshan assignment.

Chumley stayed at the top of the dock on a bench in front of the port office to wait for the floatplane, leaving Jenny and Jonah alone. "I enjoyed working with you," Jenny said.

"I hate to see you go." He was surprised that he had admitted it; the words coming out before he gave it any thought.

"Maybe our paths will cross again. After all, I'm just a short plane ride away."

"Yes." He wondered if she expected him to say more or if she was just being polite. At that point, the plane appeared in the distance, and Chumley got up and headed in their direction.

"Give me a call when you're in Juneau," Jenny said softly.

After Jonah helped secure the plane to the dock, he said his goodbyes and headed back into town, not looking back. It was easier that way. As he drove to the village, he thought about all the people who came and went in your life. At the time, you didn't always realize they were making an impact. Relationships had a way of sneaking up on you, like a high tide that covers the shore for a time, then recedes, leaving things slightly altered, but not perceptibly different. Sometimes you had to look closely to recognize the changes.

He stopped by the jail to check on North. Earlier he'd asked him questions about the theft and the threats made to Ellen, Lou, Mike, and Mike's family. North had refused to talk about any of the issues relating to criminal acts. He'd said, "I'd ask for a lawyer but doubt there is one here."

He found North drinking coffee from a thermos cup.

There was a sandwich on a plate next to him. "Sue stopped by?" Jonah asked. North nodded. "Need anything else?"

"A shave and a haircut." He rubbed his chin.

"Afraid those amenities aren't part of the jail service."

"When will you be sending me back to Juneau?"

"Tomorrow."

"How about Elliot?"

"Sue will let me know when it's okay for him to travel." He had decided to send them separately so they wouldn't have time to talk. It probably didn't matter, but it would be easier for everyone if they were transported one at a time. He would have sent North back with Jenny and Chumley, but he was still hoping he could get some information out of him before he let him go.

"You don't want to discuss your part in the theft, but could you tell me about what happened the night someone attacked you? It might help me find the person who did that."

North seemed to consider the request. Then he sighed and said, "I want that bastard caught."

"So, tell me everything you remember."

"I'm not sure what happened. We were laying there next to the campfire. I was asleep or almost asleep. The last thing I remember was Elliot crying out. Before I could react, someone hit me. When I came to, I was tied up, gagged, and blindfolded. We were piled on some kind of ATV. It was a bumpy ride.

"When we got to the cave, he dragged us over and . . ." His voice started to shake.

"Take a deep breath."

"It was terrible. He took off our blindfolds but left us gagged. He was wearing a mask. One of those ski things with eye holes. He put Elliot in first, then shoved me in alongside him. I tried to get free, but he had us tied up pretty good."

"Did he say anything?"

"Not a word."

"What happened next?"

"At first there was some light; then he covered the entrance and only an occasional flicker of light came through."

"Is there anything else you can tell me that might help identify him. Was he tall? Short? Slim? Muscular? Did you see his hair? Eye color?"

"Average height, maybe a little extra around his belly. He had on a mask, gloves."

"What did the mask look like?"

"One of those knit things, like bank robbers use."

"What color were his eyes?"

"Dark, I think."

"Gloves?"

"Leather."

"Was he wearing a jacket?"

"Your standard puffy blue rain jacket. Jeans, I think."

"Did he walk like a young person or older?"

"I didn't see him moving much, except for when he was dragging us into the cave. He was bent over, and breathing heavy. But then it's probably hard to drag a heavy person across rough terrain."

After questioning North, he went by the clinic. Mike was waiting in the small room that served as a lobby, sitting on a battered wood chair, leaning back against the wall beneath a poster that provided health service information. When Jonah came in, he leapt to his feet. "Sue won't let me talk to him; said you have to approve it."

"Why do you want to talk to him?"

"To ask about the artifacts and the money, what else?"

"You think I'm not doing my job?"

"I thought he might be more open with me, given . . . ah, our history."

Jonah thought for a moment. "I can't let you have a conversation with him on your own, but if there is something specific you want me to ask, tell me."

"I want to know why he thought Lou and I had the artifacts or knew where they were. And the money, of course."

"Okay."

"Do you think they beat up Will?"

"I doubt either one will confess to that."

"But what do *you* think?"

"I think there is someone still out there sitting on the artifacts and the money. Maybe the person who attacked these two guys. The only question is whether one or both know who that person is. Although if they do, then why harass you and Lou?"

Sue came into the room looking brisk and efficient. "I thought I heard your voice out here, Jonah."

"I wanted to thank you for taking North some food. And, I'm wondering if Elliot is doing well enough that I can ask him a few questions."

"He's doing okay. It's taking him longer to rehydrate and come round. I don't think there's anything wrong with him that a little rest and nourishment can't cure."

"Can he travel back to Juneau on Monday?"

"I don't see why not."

"Can I leave him here until Sunday evening? I don't want the two of them talking to each other."

"No problem."

Elliot was laying on the narrow examination table

covered with a thin blanket and propped into a half sitting position with a pile of pillows. He frowned when he saw Jonah. "When do these cuffs come off?" he asked. He sounded peeved and a bit weak.

"When the police in Juneau decide you are safely tucked away."

"I haven't been charged with anything."

"I'll be glad to make it official before you leave." Jonah pulled up a chair. "Now then, what do you want to talk about first—beating up Lou, threatening half a dozen people, stealing priceless artifacts, or leaving Will to die a horrible death?"

"I want a lawyer."

"We don't happen to have one in Koloshan, but I'm sure they will be able to accommodate you in Juneau. Meanwhile, let me advise you of your rights." He went through the familiar litany, enjoying the growing discomfort on Elliot's face. When he finished, he said, "Just one question that you don't have to answer, but I'm curious— does the name Bill Daniels mean anything to you? By the way, *he* didn't lawyer up."

One of Elliot's eyelids twitched, but he remained stubbornly quiet.

"If you want to be the one left holding the bag, fine. I just thought I would give you a chance to tell your side of the story." He wished he had some leverage to get answers from the two men. The way criminal prosecutions worked, they often took months before anything was resolved, whether through a plea agreement or a trial. And sometimes the truth didn't surface. They might never learn what had happened to Will and why. And they might never recover either the artifacts or the money.

Jonah stood up. "You can thank me any time for saving

your life." He started to turn away.

"It was horrible," Elliot said. "I couldn't move."

"When you were in the cave, you mean."

"I'm slightly claustrophobic. And after it went dark, I panicked. Almost strangled myself on that damn gag."

"What can you tell me about the person who put you in there?"

"I don't remember how we got there. But while he was . . . stuffing us in that hole, he didn't say a word."

"Do you have any sense of his height? Weight?"

"Not really. I was too panicked to notice."

"Did you see what he was wearing?"

"All I saw was a dark ski mask."

"Was he wearing a jacket?"

Elliot closed his eyes. "It was blue, I think."

"Anything else?"

"Sorry, I wasn't thinking clearly at all. At first, when he didn't kill us, I thought he would come back. But he didn't."

"I understand why you want a lawyer present to make a statement. But keep in mind, if you aren't responsible for Will's death, you might be able to get out in front of this. Either way you'll serve time; the question is, how long? And if you cooperate—"

"There isn't much to tell. Dick and I were just drivers." He paused. "You'll say I cooperated if I tell you what we did?"

"Yes. I already have a pretty good idea, but there are some gaps."

"We picked up the truck and went to the Center at the agreed upon time. Three local guys were there to help us load."

"Lou, Mike and Will."

"I think so; we didn't use names and we'd never met them

before. Problem was, they hadn't thought it through so good. They had a hard time removing the screen and those corner posts from the wall and getting everything into the truck without damaging anything. So, while they were working on that, the third guy put the smaller stuff in his pickup. We didn't want to hang around any longer than we had to."

Once he started reliving the evening, he just kept spilling details. A good lawyer might get his confession thrown out, but Jonah silently begged him to continue.

"The guy with the pickup truck full of artifacts said he could meet us on a side street near the ferry. The other two local guys rode in back with the screen. Dick was up front with me. When we got to where we'd agreed to meet, the pickup wasn't there. We hung around for as long as we dared; we couldn't afford to miss the ferry. Dick thought maybe one of us should stay behind to see what had happened to the artifacts and the money—we'd already paid for everything at the Center. Like we'd been told to do. The other two seemed as upset as we were when he didn't show, and we finally decided to leave without the rest of the artifacts. We got a telephone number and told them we would be in touch."

"We delivered the screen and were on the hook for the other artifacts. Promised we'd pick them up right away. But when we got in touch with the two locals, they claimed their friend was still missing, along with the rest of the load and the money. They acted really mad about the missing money. But Dick and I decided the three of them were in cahoots, and we weren't going to let them make us the patsies."

"How do I know one of you didn't stay behind and track down Will?"

"Someone probably saw us either getting on or off the ferry. We weren't invisible."

"So as far as you know, the last one to have the artifacts and the $500,000 was Will?"

"The guy with the pickup truck. Yeah."

"What about Daniels, do you know how he got in touch with Will in the first place?"

"All he told us was what we were supposed to do."

"You didn't see anyone showing interest in you or the truck the night of the theft, did you?"

"No. Not that I noticed."

"What about the driver you replaced? Any reason to think he double-crossed you?"

"He was too concerned for his family to try anything. Not smart enough either."

"Did you talk to anyone else in the village?"

"Just that teacher in charge of the co-op truck."

"What do you think happened to the artifacts?"

"I have no idea. We've looked everywhere. Couldn't get anyone to admit anything."

A raven outside the window took to the air, its dark shape momentarily casting a shadow across Elliot's face. Someone had left North and Elliot to die. Maybe the same person who caused Will's death. Perhaps he got what he wanted from Will and was tired of having the two men stirring up trouble. But why not just kill them outright? What had been done to them seemed personal.

"Did you bring a car the last time you came here?" He wanted to see if Elliot's story was the same as North's.

"Yes, a rental. It's parked on one of those logging roads."

Sue poked her head in. "He's still a patient; he needs his rest."

"You're absolutely certain you have no idea about who attacked you?"

Elliot leaned forward. "I wish the hell I knew. I'd . . ." He left the threat hanging.

Mike was still there when Jonah came out. "Well? Did he tell you anything?"

"Nothing we didn't already know. But your stories all jibe."

"What's going to happen to Lou and me, Jonah? I hate to leave Laurie now, her being pregnant and all."

"She won't be alone."

"No, but I should be with her."

"With no previous record and people speaking on your behalf, you might not be away too long."

"With a kid, a few months is a lifetime." Mike shook his head. "It seems so stupid now, looking back. But I thought that with the money we could go somewhere, start fresh, give the kids a chance at a better life. Instead, everything's gone to hell."

"It could be worse, Mike. At least you're alive."

TLEIḴÁA ḴA DAAX'OON

(TWENTY-FOUR)

In a large city, or maybe even in a small one, Jonah was aware that a police officer would never keep two thieves under lock and key while letting their two co-conspirators continue living their lives as usual. The fact that Lou and Mike were willing to assist in the investigation didn't necessarily entitle them to remain free. But Koloshan was a small community. And Jonah felt confident that neither man would run. In fact, he was counting on it. Otherwise, he would have a lot of explaining to do.

When he got back to the jail, North was taking a nap. There was a note on his desk. Jacobson wanted him to call. Undoubtedly, he was going to insist on picking up North and Elliot immediately. If he wanted to send someone to accompany them, more power to him. Let him deal with Sue directly. Another concern was that as soon as Jacobson had access to North and Elliot, he would undoubtedly demand that Mike and Lou be put under arrest too.

He set the note aside. He would call later. After a stroll through the village, maybe a stop at The Café.

It was another sunny day, unusually warm for that time of year. Probably in the low 70s. Practically a heat wave for Koloshan. He saw a couple of youngsters on bicycles wearing bathing suits. Probably on their way to the airport. There were a series of tide pools there that washed in along the landing field. They were shallow and warmed quickly in the sun. It was a favorite gathering place for kids. Jonah remembered many pleasant hours spent there with Dan,

Dennis's grandson, and his best friend from his early days in Koloshan. Between swims, they'd watch the occasional plane land and take off.

There was a bench in front of the grocery store underneath a painting of two lovebirds, eagle and raven intertwined. Two middle-aged women were seated there while a couple of children played off to one side, oblivious to the cloud of dust they were creating. Jonah stopped for a minute to say a few words to the kids, squatting down to their level.

It was then that he noticed the footprints in the road. They were from those same leather dress shoes that he'd seen before. And they hadn't been there long; otherwise, they would have drifted away.

Jonah stood up and turned to the two women. "Did someone pass by since you were seated her?"

"A couple of people."

"I'm looking for someone wearing leather shoes."

"I wasn't paying attention," one of the women said, and the other nodded.

"Anyone you know pass by?"

The two women looked at each other, then shook their heads. "Sorry."

He tried to track the prints, but quickly lost the trail amidst swirling dust particles and overlapping impressions from foot traffic, cars, and bikes. But at least he knew the person in the city shoes was still around. The other thing he was sure of was that the person was no stranger to the village. If he had been, someone would have mentioned it. That made Jonah sad, very sad. He had desperately wanted him to be an outsider.

Instead of stopping at The Café, Jonah decided to keep walking, hoping to get his head wrapped around some of the thoughts that were slowly taking shape in his mind. Without really thinking about it, he found himself at Dennis's. Esther was just leaving when he arrived. "Dennis is taking a nap," she whispered. "If you want to wait, there's a fresh pot of coffee in the kitchen."

Jonah poured himself some coffee and took the chair opposite Dennis with a view of the mountains across the blue-gray stretch of water. The spectacular landscape was a part of his life, but his world wasn't shaped by the people who had lived here for as much as 11,000 years. His was a world of painted walls and written rules alien to the Tlingit elders. Although he wasn't sure what the Tlingits of the past would make of today's village either. For the most part, they had given up a way of life unique to them and to their geography as their relationship with nature had shifted from efforts aimed at harmony with their environment to taming or controlling it.

"Jonah," Dennis said, bringing him back to the present. "It's good to see you."

"A lot has happened since my last visit."

"I hear you caught the outsiders who stole the screen."

"They had help from locals."

"But outsiders made it all happen."

"I don't think they were responsible for Will's death though."

"Really? That's unfortunate."

"You heard that the two men were tied up and left in a cave?"

"Yes, I heard."

"Who could have done that to them? And why?" He didn't expect an answer. Even if the instigator was local, he doubted that Esther's sources knew who had committed the despicable and cruel act of violence against the two men.

"People seek revenge for all sorts of reasons."

"But to leave someone there like that—"

"Death is death. What does it matter whether you kill an enemy face-to-face or leave them to die slowly, giving them time to suffer and repent. Quick or slow, death is death."

"But you don't kill someone because . . ." Jonah stopped. He didn't have any theory about why North and Elliot had been left there to die like that. Was it because of the theft? Or did someone think they were responsible for Will's death—an eye for an eye? One slow, gruesome death for another?

"Why does anyone ever seek revenge?"

"What makes you so certain it was an act of revenge?"

Dennis leaned back and closed his eyes. "Why indeed."

Jonah finished his coffee, waiting impatiently for Dennis to speak again. It seemed like a long time before he did.

"Remember the story about the daughter of East-wind?"

Jonah had to think back; he only vaguely remembered a long, meandering story about Sa'n Axet, daughter of East-wind.

"It happened a long time ago." Dennis's soothing, storytelling voice took him back in time to when Tlingit legends had created a bond between them.

"Sa'n Axet was a very pretty, young girl, with long shiny hair that she wore lose like a soft breeze. When a high-caste man wanted to marry her, she was very happy. But the honeymoon was short-lived."

Jonah smiled to himself. More and more often of late, Dennis added phrases to his stories that he picked up from television. Jonah was fairly certain that a short honeymoon was not part of Tlingit legend.

"The man heard of another very pretty, young girl, Xun, daughter of North-wind. He left his wife and went north to see her for himself. And sure enough, Xun was lovely. So, he married her too.

"The problem came when he returned to the village of his first wife with the second wife in tow. Everyone agreed that Xun was attractive; her clothes sparkled and made a noise like tiny bells chiming. East-wind's daughter was jealous. 'I will fix that girl you all talk about,' Sa'n Axet boasted.

"Not too long afterwards, it began to grow cloudy and warm. The snow on the ground melted and new shoots appeared everywhere. The daughter of North-wind lost her beautiful clothes. The icicles and frost that were so alluring disappeared. And without these she lost her beauty. Such a sad story."

Jonah knew he was supposed to understand the meaning of the story. It was like a joke, if you had to ask why it was funny, you were never going to laugh. Was the point of this story that nothing lasts forever? No, it had to be something about revenge.

When he realized Dennis had fallen asleep, Jonah quietly got up and left. It worried him that Dennis tired so easily of late, but at least he was lucid.

Still thinking about the story, Jonah walked back to the store and made his purchases. He put everything away at home, then returned Jacobson's call.

"I understand you have two suspects in custody."

"Yes, I'd like to send one of them to you tomorrow and the other on Monday. Can you arrange that? Or do you think I should involve the State Troopers?"

"Why not transport both at the same time?"

"One is still in the clinic, recovering. Also, I think we should avoid giving them a chance to talk to each other. But if you can keep them apart, Sunday afternoon would work for both."

"Maybe they should be getting medical attention here in

Juneau. Or I could have the Troopers take them to Anchorage."

"They should definitely be checked out by a doctor. But our nurse concluded they were mainly dehydrated, no life-threatening injuries."

"And she's qualified to make those kinds of assessments?"

"Yes." He resented Jacobson questioning his judgment and Sue's competence, but he wasn't about to give him the satisfaction of defending her beyond a simple "yes."

"Have they confessed?"

"There are too many witnesses for them to deny their involvement in the theft. But they claim they had nothing to do with what happened to Will. And they say they have no knowledge as to the whereabouts of the money or the missing artifacts."

"And you believe them?"

"Their stories hang together, and their actions suggest they were still looking for the artifacts and the money when they were assaulted. But you can decide that for yourself."

"Your prisoners are safe there, aren't they?"

"What do you mean?"

"I understand the locals are upset. Things won't get out of hand, will they?"

"Are you asking whether some of the villagers will bust them out and string them up? Don't worry, they will arrive with their scalps intact." Jonah knew he was overreacting, but Jacobson's prejudices always seemed to simmer beneath a polite exterior.

"That's not what I meant."

"Sorry. I do appreciate all your help."

After he hung up, he checked on North, then went for another walk, keeping an eye out for the city shoe prints. He took a side street up the hill to what the villagers referred to as the high road. Most of the newer, more modern houses were there, not far from the older, government-built homes. In Koloshan, there weren't large income gaps. Those with higher-paying jobs lived side-by-side with those of more limited means.

Much of the land along the road had been cleared as houses had gone up, but there were still a fair number of tall evergreens on the hillside. Through the trees he could catch glimpses of water, rocky shorelines, rolling forested hills, and distant snow-capped mountains. It was easy to become so accustomed to these amazing landscapes that you took them for granted. The occasional unobstructed views were magnificent.

A breeze skittered across the road, raising tiny trails of dust. Dust danced around his feet as he walked. The dust was a part of summer that they had to accept— even if it did clog up the air filter on your car. When and if they ever got their roads paved, it wouldn't be the same.

As he walked, Dennis's story kept coming back, its message still eluding him. Dennis had a story for every situation, every occasion. The characters and settings were unique to the Tlingit culture, but many of the lessons were the same as those of folktales from other places, stories used to reinforce cultural values or traditions. Good and evil, bravery, loyalty, honesty, behavioral consequences— social conditioning in a memorable and entertaining format.

Was the story of East-wind's daughter the ramblings of an aging mind, or had Dennis been guiding Jonah's thoughts toward a solution to the puzzle before him?

TLEIK̲ÁA K̲A KEIJÍN

(TWENTY-FIVE)

He knew he was dreaming, but he couldn't make himself wake up. The dream world was too strong; it wouldn't let go. He was being chased, and he couldn't get way. He had to escape, or they would kill him. Shots were fired. He could feel them hit the ground nearby as he ran . . . on all fours, heavy, ponderous, but fast. The fur on his back was stiff with blood. He'd been hit. The pain was tremendous. But it wasn't going to stop him.

On and on he ran, faster and faster, the voices fading in the distance but never completely going away. Another shot rang out. Was he hit . . .? No, but it had been close. He could feel himself begin to sweat. If he could only wake up. But he didn't really want to wake up until he was safe—

The alarm went off. Jonah's heart was racing, and there was sweat on his forehead. His mind clung to the dream, willing an end to the chase. He didn't want to think about anything else until he knew the chase was over.

Slowly, reality intruded and the powerful enticement of the dreamworld vanished.

The bear. The bear that had killed Will was dead. A hunter had shot it late yesterday afternoon. They had found a recent bullet wound in its left shoulder, just as the two boys had described. And no one else had reported taking a shot at a bear lately. There was one less thing to worry about. So, why was he reliving it in his dreams? The bear was dead. People could let go of their fear. That was a good thing. But ultimately, it wasn't a bear that had killed Will, it was the person who had struck him, thereby indirectly sentencing him to death. Until Jonah found that person, the case wasn't closed.

He'd questioned North again last night, but he was no closer to discovering the identity of either the person who had fought with Will or the person who had attacked North and Elliot. Although he was becoming more and more convinced that they were the same person in both instances, he still could not link the two incidents with a common motive.

After putting Mann off several times, today was the day he was finally taking the persistent archeologist to the site of the old village in order to fulfill his part of the agreement about Conn and Eddie. Still haunted by the dream, he forced himself to get up and get dressed. While brewing his coffee, he relived some of the dream sequence. It had seemed so real, even after he knew he was dreaming. He didn't understand why some dreams were like that, staying with you as you left the dream world and still clear after you were fully awake, while others vanished at the moment of wakefulness.

He fixed himself a hearty breakfast and packed a lunch. Would Mann think to bring something to eat, he wondered? He added some extra food just in case.

Before going to meet Mann, he had to drop North off at the airport. The plane was due at 8:00 a.m. After stopping at The Cafe to pick up some coffee and a breakfast sandwich for North, he swung by the jail to get him. The man seemed eager to leave, even though he was headed off to another jail where he would be formally charged with several crimes.

"Your buddy will be along tomorrow," Jonah told him.

"I won't miss your hospitality," North said. "Although the coffee's been good."

"Daniels will be disappointed. You'd better be prepared for him to deny everything. I'm pretty sure he intends to lay all the blame on you."

"The wealthy always get away with things."

"I don't sympathize with what you did, but I hope you get a good lawyer. I wouldn't mind seeing Daniels get what he deserves."

"For a backwoods cop, you expect a lot from the justice system."

Jonah let his comment slide. North wasn't too far off the mark. But he'd been let down enough times to have become cynical in the midst of hope.

The handoff at the airport went smoothly. The officer Jacobson sent to pick up North yawned with his mouth open as he accepted his charge. "Early morning for you?" North said.

"Not a morning person," the officer replied.

At the last minute, North turned back to Jonah and said, "Thanks for saving my miserable life." Then he disappeared inside the plane.

Jonah rushed off to meet Mann at the marina. Mann was waiting on the dock next to Jonah's boat. He was wearing a large pack with some digging tools strapped to it. "Good morning," he said cheerfully before adding, "I hope I brought everything I need." Jonah eyed the digging tools but didn't say anything.

They climbed aboard Jonah's twenty-four-foot boat, a recent purchase powered by two outboard motors. He intended to spruce it up a bit one of these days. But for now, it was enough that it was reliable.

"Do I smell coffee? I didn't think to bring any."

Jonah nodded. "Ready?" He started his engines and tossed off the lines, then slowly motored out into the harbor towing an 8' dinghy behind. When they were far enough away to avoid causing problems with their wake, Jonah pushed the throttle forward and the boat picked up speed.

It wasn't a long trip. What everyone referred to as the "old village" site wasn't far from Koloshan, but it was difficult to get to through the forest. Like Koloshan, the "old village" was on the water, but on the opposite side of the peninsula. If its residents hadn't been ravaged by disease and death, it would probably still be a thriving community. According to Dennis, the survivors deserted the village in order to leave the evil spirits behind. That was also the reason they didn't say its name and only referred to it as the "old village."

They anchored in a small inlet close to the beach and rowed the dinghy ashore. The water was calm, but the beach was rocky, and the gray sky cast a shadowy pall on the narrow strip of grasses that covered the land between the beach and the woods.

"You sure this is the place?" Mann asked.

"The old village site isn't far from here. This is the easiest way to get there."

They pulled the dinghy up into the grass, and for good measure, Jonah tied a line to a tree. Then he looked around. It had been a long time since he'd last been there. He didn't remember it being so wild looking, and so quiet. Suddenly his dream came into sharp focus. Why wouldn't it go away? He didn't want to think about bears or Will's death. Today he was repaying a debt. Tomorrow he would worry about finding the artifacts and healing the rift between villagers over the theft.

"Well?" Mann was standing there, waiting for Jonah to show him the way. Jonah roused himself and started off through the tall grass on a trail that was barely visible through the new growth. Little remained of the once well-traveled path. They also had to get past several fallen trees, and once Jonah lost the trail completely. It felt to him as if the forest was trying to prevent them from reaching their destination. He paused to get his bearings.

"What's wrong?" Mann asked.

"Nothing." He started wending his way through the heavy underbrush. This is ridiculous, he told himself. First, he identified with the bear as a victim in a dream, and now he was acting like some sort of superstitious fool. Still, he could not shake the feeling of dread, like they were entering a space where they weren't welcome.

Mann sounded peeved when he asked. "How much farther? I would have thought the village would be near the water."

"We're on a peninsula. The old village was closer to the other side."

"Then why didn't we go there by boat? If I find things to take back, I don't want to carry them through this mess."

Jonah didn't want to admit why he didn't want to approach the village from the other direction. When the villagers had abandoned the site, they had left a warning to others on the shore to stay away. It may have been because they feared the site might still be unhealthy, but for whatever reason, the spiritual legend persisted. Instead of explaining, he said: "The anchorage on that side is iffy."

"Maybe next time you could drop me off from there and let me work the site for a couple of days. Assuming it looks worth the effort."

"Some say it's bad luck to visit the old village site."

"If there's anything there, this could be good luck for me."

"If you find something, it wouldn't belong to you, you know that, right?"

"This is federal land. I checked."

"I doubt they will have left anything of value behind."

"I'm not interested in making money off of this. I want to preserve anything that's still there. Leaving the village to revert back to nature doesn't do anyone any good."

"Did you feel the same way about the screen?"

"You mean the one that was stolen?"

"Yes."

"Well, I do hope it ended up in the hands of someone capable of preserving it."

Jonah stopped and turned back to Mann. "You think that's more important than letting it remain with the people whose ancestors created it?"

"In my opinion, most of the villagers fail to recognize the significance of artifacts such as the Raven House screen. I believe that they belong to a larger body of knowledge about the past, not to a handful of people with dubious claim to them."

"So, you're in favor of museums or individuals keeping artifacts pilfered from other countries? Like the Elgin Marbles or the Koh-I-Noor Diamond."

"As a general rule, I believe original ownership should be honored, but provenance isn't always clearcut, and there are other considerations."

"Like whether the rightful owners are in a position to care for the pieces."

"I feel that should be taken into consideration."

"And who do believe should decide that?"

"Times have changed. History is no longer a single story but part of a larger perspective. Take the situation in Koloshan, for instance. The Tlingit language is almost extinct. Their ceremonies are performed mainly for tourists. Only the elderly engage in some of the traditional crafts.

Some of the native wood-carvers get their designs out of a book written by a white anthropologist. You know all this— so why fight with me about it?"

"You're saying, the past is the past; let it go."

"I wouldn't put it quite like that. Honor it. Preserve it. And move on."

"What nationality are you?" Jonah asked.

"What does that have to do with anything?"

"Do you have any traditions you associate with your ancestors?"

"My grandparents were from Scotland. Things have changed there too, but they have a written history. That makes it different."

"The Tlingits have a robust oral history. And a history preserved in these artifacts. All they are asking for is the right to control their own past."

"Don't future generations have some rights too? What about preserving the past for them? You know the Center can't adequately preserve or protect their possessions. And Koloshan is largely inaccessible to the rest of the world."

"I'm not sure I care about the rest of the world." With that, Jonah started pushing forward again. He would show Mann the site, but he regretted that he hadn't taken the time to check with council members on his own to find out what they'd told Mann about the visit. And to make sure he'd asked permission in the first place. He picked up the pace, knowing Mann was struggling to keep up.

When they reached the old village site, the clearing was barely recognizable as a place where people once lived. Although it was surprising how few trees had taken hold in the area, most of them stunted and unhealthy looking, almost as if the site was being protected by nature. There was, however, a lot of salal intertwined with blackberry vines.

Digging anywhere in the area would be a challenge.

"This is it?" Mann asked. They could see the expanse of dark water through a row of tall evergreens, vying for sunlight with each other. In the distance low foothills disappeared into a stone-colored sky. "Not exactly a hospitable place."

"A lot of people died here."

"You don't believe in evil spirits, do you?"

Jonah closed his eyes and listened. All he heard were his own misgivings about the place echoing in his brain. It was a calm day, but overcast, the surrounding trees casting ominous shade over everything. "Inhospitable—I agree. Maybe for a reason."

"I would say it feels downright creepy." Mann looked around as if expecting ghosts or monsters to be hiding behind trees, ready to jump out at any moment. "But now that we're here, I want to have a look around." He dropped his pack and began pushing his way through the brush along the perimeter.

Jonah left him and made his way out to the beach. It had been a good place for a village, he thought, but Koloshan was better. The wooded hillside behind their village blunted the impact of heavy winds, and the harbor was tucked into a cove that froze in the winter but provided some limited protection from summer storms. Here, the surrounding country was flatter. Less interesting terrain. And the exposed water was unpredictable. Still, the steep, gravelly beach would have made it easy to launch small boats, at least in good weather. When the village was occupied, the shoreline had likely been lined with seaworthy dugouts. Jonah remembered Dennis telling him that not only did the Tlingits decorate their canoes but often named them. Like Yáxwch'i Yaakw or Sea Otter Canoe. The transition to larger, powered vessels made a well-protected place to keep boats even more important.

Mann was right in many ways. Oral history was generally less reliable than written history, certainly less easily preserved. And with the village culture changing so rapidly, their history was no longer connected to the daily lives of the new generation. Still, wasn't that all the more reason for villagers to hang onto the remnants of the past?

He had only agreed to bring Mann here to give Conn and Freddie a break, so that they wouldn't be prosecuted for vandalizing his office. No one else came here. And one day in the not-too-distant future, the site would be entirely enveloped by nature, descending into oblivion like one of the lost Mayan cities. Perhaps some professionally responsible non-native's record was better than no record at all. Did it matter that Mann would enhance his professional reputation *if* he found anything of interest? *If* there was anything left to find.

After a brief walk along the rocky shore, he rejoined Mann. He found him hacking away at some brush, trying to clear a space so he could take a better look at what might be buried near the surface. He looked up from his work and swiped a hand across his sweaty brow. "You've got me spooked."

"How's that?"

"The place has a weird vibe."

"How about something to drink? Maybe a sandwich?"

"I could use some coffee. But let's hold off on the food." Then he added, "You brought something to eat?"

"I get hungry." He shucked off his pack and pulled out a thermos and two cups. When he removed the lid, steam from the coffee curved upward, disappearing into the grayness overhead.

"Think this place might feel better on a sunny day?"

Ignoring his question, Jonah said: "I had a dream last night. I was a bear trying to escape from some hunters, but I couldn't get away."

"Inspired by the injured bear they were tracking?"

"Maybe."

"Trapped by destiny, huh?"

"Something like that."

They drank coffee in silence, both men ignoring the sense of gloom that permeated the overgrown clearing, almost a palpable force. Maybe it *would* look different on a sunny day, but today—

"I'm sorry about the artifacts that were stolen," Mann said. "The screen was a particularly nice piece."

"You're on our list of suspects, you know."

"Me?" Mann seemed genuinely surprised.

"You inquired about buying the screen."

"Oh, that. Yes, I did."

"Were you acting on someone else's behalf?" Something just occurred to Jonah; he should have thought of it before.

"No. I was just curious. It's worth a lot of money."

"You weren't asking for Bill Daniels?"

Mann hesitated. "I have talked with Daniels about the artifacts. He approached me. He was interested in their history."

"And it didn't occur to you to mention that to me after they were stolen?"

"Someone like Daniels doesn't get mixed up in selling illegal artifacts."

"Are you sure you didn't supply Daniels with information as to the security, or lack of it, at the Center? Maybe you even suggested the names of a few people you thought might be receptive to 'selling' the artifacts?"

"That's ridiculous."

"Is it?" Jonah drank down his coffee and set the cup aside. "I've talked with Daniels, you know."

"So?" A tiny bead of perspiration appeared along the edge of Mann's upper lip.

"He was definitely involved."

It all seemed so obvious now that Jonah had put it into words. And it explained why Mann had agreed so readily not to prosecute Conn and Freddie. He might not be legally culpable, but the trail circled back to him. Jonah noticed that Mann's hand holding his coffee cup was trembling.

"In retrospect, I might have said some things that I shouldn't have, but to someone I assumed was a *reputable* art dealer. That doesn't mean I participated in any way in what happened. I wouldn't do something like that."

"For your information, I've located the screen, but I don't know what happened to the money or to the rest of the artifacts. You want to tell me what you know about them?"

"As I said, I wasn't involved."

"But you've suspected Daniels was, haven't you?"

"I admit it, I got a finder's fee from him, but that was the end of it."

"So, it wasn't a noble 'save the artifacts' act of charity?"

"You can believe me or not, but I truly was thinking about how important it was to preserve the artifacts, particularly the screen. But he's a dealer; I certainly didn't think he would steal them."

Jonah looked at Mann's hiking boots. "What size are your boots?"

"Why?"

"About ten?"

"Yeah."

"Have any leather-soled shoes?"

"Dress shoes, sure. But I didn't bring them with me. Why would I? And what does that have to do with anything?"

"Just wondered."

Mann dumped out the remains of his coffee. "Look, if you don't think I should do any digging here today, that's fine by me."

"It doesn't seem like such a good idea." Jonah wasn't sure it would ever be a good idea.

They pulled on their packs and gave the site one last look. Mann shuddered. "This place is enough to make *me* believe in evil spirits."

Jonah's eyes moved slowly across the space where the former village once thrived. Goodbye, he silently said. Rest in peace. I don't think I'll be back.

TLEIK̲ÁA K̲A TLEIDOOSHÚ

(TWENTY-SIX)

Mann's role in the theft had filled in some gaps, but it was Dennis's story about the daughter of East-wind that had helped him see what he needed to do. Dennis had guessed the truth before Jonah. When the daughter of North-wind lost her beauty, it wasn't simply an act of revenge. It was because she had been stolen away from her home in the north. If she had stayed home, the icicles and frost would not have melted, and the story would have had a different ending.

Will had made off with the artifacts and someone had abandoned him in the wilderness and had also been ruthless enough to tie up and leave two men in a cramped cave to die a slow, terrifying death. The idea that these horrific acts had been committed by a villager rather than by a stranger had been haunting him, and he could no longer remain in denial. It was time to face the truth, no matter how unpleasant.

He spent the late afternoon going from one house to the next, halfway hoping that he wouldn't find the leather shoe prints he was searching for. Proceeding methodically, he worked his way up and down the hill behind the village and walked the upper road until it ended. It was getting late. Daylight was beginning to fade. It was time to quit for the day.

On his way home he ran into Phil returning from an evening stroll. Jonah joined him on his front porch for a friendly chat. He was fond of Phil, the memories of his kindness when he and his father first came to Koloshan were an integral part of his first impressions of the village.

Relaxing with him at the end of a hard day was a pleasant reprieve. Until Phil leaned back and stretched out his legs—

Jonah felt the life force drain out of his body. He wanted to look away, to forget what he had just seen. Instead, he continued to stare at Phil's *leather shoes*.

He could be wrong . . . couldn't he? Besides, he hadn't shared his observations about the footprints with anyone; no one else would ever make the connection.

Even as thoughts of a coverup flashed through his mind, deep down he knew it wasn't in him to simply walk away. Too many people were already suffering as a result of the theft, and Will had died for the part he played in it. Jonah had an obligation to uncover the truth, no matter where it led, no matter how hurtful it was to him personally.

Suddenly, he realized Phil had asked him something. "What did you say, Phil?"

"Is something wrong?"

Jonah took a deep breath. "Yes, Phil, something is terribly wrong." He looked Phil in the eyes, desperately wanting to believe that Phil wasn't the person he'd been searching for, that wearing leather shoes didn't prove anything.

For an instant, Jonah thought Phil was going to say that he didn't know what Jonah was hinting at. But rather than looking innocent or alarmed, the man seemed almost relieved.

"You've figured it out," Phil said. "How?"

"It's your shoes. Why leather-soled shoes in Koloshan?" Jonah's calm question masked the inner turmoil he was feeling, the desire to rail against his own investigative success.

"Leather breathes. And it molds to your foot. I was having some foot problems; my doctor suggested I try them." He looked down at his shoes. "They were expensive."

"I know you didn't mean for Will to die like he did." Jonah's entire body was tingling with disappointment; at the same time, he wanted to know *why.*

"No, I liked Will. He was a good person. When I left, he was in his pickup. I don't know how he ended up on the ground."

"Maybe he was more confused by the blow to his head than you realized." Jonah found it difficult to fathom why Phil would have struck Will like that.

"I didn't mean to hurt him. I just didn't expect so much resistance. He charged me in spite of the gun I was holding."

Phil was holding Will at gunpoint? Why? "Tell me what happened."

Phil sat up and leaned forward, staring off toward the water. "The night of the theft, I couldn't sleep. I was out walking around when I saw them at the Center. I got close enough to hear them talking and realized what was going on. I didn't know what to do. Before I could figure out how to stop the truck with the screen, they took off. I knew Will had the rest of the artifacts, and he was about to take off too. I only had one chance to stop him.

"I always carry a gun when I go for a walk, in case of running into a wild animal. So, I got in the passenger side of Will's pickup truck and forced him to take the money and the artifacts to my place. I had him put them inside, then toss my bike in the back of his pickup so I had a way to get home. Keeping the gun on him, I made him drive to where you found him and disabled the truck's engine. I was going to leave him there as a lesson, make him walk home. I also needed to give myself time to figure out what to do with the artifacts and the money. But he suddenly charged me; put up a fight. I hit him with my gun and he went down. He didn't seem to be badly injured, but he was groggy. I managed to coax him back into his truck. Then I left.”

“Maybe he was concussed and didn’t realize what he was doing when he got out of the truck. That makes sense. But there was a shaman’s amulet near the cache. Any idea how it got there?”

“I don’t know. Maybe Will kept one of the artifacts for himself. I did. When I opened the first box to see what was inside, I recognized something I’d given the Center, a carved horn spoon that had been in my family for generations. I decided to keep it, and I had it in my pocket when I went looking for the two men. I thought it might bring me luck . . . At some point it must have fallen out of my jacket pocket.”

“It was found by two kids near the camp where North and Elliot were.”

“Careless.”

“But fortunate. Otherwise, I wouldn’t have searched the area and found North and Elliot. That’s something I don’t understand at all—how could you leave them there like that?”

“I didn’t mean to. I’m so very sorry about that. I’d heard they beat up Lou and threatened Ellen and Mike. And I knew they were still looking for the artifacts and the money. I didn’t think they were staying in town; someone would have seen them. So, I guessed they might be camping out somewhere. The most logical place seemed to be up in the hills off some logging road, but not too far from the village.

“It took me a while, but I found their car. After that, it didn’t take long to find their camp. I decided to ambush them and scare them, really scare them, let them know it wasn’t smart to steal from us, to terrorize our village.

“When I was a kid, we used to hang out in that cave. It seemed like the perfect place to leave them overnight. Caves are scary even when you can see light through the entrance.

I meant to go back the next day and set them free. Give them some food and drink and let them walk back. I wanted to make the point that we villagers don't mess around when dealing with people who take what's precious to us. I drove the stakes in the ground so no wild animals could get to them. Then I wove a screen to hide the entrance."

"If that was your plan, why didn't you go back?"

"I have congestive heart disease. And even though I walk every day, between the bicycling, hauling that ATV around, getting those two into that cave, and moving their car and equipment, I ended up having an attack. I barely made it back to the village, and Sue insisted I stay overnight at the clinic. By the time I felt good enough to go back up there, you'd found them. I'm thankful for that. It's bad enough having Will on my conscience."

"Why didn't you just come to me in the first place?" If only—

"I considered it. But at first, my main concern was for Will. I didn't want him sent to jail. He might not have understood why we shouldn't sell our heritage, but I thought if I 'found' the artifacts somewhere, it was possible outsiders would be blamed for the theft. I was sure I could come up with a plausible story."

"And the money?"

"I admit I've spent a little. But it was never about the money. In fact, I didn't realize I had it until I got back to my place the evening of the theft. I was going to figure out a way to make an anonymous donation to the Center. Something like that."

Phil suddenly put his face in his hands and began sobbing. "I didn't mean for Will to die." Jonah's heart felt like it was being squeezed. Like Phil, he was caught in a backwash of regret. Regret for the changes that were dividing the village.

Regret for the loss of culture. Regret for his role as an officer of the law that pushed him to punish someone who hadn't meant to harm anyone.

"I understand that you were trying to help Will and had no way to anticipate how things would end." He put his arm around the man's shoulders. "Sometimes even when we try to do the humane thing, things go sideways."

"God how I wish I could undo it all. There must have been another way to save the artifacts and to avoid what happened to Will. I could at least have stayed with him until I was sure he was alright."

"I'm just sorry I figured it out," Jonah said truthfully.

"You do what you have to do. We all have to live with the consequences of our actions."

Phil didn't know how right he was. This was not the first time Jonah had been forced to choose between friendship and his commitment to upholding the law. Even believing that the community had a right to know what had happened didn't ease the anguish caused by the role he felt compelled to play. He was certain that most of the villagers would understand and forgive Phil for his actions. But if they never learned the full story, it would deepen the gap between locals and outsiders, between young and old. Fingers might be pointed at the innocent. There needed to be an open conversation about the relationship between the past and present, about what it meant to remember the past while going through a time of rapid change.

Will had paid the ultimate price for trying to rob the past to make a better life for himself and his family in the future. Mike and Lou had lost a close friend and were about to have their lives disrupted by having to face legal consequences for their actions. Jonah would speak on their behalf, but testimony from North and Elliot would clearly label them as thieves.

Phil looked up, tears of regret streaking his face. "I remember the Raven House screen from when I was young. How it felt to be in its presence. It was so beautiful. So powerful." He closed his eyes, perhaps in his own mind seeing the screen as it once was. "In some ways I think the past is more real to me than the present."

In the oral tradition, the Raven was the trickster who regularly found himself in trouble or tried shortcuts that backfired. But he was still the symbol of hope, forgiveness, and sacrifice. For Phil, the artifacts had spiritual significance. He'd been willing to take risks to preserve them and to save Will from his own criminal acts. But, like what so often happened to Raven, the consequences of Phil's actions were not what he intended.

This time the Raven's Legacy was death.

TLINGIT LANGUAGE REFERENCES

Although I have spent many hours listening to people conversing in Tlingit, enjoying the unique cadence and intonation, I do not speak even elementary Tlingit. I have relied on three excellent sources for the bits and pieces of the language used in the book to create the sense of place and to honor the culture.

Beginning Tlingit by Nora and Richard Dauenhauer, produced by the Alaska Native Education Board and the Alaska Native Language Center, Tlingit Readers Inc. (1976).

Dictionary of Tlingit by Keri Edwards and Anita Lafferty (Contributors: John Marks, June Pegues, Helen Sarabia, Bessie Colley, David Katzeek, Fred White, and Jeff Leer), Sealaska Heritage Institute, Juneau Alaska (2011).

Say It in Tlingit: A Tlingit Phrase Book edited by Nora and Richard Dauenhauer, Sea Alaska Heritage Institute (2002).

MISCELLANEOUS REFERENCES

Over the years I've read quite a few variations on traditional Tlingit stories. Although I have adapted some of these stories to fit the themes of the book, I have tried to be true to the flavor and characters in Tlingit literature. My hope is that my respect and admiration for the Tlingit culture makes up for any inaccuracies that may have slipped by me. A few of the books that were particularly helpful include:

Alaska Bear Tales by Larry Kaniut, Alaska Northwest Publishing Company (1983).

Cultures of the North Pacific Coast by Philip Drucker, Harper and Row (1965).

Haa Shuká, Our Ancestors: Tlingit Oral Narratives (Classics of Tlingit Oral Literature) by Nora Marks Dauenhauer and Richard Dauenhauer, University of Washington Press (1987).

Northwest Coast Indian Art: An Analysis of Form by Bill Holm, J.J. Douglas LTD (1978).

Raven's Bones, Sitka Community Association, edited by Andrew Hope III (1982).

ACKNOWLEDGEMENTS

I once participated in a corporate workshop where we were asked to close our eyes and remember a moment in time when we were totally at peace and completely happy. It didn't take me long to transport myself back to being at anchor after a long day of commercial salmon fishing in SE Alaska. Going from ocean swells to flat water was enough to make someone prone to seasickness happy. But I also loved being in harbors surrounded by Alaskan wilderness, the setting sun reflecting off the calm surface of the water, with occasional glimpses of wildlife on the beach or an eagle flying overhead— the moment enveloped in a glorious silence after hours of listening to the steady strum of a Jimmy diesel engine.

My husband and I fished for nine seasons, often anchored at night in a harbor, although not always in perfect weather. Our home base was a small native village. It was this experience that inspired my two "Raven" books. Although both are fiction, I wanted to capture a time when the challenge of maintaining a culture was in conflict with increased exposure to outside influences and competition for resources. Inevitably, trees are sacrificed for profit. Art gives way to crafts that can be made in mass and sold to visitors. Tourist boats frighten and sometimes injure or kill whales. Glaciers melt. Young people leave for the glamor of the big city. Some changes happen overnight, others sneak up slowly.

Rural Alaska of the late 70s and early 80s was a snapshot in time that is singular because it was the beginning of major lifestyle changes brought about mainly by technological advances that provided a virtual bridge to the rest of the world. Like some of the characters in my book, I often feel as though I have one foot in the past while being propelled into the future.

ABOUT THE AUTHOR

Award-winning author Charlotte Stuart PhD writes mysteries that fall into a number of different sub genres: cozy mysteries, character-driven mysteries featuring a female PI, a laugh out loud comedic series, as well more traditional mysteries. She also co-authored a legal thriller with Don Stuart. In general, she favors twisty plots with a dollop of adventure. Before she started writing full time, she left a tenured faculty position to go commercial salmon fishing in Alaska, spent a year sailing in the Washington and Canadian San Juans, became a partner in a management consulting group and later a VP of HR and training. After living on boats for over a decade, boating and forays into wilderness areas often find their way into her stories.

Charlotte lives on Vashon Island in the Pacific Northwest and is the past president of the Puget Sound Sisters in Crime and a member of the Mystery Writers of America and the International Thriller Writers.

To my readers: *Thank you for giving me the excuse to live part of each day in a world of memory and make believe.*

Other books by Charlotte Stuart include:

The Discount Detective Mysteries
The John Smith Mysteries
Bogged Down (A Vashon Island Mystery)
Raven's Grave
Midnight for Justice, a legal thriller by Charlotte Stuart and Don Stuart

You can visit her website or contact her on social media:

Website: charlottestuart.com
Facebook: charlotte.stuart.mysterywriter
Goodreads: goodreadscomclstuart
Instagram: cstuartauthor
BookBub: bookbub.com/authors/charlotte-stuart

READER DISCUSSION GUIDE

1. In the book, Jonah struggles with the question of whether artifacts belong to future generations or to the individuals who inherited them. Do you think the Raven House screen should be returned to the Native Arts Center even if they cannot properly care for it?

2. How important do you think artifacts are for documenting a culture's history?

3. Do you agree with the assertion that the past is less important to younger people today than it used to be? If so, what is the significance of this change?

4. Do you feel that Jonah was acting responsibly when he held off charging Mike and Lou with theft while he was trying to find the missing artifacts and money? In what ways did knowing most of the villagers make his role as a police officer more difficult?

5. How does Jonah's emotional link to his adopted grandfather and the Tlingit culture shape his approach as a police officer? How do Dennis's stories function as catalysts for helping him solve crimes?

6. Do you agree that native cultures of the past are often romanticized while their current culture is seen through a less flattering filter? What are some examples from the book where descriptions of the village values are in conflict with city standards?

7. Cultural preservation in a world where rapid change is the norm presents many challenges. Koloshan is on the tipping point in 1980. How do you decide what part of a culture can and should be preserved? What role does language play in preserving a culture?

8. Phil's good intentions resulted in one death and almost killed two others. If his original plan had worked, do you feel it was justified?

9. Did the villagers have the right to keep secret the recovery of a headless slave skeleton?

10. The wounded bear is a minor character in the book, always in the background. What does the bear symbolize in the story?

11. Some museums have refused to return stolen artifacts that were acquired under questionable circumstances in the past. After years have passed, do they have the right to keep them?